KYREEN
Chronicles of Calan: Book I

Written by Nikki Moore
Illustrations by Ryann Armstrong

For my family

PART I

Chapter 1

Whether it was the soft breeze from the open window or a stray noise from the courtyard below, something drew the child from her slumber. She woke slowly, green eyes fluttering open. The child, still too young to grasp the concept of time, furrowed her brow at the sliver of pale light cast by the crescent moon. When one awoke from sleep, it should be morning and the sun should be shining. She was awake, but night still lingered about her bedroom.

With the ease of a child's mind, her thoughts turned from the worries about night to her bed. Her bed! She stretched, smiling at the memory. When the sun did finally arrive in the morn, it would be her and Quillan's third birthday! Mama had surprised them with the early gift yesterday after naptime. Gone were the cramped baby cribs. Instead real feather mattresses with carved wooden headboards and footboards had been set up in the nursery. The beds were tiny replicas of the bigger bed Mama slept in down the hall.

"After all," Mama had said, ruffling Kyreen's ebony curls, "we cannot have the princess and prince of Calan sleeping in cribs when they are practically grown up now!"

Kyreen had known Mama was teasing, but still it felt good to be in a real bed, snuggling into the soft luxurious linens under a down comforter. Absently, the toddler reached back to scratch her right shoulder blade, tiny fingers falling short of their mark. The cotton nightgown chafed her where the strange man, pictures drawn over every visible spot of his own skin, had drawn a picture on both of the children just a couple of days earlier.

Kyreen worried her own picture was not as pretty as that of her brother's, a red rose in full bloom, its verdant stem entwined around the blade of a sword.

Thinking of Quillan, she smiled again, allowing her mind to gently reach across the room. Caressing his drowsy thoughts, the girl assured herself that her twin still slept. Even in the dark she pictured him—curled on his side, rosy lips pursed, golden locks damp with sleepy sweat, one small fist bunched with his blanket. Kyreen wondered if Quillan had ever wakened during the night. She must remember to ask him at breakfast. Their birthday breakfast!

The child slipped from beneath the covers and padded to the open window to search for a sign of dawn. As the soft breeze caressed her cheek, she gazed down. Sleeping shadows littered the hushed courtyard. For the last two days people had been pouring into the castle in anticipation of the annual festival marking the birth of the royal twins. Quillan said the festival had been going on forever, even before Mama was born. Kyreen thought this to be a silly notion. As remarkable as the Calanian people were, how could they have known when Kyreen's and Quillan's birthday would be way before Mama was born? Quillan had then explained, more than a little impatiently, that the festival was really to celebrate the beginning of the foaling season. To which Kyreen had pointed out many foals had been dropped already, long before the festival was scheduled to begin.

Mama had simply laughed, a real laugh that sparkled all the way up to her green eyes, saying, "If Kyreen wants the festival to be a birthday festival that is fine with me."

As she was the older of the twins and almost three years old, Kyreen had maturely ignored Quillan when he stuck his tongue out at her. She had, however, crossed her eyes at him later during dinner. That always made him mad, because no matter how hard he tried, Quillan could never get his own blue eyes to cooperate.

Even as she giggled at the memory, a subtle motion caught the girl's attention, pulling her gaze back down to the courtyard. A wraith-like shape, an inky stain against the other shadows, moved against the stonewall surrounding the courtyard. Instinct more than training urged the girl away from the open window, her body hugging against the wall. She peered around the corner, inspecting the shadows below. A man, his black armor dull, crept towards a sleeping form. The hand encased in shadows rose slowly, pausing a heartbeat, the glint of steel reflecting in the moonlight, before plunging downward.

<hr />

The hounds' mournful baying floated across the valley, carrying farther than usual on the crisp air of the late harvest season. Pausing from his duties, Jorn ran a gnarled hand through his thinning hair. Who would be on a hunt at this time, he wondered. The woods had reeked of the first snows of Fallow for many days. After listening a moment longer, more to catch his breath than for curiosity's sake, Jorn turned his attention back to the felled oak tree. With so much woodcutting to do, he had no time to wonder about a rich nobleman and his entourage frolicking about the woods. Most men his age were warming their bones by the lodge fire while the younger men finished preparations for the long winter season.

"Those men have children," Jorn's voice rang hard in the clearing.

He split another log and attempted to force back the all-too-familiar bitterness welling up inside. Old resentments would not get this work done.

Groaning as he bent over, Jorn picked up another load to carry to the waiting wagon. The mule, hobbled nearby, paused in its rooting for the last green grasses to watch him with dark mournful eyes. Even working as hard as he was able, Jorn had failed to gather enough wood to keep the cottage warm and food cooked for even half of the upcoming winter. This meant he would have to venture forth during the snows if he and Ildri were to survive the Fallow.

Returning to the tree, every muscle and joint in his upper torso protesting, Jorn bit back a curse as the axe slipped from his grasp, bounced roughly on the ground. In his current ill mood, the old man was mildly surprised the blade had not fallen straight down and severed his foot. Used to be woodcutting had been a pleasant chore, time alone in the woods, time for mindless labor which allowed his thoughts to roam free, to make plans, mighty plans. Once, Jorn had fostered many mighty plans.

The land he had inherited from his father was good fertile ground. With sons at his side, Jorn had planned to plant the extra fields, the ones that had lain fallow after Jorn's father and brother had both crossed over at much too young an age. Once this piece was properly tilled, Jorn and his sons would clear out the land Jorn had received from Ildri's father, a woodcutter by trade. It had been this land that would make Jorn a rich man. Dark, fertile Hanorian soil that had never been tilled would surely bring forth bountiful crops. This land from Ildri's father, however, had trees. Trees needed clearing. Clearing needed brute strength. Brute strength came from young strong men, from sons, sons that had never appeared.

All through Ildri's bearing years, the couple had remained childless; Jorn's mighty plans dimming with each passing season. Now it was all Jorn could do to keep up with a small garden and two alfalfa fields.

Bending over to pick up the axe, Jorn's mind vaguely registered the baying had moved a little closer, maybe just one valley over now. Thus, he was quite startled by the appearance of the woman a few moments later, the slight swaying of bushes behind her the only testimony of her entrance into the clearing. The hand that emerged from beneath the cloak was grimy and dirty, her nails torn and ragged like the cloak hanging from her thin frame. Yet somehow Jorn knew instinctively that once the hand had been soft and white. Pulling back her hood, she released masses of curls, as dark as the raven's wings, which spiraled wildly about the tattered cloak with a life all their own. As the woman approached, Jorn could tell from the deep burgundy velvet and elaborate gold stitching this cloak had once cost more dinars than he, a simple farmer, had ever possessed. The collar, while dirty and worn, still had patches of luxurious brown fur. Jorn, one of the tallest men in the village, found he had to look up to see the woman's face. Alabaster skin, drawn taut over sharp cheekbones and a strong jaw, made her face look like it had been carved from granite. It was her eyes, however, that most mesmerized the old man. He found himself drawn into green so deep and vibrant he had difficulty breathing. The woman's breathing, though silent, was accelerated, her pale nostrils flaring; and Jorn could see the steam rising from her form.

"Please," the woman whispered, her voice deep with a melodic accent, "if they find her, they will kill her. You must help us, Jorn."

Jorn recoiled when the stranger used his name. How in the name of the Ten Lords of Hayrik could she…? A sorceress! She must be a sorceress! That would explain her silent approach, her hypnotic eyes… yes, a sorceress! Jorn took a fearful step back, his grip tightening upon the axe handle.

A mix of emotions flashed in the woman's strange eyes, but her tone remained calm and even. "Jorn, please!" she urged once more. "If they take her, all will be ruined!"

Belatedly, Jorn realized the woman was gesturing to her cloak. Her form expanded, mutating and growing. Jorn tensed further, ready for flight, positive the sorceress was changing into a hideous monster. Then, pulling back her cloak, the woman revealed a sleeping child, hanging about her body in a homemade sling. The child clearly belonged to the woman… ebony curls peeked from beneath the knitted cap and the woman's sharp features lay hidden just below the surface of alabaster baby fat. Jorn would wager both his mule and wagon that when the child awakened, her eyes would be the same bewitching green as her mother's.

"Please watch her. Without Kyreen's weight, I have a chance to lose the hounds," the woman pleaded a third time. Stepping forward, she thrust the child towards the old man.

Reflexively, Jorn took the sleeping child, the forgotten axe slipping to the ground. He nearly staggered beneath the child's weight that the woman had appeared to bear so effortlessly.

"I cannot take her," he protested feebly.

The woman glanced over her shoulder, listening for the position of the hounds. She returned her gaze to Jorn with a gentle smile. "After the draught wears off and she awakens, Kyreen will be of no trouble to you, dear man." She placed a gentle hand upon his arm. "I am sorry I do not have time to explain. Just know these men who pursue us are evil. I should return in three days, six at the most. Please keep my daughter safe."

Jorn began nodding at the word 'evil' and tightened his hold on the sleeping child. "Aye, I shall keep the girl safe until ye return," he promised, his eyes scanning the bushes, as though he fully expected the apparitions of evil to suddenly burst forth.

On cue, a lone hound's bay rang forth, announcing the scent had been reacquired. Panic washed over Jorn. "Go," he urged, promising once again, "I shall watch over the lass until your return. Ye have my word upon it, m'lady."

With a final caress of lips upon her daughter's smooth brow, the woman drew the hood over her head once more. At the edge of the clearing she paused, glancing back at her child resting in the arms of the old man. "Do not fear, Jorn, I shall lead them from here. You will not even see these men. Just protect Kyreen. And, thank you."

As she disappeared into the bushes as silently as she had appeared, Jorn's gaze turned to the child. He sent a silent prayer to the Ten Lords of Hayrik, asking for the woman's safe return. Slowly shuffling to the wagon, he gently eased the sleeping child down. The sun had barely reached mid-sky and Jorn still had much work to complete before dusk. Resuming his chore, it never occurred to the old man that the beautiful stranger could have been lying to him.

Chapter 2

One moment there was warmth and hope, the next complete emptiness. Because the young child's entire focus was directed towards the event, Kyreen felt the life drain from the sleeping Calanian as the assassin's blade did its work, experiencing a void vaster than anything else she had ever felt in her young life. The intensity washed over her and she stumbled against the windowsill, her mind screaming in protest. One small fist covered her mouth, silencing a verbal cry that never transpired.

A mere instant later, Mama burst into the room, scooping the girl up, away from the window. The woman's keen gaze quickly found the shadow in the courtyard, now working towards its next sleeping victim. The little boy, also alerted by his sister's silent scream, sat up, tiny fists wiping sleep from his eyes.

"Quickly! Sound the alarm!" Tyra commanded the pair of guards who had trailed her into the twins' room. Even as she spoke, the queen crossed to the chest of drawer, adding, "Have the Council join me in the war room!"

Afraid she had done something wrong, the girl nibbled at her bottom lip as the cotton shift is slipped over her head and deft fingers fasten clothes about her body. Mama's voice was tense, the fun and laughter from the previous afternoon when they were discussing the festival gone. And Mama had closed her mind. The girl tried once more, frantically searching, but could not read anything from her mother. Blinking back tears, Kyreen followed her mother into the hall, falling into step with her brother. Instinctively their small hands reach out to clasp together. Quillan's blue eyes, wide with fear, seek Kyreen's emerald eyes, wordlessly asking for guidance. She was always the quick one, the one with ideas, with plans. This time Kyreen merely shook her head, sending calming thoughts to her brother.

Grey clouds filtered the final rays of sunlight as Jorn led the mule and wagon out of the woods. Silently he gave thanks that Ildri was not waiting at the cottage door for him. He was home earlier than normal, partially due to the child, but mainly because of the biting cold wind that permeated the valley. The first snows were imminent. If not tonight, Jorn reckoned they would arrive within days, blanketing the entire province until the thaws of Sowing.

The child... Kyreen was her name he reminded himself... had slumbered until Jorn broke for his mid-day sup. By then the sound of the hunt had faded away into the west. Upon waking the child had sat up in the wagon bed, silently perusing the clearing until her gaze, as vibrant green as the woman's, had rested upon Jorn.

"Mama says I am to stay with you until her return." The voice was higher pitched than her mother's with the same melodic accent.

Caught in mid-bite, Jorn had merely nodded. He doubted he would have been able to speak even without his mouth full. This was not the reaction he expected from a small child left in the care of a complete stranger. Jorn had been bracing for tears and screaming. In sleep, Jorn had judged the child to be seven or eight summers old, allowing for the woman's height. Now he did not know whether to guess higher or lower.

The child had climbed out of the wagon and, before Jorn realized her intention, had moved towards the mule. His protest fell silent as he watched her softly stroke the animal's muzzle, her voice murmuring quietly. After length, she had looked over at the incredulous man.

"My name is Kyreen. I am five summers old," she paused, small white teeth nibbling her bottom lip in obvious conflict. "Mama says it is rude to ask, but my tummy hurts when it is hollow. Do you have any more food?"

Jorn had readily shared the remainder of his bread and cheese. Then he had sliced up both sweet red apples for the child before returning to his work. Kyreen had watched him silently as he moved the cut wood to the wagon. After she finished eating, the girl had wordlessly begun carrying logs, one by one. With her help, Jorn had managed to get the entire day's work loaded before the cold wind became too bitter.

Currently the child was sitting beside Jorn in the wagon, quietly taking in her surroundings. Of average size for this province, Jorn's homestead included the cottage, one barn, and two nearby fields which were furrowed under in preparation for the Fallow. The barn dominated the clearing, more than big enough for Jorn's few animals, a cow, a goat, the mule, and a handful of chickens. Across the yard stood a small thatched-roof cottage, smoke curling from its chimney, and lantern-light twinkling from behind the oil-cloth windows.

With a sigh, Jorn clambered down from the wagon. Slipping the flask from a pocket, he took a sip and settled on an old stump, resting his aching joints before tackling the evening chores.

"Ah, quit your complaining," he cursed the mule, which had begun braying loudly.

Jorn did not know what he was going to tell Ildri. She would be ecstatic when she saw the child. How would he explain her arrival? He must stress this was temporary, but he was loathe to once again see disappointment in his wife's beautiful blue eyes. For so many seasons they had prayed to the Ten Lords of Hayrik for a child. How many special offerings had Ildri presented Sevan over the years? The Lady of Fertility, however, had remained unmoved and the couple had remained childless. Jorn hated getting Ildri's hopes up, even for an instant.

The mule's silence brought Jorn from his reverie. Glancing up, he was surprised to see the wagon harness empty. Whilst the old man was lost in thought, the child had taken the mule into the barn. Gritting his teeth against the pain, Jorn rose and moved his aching body inside, grateful for reprieve from the biting wind. The child was standing upon an upturned bucket, wiping the animal with a soft rag. She looked up and met Jorn's gaze across the back of the mule, which was contentedly munching on the flake of sweet hay that Kyreen had placed in the trough.

"He was hungry," The words were simple, but Jorn recognized the tentative question in her tone.

"Ye did right, chil… Kyreen. Now the wood unloading and other chores can hold. We… I have some explaining to do and explaining is best done on a full stomach."

The girl's face lit up. "You mean inside? The house? Real cooked food?"

Jorn chuckled, "Aye. Inside the house and some of the best real cooked food ye shall find in this province."

Placing a gnarled hand upon the girl's thin shoulder, Jorn headed towards the cottage and his wife of forty-three full seasons. Not for the first time that day, he wondered how long and from whom had the pair been running? Who was the mother? From where did they come? When, if ever, would the woman return? Those were questions he suspected would not, could not be answered by the child.

Sometime later in the cottage, the elderly woman backed down the ladder. She stood there a moment, her pale blue eyes gazing tentatively up into the darkened loft. Satisfied the child was indeed settled, Ildri turned towards her husband, who was standing in the open doorway. Her brow furrowed at the pipe in his mouth, but the words of reproach died unspoken. There were more important matters to discuss.

"Jorn," she lamented, her voice quiet so as not to disturb the child, "What if her mother has crossed over?"

Jorn drew heavily on his pipe, thankful for Ildri's distraction. Not that he would have budged and stepped out into the cold. After all, he reasoned a man must have some pleasures in life and tobacco was about all he had left. His gaze locked upon the snowflakes slowly drifting down.

"Ildri, this is temporary," he spoke gruffly, his heart not sharing the confidence of his words, but he did not wish to worry or encourage his wife any more than necessary. After so many years of marriage, he knew she was already making plans.

Her steps light despite the bulk of her frame, Ildri quickly crossed to place a soft hand upon his arm. "But ye heard what the lass said, Jorn. If her mother is alright, why cannot the child hear her? She claims to be from Calan and it is said the Calanians have special powers. They read minds and converse with animals. It may not be safe to harbor the child, especially if her mother is a sorceress. What if she is evil?"

With a snort, Jorn pulled the pipe from his mouth, waving away his wife's notion. "Posh and be gone with ye thoughts of evil, Ildri. That child could no more be evil than ye could."

Glancing over her shoulder towards the loft opening, she sighed. "She is quite a lass, but still…"

Ildri's grip on Jorn's arm tightened and her gaze snapped back to him, exclaiming, "The lodge!"

"Eh?" Jorn's unruly brows arched.

"The lodge. If any strangers have come through the village, especially tonight with the first snows, they would be at the lodge. Quick! Go to town, have some ale and see what ye can find out."

Ordinarily a tankard of forbidden spirits would have been just the thing, but tonight, the first snows of Fallow? Jorn had been looking forward to collapsing into his bed early. Then again, he knew his wife well enough to know he would get no rest tonight until Ildri knew what was going on with the child and her mother.

Grudgingly, Jorn nodded, leaning over to empty his pipe bowl against the doorstep. "Aye, woman, ye are correct. If anyone would know,

Havard would."

So, it was that, after rousing a very reluctant mule from its warm stall, Jorn arrived in the village, half-frozen himself. Silently he cursed the strange woman, her child, his wife, and the whole Fallow season as he entered the jovial atmosphere of the village lodge. Though a fire crackled in the hearth, it was the numerous men who nourished the room's almost smothering warmth. This Harvest, officially brought to close by the first snows of Fallow, had been especially fruitful and many celebratory toasts were being hefted to Kevork, the Lord of Harvest, Second Lord of Hayrik.

While on the surface, no notice was made of the elderly man's entrance a spot was quickly cleared at a center table, a spot of honor. Though a childless man, Jorn did hold an office on the village's Council of Elders.

He grunted softly as his weary bones settled, blue eyes subtly scanning the crowd.

"Jorn! Out on the first snows of Fallow? Ye have stuck your ancient friend speechless!" roared a rotund man with a bushy gray beard, weaving through the tables with agility defiant of his bulk. Trailing behind the older man, an extremely harried looking young man carried two foaming tankards.

Jorn snorted, his eyes twinkling merrily. "Ye speechless, Havard? I did not know that word was in ye vocabulary!" Even as he spoke, Jorn took one of the tankards from Havard's son-in-law, resolutely quelling the resentment rising in his mind. Havard, father of five sons and a married daughter, had most likely spent the majority of today in this lodge, as had most of the men of their age.

"Move, move, move," Havard commanded, creating a spot for himself before settling heavily on the bench beside Jorn and seizing the other tankard. Simultaneously taking a deep drink and wrapping a meaty arm about Jorn's shoulders, Havard swallowed before declaring, "Jorn, my dear old friend, we have missed your sorry face this Harvest. I kinnae believe that wife of yours allowing ye to venture forth on this night."

Jorn shrugged, "Sometimes a man must have male companionship. Fallow is a long season to be cooped up with only a woman for company."

Havard threw back his head, laughing. "Ack, Jorn, we surely must be getting old! I remember when we looked forward to Fallow just to be cooped up with a woman." Those close enough to hear burst out in boisterous laughter.

Once more Jorn worked to control his features, unable to stanch the words flowing through his mind. 'Used to be Fallow was easier to prepare for when the body was young and fresh,' he thought, but did not speak out loud.

Instead he chose to get directly to business. "Tell me about the strangers," he commented casually.

"Strangers, Jorn? How did ye…?" Confusion clouded Havard's blue eyes. He glanced around, lowering his voice conspiratorially. "By the Lords of Hayrik, Jorn, what do ye know about them yourself? These are not nice men."

Now it was Jorn's turn to laugh, although his stomach twisted uncomfortably. "If ye do not have strangers boarding, then who belongs to yonder hounds? Strange dogs I have never seen before, eh?"

Relief flooded Havard's features and he leaned back. "I never could put one over on ye, old friend. Aye, we have boarders this eve. They showed up around suppertime, took dinner in their rooms and we have not seen them since. I will rest more comfortable tomorrow when they leave." Once again, Havard leaned forward, voice lowering below the general conversations. "They claim to be of the west from Myrddin, but I tell ye, Jorn, I recognized the crest of Faldor upon the leader's scabbard and their coinage is not from the capital city. I have only seen its crest once before. It looks to be of Galor, which is very far north."

Jorn nodded, saving himself from comment by drinking more of the warm ale. Faldor to the west was renowned for mercenaries, assassins and thieves. The small far-away Galor was a mystery to Jorn. Havard's father, however, an emissary for Hanoria, had often taken Havard, his first-born son, with him during his travels. There was no one else alive in Hanoria who had traveled more, or knew more of the outlying provinces, than Jorn's lifelong best friend.

"They are not nice men," Havard repeated, scooting closer, his voice lowering even more. "The young one stayed down to care for their dogs while the others went up to bathe. He was boasting that they had captured and burned a witch, an evil sorceress. But I tell ye, my friend, those men are not to be trusted. It is they who are evil. Their eyes are dead, like those of the serpent."

Once more Jorn stalled by hoisting his drink, attempting to quell the rancid acid rising from his stomach. The beautiful woman was dead. He found it hard to believe. He had wanted so badly to believe she had escaped the hounds. But he could not waste time mourning a woman he had met for a mere moment. Now he must provide for the child. He had given his vow to the girl's mother.

As Jorn drained the last of his tankard, preparing to leave, the room grew quiet. Looking around, he saw three strangers descending the stairs. Dressed in dull black armor, bulky swords hanging by their sides, the trio presented an ominous and deadly picture. Goosebumps broke out on Jorn's body, the stuffy room immediately chilled by the strangers' appearance.

One man, a half-healed gash traversing the left side of his face, leapt on top of a table and surveyed the village men. A dirty bandage covered his left eye. When he spoke, his deep voice rumbled to every corner of the room, sending fresh chills down Jorn's spine.

"Greetings, fair Hanorians! For many seasons my friends and I have ridden in pursuit of a vile creature, a witch of black magic. Finally, today, we captured and dealt with the sorceress!" Here the man paused, his one remaining eye continuing to peruse the room, searching. For what no one knew, no one except Jorn. He sat unmoving; afraid even to raise his tankard for fear the action would call deadly attention to himself.

"As I said," the man continued, the angry red welt on his cheek adding to his menacing looks, "we have taken care of the woman. She will not be hurting any more people, but she carried with her a child, her demon seed, and this child has disappeared. As is the way of the evil, this witch had us all fooled. We thought she would bring peace and tranquility to our province, but she only brought famine and death, using her magical spells to doom us to poverty."

"So, what do ye want from us, stranger?" A drunken voice rang out from the back of the room.

"We must find this demon child and destroy her before she can wreak revenge upon our province. Has anyone seen the child? I have a pouch of Salandingar gems, the best known to man, for her capture. She is four or five summers of age. We know not what her looks, but her mother was tall with ebony hair and wicked green eyes."

The men of the lodge murmured amongst themselves. The pouch of gems represented more money than most families would see in two, maybe three, generations. Jorn listened to their tones carefully; thankful most were already so drunk they would forget the strangers in the morning's light.

Abruptly a fresh crop of chills worked up Jorn's back. When he glanced up, he found himself under the scrutiny of the black clad leader. Jorn managed to meet the man's steady gaze, willing his body to remain motionless and his face expressionless until the stranger moved his inspection elsewhere.

"Can ye believe that man?" Havard whispered. "He asked me about the girl upon his arrival. Jorn, ye know that I of all people would know if anyone discovered a child in the woo…" Havard's voice trailed off, his crystal blue eyes lighting up with understanding. "Oh, Jorn, you did not…"

Jorn gave a tiny shake of his head. "Havard, quiet! Ye will learn all soon enough," he whispered, confident he could trust Havard's discretion.

Unable to discern a culprit, the leader jumped down and joined his friends by the fire where they ordered a round of ale and began to whisper furtively amongst themselves. When he once again caught the strangers staring his way, Jorn ordered another ale for appearance's sake. He managed to consume the alcohol at a leisurely pace, although his heart was racing and he was anxious to be on his way home.

Draining the last of his ale, Jorn threw Havard a wink and whispered, "Play along, old friend." He then lurched clumsily to his feet and staggered in the direction of the door.

"Havard, me old friend," he announced with drunken slurs. "I must be going home now. Ye know Ildri…hic…She… will be…hic…worried." He chuckled as Havard steadied him.

"Jorn, my friend, I believe ye are drunk." Havard played his part perfectly. "Can ye make it home?"

Jorn nodded sharply and truly stumbled. Whoa now, he warned himself. It would not do to actually fall down and get hurt. "I brough' the mule," he slurred. "Tha' beast could find its way home in a blizzard."

As the two men stepped through the door, Jorn noticed the youngest of the strangers leave the table and follow them out. He and Havard remained silent on the walk to the stable where they found Jorn's mule contentedly munching hay. The animal gave a snort of protest when Jorn loosed the reins and led it out of the warm barn into the crisp night. In the time Jorn had been inside, the landscape had been dusted with a generous coating of snow.

"Speaking of blizzards, old friend," Havard announced loudly, "there is one on its way. Ye get home before the Fallow sets and get some sleep." Havard helped Jorn onto the mule's back, making a show of fastening the other man's cloak so he could whisper urgently in Jorn's ear, "Be safe, my friend. At the Fallow's first break, I will visit. I fear ye have a story to tell and I pray to the ten Lords of Hayrik ye have made a wise choice."

Jorn nodded and silently took his leave of the village square. Drifts had already begun to form by the time Jorn entered his own clearing. By then Jorn's joints were frozen and he had trouble getting down from the saddle. Despite the pain, Jorn was diligent in his care of the mule, feeding all the animals, even milking the cow. If indeed this was the first blizzard of Fallow, it might be a day or so before he could venture out of the house. Once again, he fought the anger. If he and Ildri had children, one or more would live on the farm with their parents, clearing the snow and handling daily chores, all of which would make the cold season much more bearable on aging bodies.

"This grumbling will not get the chores done, old man," he chided himself, spreading out fresh straw for the cow. Picking up the bucket of steaming milk, Jorn began the trek to the cottage, a light in the window his beacon through the snowfall.

Later, warming up in bed, Jorn related to Ildri the evening's events. Ildri immediately resolved to protect the girl and tried, well into the snow ridden night, to persuade her husband to see her way.

"The child is a blessing, Jorn," she pleaded.

"What if she and her mother are evil as the man suggested?" Jorn shivered, torn by indecision, remembering the black armored men.

"Jorn, was it not ye who shushed me earlier this eve? I cannot believe ye would think that of such an innocent!" Ildri exclaimed sharply.

She winced and looked up at the ceiling, waiting a moment to see if she had waked the child. When she once again resumed talking, her voice was once more soft and pleading. "Jorn, we can…" she dared not complete the thought for fear the putting her wish into spoken words would curse it.

Jorn merely leaned back upon the bed and stared at the ceiling.

He, too, had always yearned for children, as fiercely, if not more than his wife, but he had never vocalized his longings. Then the seedling of an idea formed, blossoming quickly. From the looks of tonight's storm, the cold season was upon them, which meant the farm would be isolated until the thaws of the planting season. Jorn sat up abruptly, startling his wife.

"Jorn!" she whispered intensely, this time mindful of the sleeping child. "What is it? Did you hear some…?"

Jorn silenced her with his hand. "No, Ildri," he murmured, his mind a whirlwind. Though his voice remained low, his words tumbled out quickly as if he were afraid of losing the idea before it gained life upon his lips. "Ildri, what if we told everyone your cousin from Flueren had crossed over and left a child, but there were no womenfolk left to raise her or, no, there were too many children already. And, your uncle, knowing we had borne no children of our own, sent us the child to raise as our own?"

"But, Jorn, those men…."

Jorn waved a hand. "They will be gone now that the cold season has set in. The people in the village, their memories are short. None will remember the strangers by the time the snows thaw. If we keep Kyreen here at the cottage all through the season no one will be the wiser…." Here Jorn paused. "No one," he whispered, "except Havard and he is trustworthy."

The only thing Ildri heard was that the child would be staying and would be their own to raise. An intense heat radiated from her inner being, making the old woman almost giddy with delight.

"A child! A daughter!" she clamored silently, resolved to lightwax and give thanks to Veran, Hayrik's Ninth Lord, the Lord of Good Fortune, first thing on the morrow.

In the dim light, Jorn watched his wife's excitement pluck years away from her beautiful face. Maybe a child would be good for them both, he thought. Someone who needed them, to make their lives worthwhile.

On impulse, he kissed his wife's cheek before whispering, "Good night, my lovely."

"Good night, Jorn," Ildri whispered. "I want to check on the chi… our daughter," she corrected herself, numb with disbelief, as she slipped from bed and up the ladder.

As she gazed lovingly down on the beautiful sleeping child, truly a gift from the Lords, a hand slipped to her cheek. Indeed, this child was a blessing, Ildri thought, for she could not remember the last time her husband had kissed her, let alone called her lovely.

Chapter 3

Time blurred...a meeting in the massive war room, loud voices, decisions made and challenged. Kyreen and Quillan sat quietly, huddled together in a chair at the huge table, surrounded by grim-faced adults. The children knew something very important and very scary was happening, but neither child was sure what. This was nothing like the retreats into the woods. This was Serious. At one point, Kyreen's eyes are drawn to the massive painting above Mama's chair, two people Kyreen has never met, but whose lives have been retold many times as bedtime stories. Their mother's parents, Queen Ursula, beautiful and exotic with her halo of ebony curls and emerald eyes, and King Rolf, handsome and sturdy with flowing dark brown locks and a wise sapphire gaze, look down upon the girl and she drew strength from their memories.

"We knew the Galorians had been too quiet. The fight was bound to flare again..." Kyreen heard in her mother's voice an edge never before present. For years, since before the twins' birth, the two warring countries had been, not at peace, but distant, no encounters, no contact at all.

"My queen," a voice interjected quietly. The girl recognized her guardian-uncle's voice, Arvis, not a native of this country. Kyreen knew he had been her father's best friend. Had been. Their father, also named Quillan, had died before the twins' birth at the hands of the Galorian emperor, Cathal. Kyreen shifted her position to see Arvis's face as he leaned forward, lavender eyes glittering in the lantern light.

"My queen," he repeated, "Reports are coming in. Faldor mercenaries, hired by Emperor Dolan, infiltrated the courtyards yesterday afternoon. Galorian troops advanced using night and cloud cover. Our Kyreen saw the first soldier begin his attack. If she had not..." He sat back allowing his comment to fade off.

The war council, a relatively new, inexperienced council, which had operated only in peace, looked at each other. Only two advisors, one man and one woman, remained from King Rolf's council. The others had perished in the same skirmish that had taken the children's father.

Kyreen watched her mother sigh deeply then move to her feet, just as the outer door burst open. A Calanian warrior stumbled into the war room, armor and helmet obscuring gender until she spoke.

"My queen," she panted, a ribbon of blood spreading from under

the armor, leaking down her arm. "They have...swarmed...castle walls.... Cannot...hold much... longer." Her message delivered, the warrior leaned against the wall and sunk to the floor, trembling hands fumbling with her helmet. All eyes focus on Tyra, seeking guidance from their queen.

Terrified, Kyreen clutched her brother's hand even more tightly, shrinking back against her chair, eyes glued upon the wounded soldier. She desperately prayed to the goddess that this is all a nightmare, prayed she will wake and they will be back in their room, prayed to have the morning sun shining through the window with the festival set to begin. Instead, strong hands scooped her up and she clung to her mother's side. The queen hurried to the concealed panel that leads to the tunnels below the castle grounds. Kyreen peeked over her mother's shoulder, searching for Quillan, safely ensconced within Arvis's embrace. Now it was his turn to reach out, sending good thoughts to his sister.

Calmer, Kyreen peered into the darkness as they descend, looking for the pair of glowing yellow eyes which as always would be waiting for them. The group of four passed the gargoyle. Last of the official guardians of the royal family, the massive beast took its post to the rear, trailing the group as they headed for the underground stables.

⁂

Sunbeams filtered through the treetops, casting soft shadows on the tall girl, errant curls escaping the dark plait hanging down her back. With deep inhalation, she extended her arms straight above her head. Exhaling slowly, the arms lowered and the slim body pivoted to the right. For several long moments the meditations continued, the lithe form moving through the age-old forms of a Calanian warrior. Eyes closed, Kyreen's lips moved, silently reciting the words of her history, words taught her by her mother to ensure Kyreen remembered her people, words she had faithfully recited twice daily for the last six years.

When finally her body returned to center and the green eyes opened, a light sheen of perspiration glowed upon the girl's upper lip despite the coolness of the spring morn. As always the Ceremony emptied her, preparing her for the filling of the day ahead. Scooping up her cloak, Kyreen headed toward the homestead. She did not want to be late. If she hurried she would get the bulk of the chores done before Jorn emerged from the cottage.

As always, when thinking of her foster father, conflicting emotions churned within the girl. She knew Jorn loved her, yet darkness and anger so often engulfed his mind, making it painful for Kyreen to spend much time around the old man.

As she emerged from the woods, nothing from the barn other than contented animals reached her mind and Kyreen relaxed. If Jorn or, very unlikely, Ildri had been in the barn, Kyreen would have felt it.

Ildri. The girl smiled. If the emotions within Jorn were conflicting, Ildri's were unswerving. Love radiated from the old woman's entire being. Though the energy was sometimes smothering, Kyreen was grateful for the consistency and appreciated Ildri's unconditional love.

"Unlike the lot of you ungrateful animals. You just love me for your food," the girl teased, walking into the barn. Primitive emotions of contentment and love from the cow, the mule and the goat—prompted by the girl's tone, not her words—enveloped Kyreen, instantly warming her.

Once she had pitched hay for the three larger animals, Kyreen herded the small flock of chickens outside. Leaving the scrabble for corn behind, she returned to the barn to check the nests. Now that Sowing had begun with the longer warmer days, eggs would be laid more frequently. Wrapping the fragile items in her cloak, she settled into the chore of mucking stalls. The peace of the barn enfolded the girl as she worked around the cow that watched her with mournful eyes. Ignoring both the cow and the now-bleating goat, Kyreen continued cleaning. Jorn would be here soon and milking was Jorn's job.

Over the past six years, Kyreen had learned the fine balance of which chores Jorn would relinquish and which ones he firmly held onto. As she spread straw in the last stall, Kyreen felt the mood of the animals shift and realized Jorn must have left the cottage. Emptying the barrow behind the barn, she placed it and the pitchfork by the straw pile, gathered the cloak and eggs, and made her exit out the back door. Walking around the outside of the barn, she ensured she would miss seeing Jorn. Some days he was gracious and accepting of Kyreen's help, others he was brooding and resentful.

"Kyreen! Lass, ye must have risen with the First Lord Hayrik to bring up the sun this morn! Come! Break fast, child!" Ildri's greeting immediately cheered the girl upon her entrance into the cottage.

As Kyreen moved the eggs from her cloak to basket, some leaves fell upon the floor, which the girl discreetly pushed under the table with the toe of her boot. While the older woman's vision had steadily faded over the past seasons and it was unlikely she would have noticed, Kyreen did not want to take the chance. Ildri never scolded Kyreen, but the girl felt the old woman's worry over Kyreen's trips into the woods. Ildri did not understand the cleansing ritual or the meditations and Kyreen did not have the heart to tell her adopted mother that the woods were more Kyreen's home than anywhere else. Perhaps it was because Kyreen and her birth mother had spent so many seasons in the wild, but Kyreen also had vague recollections of time spent in the woods even before the flight on her third birthday, dreamy images of making nests in shrub patches with her brother and practicing Stillness.

The girl ate quickly, washing down the dry bread with warm tea sweetened with honey. Before leaving the table, she palmed a few extra slices of fruit to share later with the mule. The animal, getting on in years just as its master, loved the sweet treats.

Kyreen cleared her dishes and began the daily sweeping, her thoughts turning once again to the problem of the mule. Jorn refused to buy an ox for the heavy work, grumbling the extravagance was unjustified, as the mule had always sufficed in past seasons. As much as Jorn complained about his aging bones, Kyreen knew the mule suffered similar aches. The old man scoffed, however, anytime Kyreen suggested these things. In Jorn's mind, the mule was merely an object, a tool to be used to get a job done, not a living creature.

Kyreen finished the sweeping, making sure to remove all the evidence of her early morning outing. Ildri, humming softly, had been tinkering in the cooking area. Stifling a groan, Kyreen remembered today was baking day. That meant staying indoors all day. No matter how she tried, Kyreen could not catch onto the subtleties of baking or cooking. While her actions and ingredients mimicked those of Ildri's, Kyreen's results were always dismal.

"Now where is Jorn with my milk?" Ildri muttered wiping floured hands on her apron. "I swear that man..."

A bellow from outside stopped Ildri's next words. Before the anguished cry faded, Kyreen was out the cottage door. One of the animals, the mule she believed, had panicked a mere moment before Jorn's yell. As Kyreen reached the barn, the mule came barreling through the door. Only her quick reflexes allowed Kyreen to grab the harness and with much effort she managed to pull the beast to a halt. Murmuring quietly, she stroked the animal's neck while gathering up the long reins with her other hand. It was lucky the mule had not become entangled and injured.

"Kyreen?" Ildri had followed the girl from the cottage. Her voice was full of fear.

"Something spooked the mule," Kyreen replied, keeping her voice low, the mule's pulse still racing beneath the girl's soothing hand.

"And Jorn?"

Kyreen glanced towards the building. The old man's voice had fallen quiet, but strong emotions radiated forth, pain, fear and, as always, great anger. She handed the reins to Ildri. "Take the mule and I shall check on him."

With an expression of caution mingled with distrust, Ildri stepped forward. She was merely a woman. She had no knowledge of animals; that was man's work. Still, Ildri did not wish to investigate herself, terrified she may find Jorn had crossed, leaving his empty body in the barn.

"Mother," Kyreen spoke with a slight edge to her voice. She was as reluctant to leave the mule with Ildri as the older woman was to be left with it, "If you stroke his neck, he will stay calm. Right here." Patiently, the young calloused hand guided the trembling blue-veined hand.

Sparing a final pat to the mule and a smile to Ildri, Kyreen entered the shadows of the barn. Underneath Jorn's emotions, she could sense the other two animals. They had not been panicked, so whatever happened did not occur by the stalls on the far side of the barn. Not sensing anything or anyone else, Kyreen found Jorn lying on the ground near the door she had exited just a short while earlier. Noting the unnatural angle of the arm positioned under his body, Kyreen knelt beside the old man. Judging from the torrent of emotions, she was fairly certain he was conscious.

"Jorn?" she inquired, using the same calming tone she had used on the mule. "Aside from the arm, where are you injured?"

"Do not worry about it!" Jorn barked. "Get that confounded mule! It has lost its mind it has! Knocking me over like that, out of the blue! Just wait until I get my hands on that animal."

Kyreen tuned out the ranting, her eyes moving towards the straw pile. What would have made the customarily docile animal so spooked? To Kyreen's knowledge, there were only two constant terrors to both horses and mules. The first, fire, obviously was not the culprit here. She rose, moving further into the shadows, brow furrowed pensively. These last few days of

Sowing had been pleasantly warm while the nights had continued to hold a chill. Something must have sought reprieve in the warmth of the barn, finding sanctuary within the straw. Never taking her gaze from the pile, Kyreen picked up the pitchfork, still leaning where she had placed it a short time ago, and began to poke at the straw.

"What in the name of the Ten Lords of Hayrik are ye doing, girl?" Jorn's voice rose in volume and pitch.

"Jorn?! Kyreen?! Is everything alright?" The concern in Ildri's voice was evident.

"What craziness is going on this morn? Has everyone lost their minds?" Jorn shouted, grunting as he sat up awkwardly using only his uninjured arm. "Kyreen, stop that foolishness and get…" Jorn's next words were cut short by his exclamation of surprise mingled with fear. "A serpent! By the Lords of Hayrik, evil has entered my barn! Kill it, child! Kill it now before it spreads illness to the animals!"

"Yes, Jorn," Kyreen replied calmly, pivoting towards the barn's rear entrance. "I shall take it outside."

"Aye. Do not spill that evil within the barn! The spirit might be trapped here!"

Balancing the long black snake on the end of the pitchfork, Kyreen made her way to the newly planted garden, taking care not to injure the creature. Crossing over to the forest's edge of the plot, she lowered the snake to the ground and watched it slither into the bushes. Her foster parents' superstitions aside, Kyreen appreciated the worth of a snake within the vegetable garden, the girl's single biggest responsibility on the farm.

This creature would help keep the rodents away. Last year so many blooms had been eaten by woodland creatures that the harvest had been much leaner than it should have been.

On her way back to the barn, Kyreen walked around front to take the mule from Ildri, who was red-faced with anxiety.

"Jorn has injured his arm. I do not know what else," she explained to the older woman as they entered the barn. Kyreen tied off the reins and replaced the pitchfork before again kneeling beside Jorn. The old man, his face extremely pale, had lain back down. Ildri hovered a short distance away, wringing her hands.

"Did ye destroy the vile creature?" he asked tersely, his good hand clutching the girl's arm.

Dislodging his grasp, Kyreen ran a light hand across the injured arm. "I took care of the serpent," she replied, avoiding the man's intense gaze.

"Serpent?" Ildri asked, backing towards the door, her blue gaze casting around the shadowy barn.

Kyreen spared the old woman a glance. "It is gone, Mother," she said gently. Looking back at Jorn, she inquired again, "Have you any other injuries? The arm is beyond me."

"My knee hurts. I do not think I can stand. What do ye mean the arm tis beyond ye, lass?"

"I believe it is broke," Kyreen stated. "I cannot fix that. The knee…" she paused as her fingers explored the joint, swollen and straining tightly against the fabric of his pants, "…is merely twisted. A poultice will help. But, Jorn, you need someone to care for the arm." Kyreen sat back on her heels, gazing steadily at the man. She appeared to be waiting for something, but he was oblivious.

"That would be Yorick, the apothecary. Help me up, lass."

With a firm grip on his uninjured arm, Kyreen assisted Jorn to his feet. As he did almost daily, Jorn marveled at the girl's tallness. Whether from Ildri's love or good cooking or both, the girl had flourished and grown over the last several years. The child was now almost Jorn's height. Though her frame remained lanky, Kyreen possessed great strength and stamina, both physically and mentally. The purpose with which she faced each day was startling to her foster parents. They had never known an adult, let alone a child, with such drive. Not once in six years had they ever needed to complain or coerce Kyreen to do her chores. Yes, she disappeared into the woods whenever possible, only remaining inside during the worst of Fallow snows, but always after the work was complete. Kyreen never shirked her duty. Jorn often wondered at her forays into the woods. He hesitated to press the girl for answers, not out of respect of her privacy, however, but more from the fear he would not like the answers.

Since the girl's arrival, Jorn's farm had steadily earned profits, a feat unseen for many seasons. Last Harvest had been so copious Jorn had hired two young men from the village to gather it all before Fallow. The men, boys really, had marveled at Jorn's wheat and had wondered, quite respectfully of course, how the old man had managed the Sowing alone. Jorn had evaded their questions. The Village knew he and Ildri had adopted a child, the orphan of a cousin from a neighboring province, but other than that…

Jorn stopped so abruptly that, had she not been expecting the epiphany, Kyreen would have stumbled. The pair had just emerged from the barn, Ildri trailing behind. Kyreen helped ease Jorn down onto the stump, the same one Jorn had rested upon the night he had brought Kyreen home, the morning sunlight comforting after the barn's shadows.

Kyreen began digging into the leather pouch she kept perpetually attached to her belt, leaving Jorn's thoughts to work out the problem. She withdrew a small dark, almost black, leaf and held it to Jorn's mouth. "Here. Rest it under your tongue. Do not chew. It will help the pain."

She next pulled out a dried pink flower and a few faded yellow-green leaves. These she popped into her own mouth and began to chew. Her gaze watched the man's face as he continued to puzzle through the situation. A moment later, the herbs in her mouth a thick mush, Kyreen pulled out her dagger, mumbled something about forgiveness to Jorn and, before he could react, sliced open his trousers at the knee. Ignoring both of her parents' objections, Kyreen spit out the poultice, smoothing it across the angry red joint. Using a strip of cloth from Jorn's ruined pants, she firmly bandaged the knee before standing up.

"It will feel warm, very warm, for a while. When it cools, tell me. It will need replacing then."

Jorn nodded, his blue eyes glassy. "What have ye done to me?"

"That's the ravenvine working to ease your pain. On your knee are herbs to draw out the swelling."

When Jorn did not respond, Kyreen looked at Ildri. "The arm must be set. I cannot do that. Jorn must go to the village."

"Of course, dear," Ildri replied distractedly nodding, keeping her eyes on Jorn. "Ye hitch the mule for ye father and he can…" her words trailed off as she arrived at the same realizations of Kyreen and Jorn. A hand shot to her mouth. "Oh, my! How shall he get to town?"

"Do not be daft, woman! I am capable of driving my own wagon."

"Do not be daft yourself, Jorn! Ye can barely walk. Your arm is useless."

"Then ye shall drive the mule. It is not difficult. Why must women make difficult so simple a deed?"

"Why must men be so dense?"

Kyreen hid a smile. She had rarely heard Ildri speak so sharply to Jorn. Ordinarily the old woman was very compliant.

Ildri placed her hands upon her hips, gazing down at her husband. "I cannot take ye to town, Jorn. For one, I know not how to drive the wagon. I would just as likely run ye into the creek as get ye to town. For another, today is baking day. The yeast is set and if I leave now we shall not have any edible bread for the next week."

As though realizing what she had just said, Ildri looked apologetically at Kyreen. "I beg forgiveness, lass. I mean no foul! It is just that... what I mean...."

Kyreen smiled, shaking her head. "Tis no foul, Mother. You only speak the truth. My cooking is not good enough to feed swine."

"Fine wife ye are! While ye are baking, my arm shall rot away!"

"Quit behaving like a squalling bairn, Jorn! Kyreen shall take ye."

Jorn looked at his wife, then Kyreen, then back at Ildri. His mouth opened, closed, opened again, and then closed once more. Many intense emotions radiated from the old man...fear, apprehension, and shame.

This last emotion struck Kyreen with such force it took all her will not to react visibly. Jorn was ashamed of her! Ashamed to take her to the village. Ashamed to let the villagers see her. After a moment, unable to stem the emotions shimmering in her eyes, Kyreen turned back towards the barn.

"I shall hitch the mule," she mumbled, anxious to escape the proximity of Jorn's emotions.

Oblivious to the conflict, Ildri called out, "Hurry, lass! Ye must change before heading to town!"

Kyreen frowned. She had hoped Ildri would not have remembered.

The first Fallow after Kyreen's arrival, while the family was confined during the snows, Ildri had sewed a wardrobe for the young girl. The first time the five-year-old Kyreen had donned a dress, it was only her natural reflexes that had saved the child from tumbling down the loft's ladder.

Despite practicing the entire Fallow season, the child had been unable to master the art of walking in a skirt. When Kyreen had burst forth from confinement when the last of the snows cleared, she had promptly tripped, her long strides tearing the skirt. Pride injured more than body, the girl had ripped slits in the front and back of the ruined dress before jumping up and disappearing in to the woods. Ildri, not having the heart to scold Kyreen, had eventually given up on making Kyreen dress like a girl. That did not prevent Ildri from sewing a new dress for Kyreen every year, just in case the girl had a change of heart.

When Kyreen climbed into her room in the loft a short while later, she found a dark blue dress, an apron of yellow and a sky-blue cap set upon her pallet. Ildri had also thoughtfully prepared a basin of warm wash water. Kyreen quickly bathed off the dust of the barn and began to dress.

"Mother? May I bother you?"

The strangeness of Kyreen's tone caused Ildri to ascend the ladder quickly. The dress bodice stretched tight across Kyreen's torso, the sleeves straining against her thin muscular arms, and the skirt fell quite short of the floor. When Ildri stubbornly attempted to fasten the bodice, a button popped off, clattering down the ladder.

"Oh, lass! What shall we do?" Ildri's eyes filled with tears.

"You feed me too well, Mother. It appears I grew a bit over Fallow," Kyreen commented, attempting to look disappointed while holding back a fit of laughter. "My other clothes are clean and fit well."

"Oh, lass!" Ildri repeated, sitting down on the edge of the pallet. "We cannot allow ye to go to town dressed like... like a..."

"A boy?" Kyreen offered, already tugging on her clean tunic.

"This is not a laughing matter!"

Kyreen recoiled, startled by the sharp tone in Ildri's voice, a tone the woman had never taken with the child before. Then the girl resumed dressing, sitting down to tug on her boots.

"It is an emergency, Mother," she finally said, "I do not see what it matters what I wear. It is Father who needs attention, and quickly."

"Ye are correct, lass," Ildri surrendered with a sigh, starting down the ladder. "Let us make haste."

Chapter 4

Two horses emerged from the labyrinth maze of tunnels and begin galloping madly into the early morning mist. Though only two hours had passed since Kyreen had awakened, the child remembered the predawn events vaguely as though a week had passed. The moon was no longer visible, having set while the sun announced its impending arrival with flashes of pink and gold across the eastern horizon.

Kyreen, riding behind her mother, gazed back at the gargoyle standing at the passageway opening, forbidden to leave the tunnels. Tentatively Kyreen raised a hand, waving farewell, not only to the creature but also to all that was familiar. The child leaned a cheek against her mother's back, ignoring the restless rumblings of her empty stomach, and allowed her eyes to close without complaint.

Mama was tense, filled with a strange emotion, something Kyreen had never felt emanating from the young queen. A part of the child worried about her own role in these recent events. Was it her fault? Did she start the fighting? Was that sleeping peasant killed because she was watching? What about the soldier in the war room? Did Kyreen cause her injuries, or worse, her death? As the anxiety built within, Kyreen recognized the icy tendrils snaking through her veins and was then able to give name to Mama's emotions...Fear. Mama was afraid. Arvis, as always, was unreadable. Instead Kyreen concentrated on the comfort of her twin's familiar essence radiating from his perch behind Arvis on the galloping horse, mirroring Kyreen's position behind their mother.

Unable to physically clasp hands or talk, the two continued to console each other. For although this dawn marks only their third birthday, both children fathomed the seriousness of the situation. This was a race for their lives. There will be time for comfort, food and rest later.

The sun was approaching midday when Kyreen drove the wagon into the small village of Hanoria for the first time. The girl's stomach fluttered with nerves and anticipation. A trip to the village was not something the family had ever discussed and Kyreen had never expressed an interest in visiting the village, preferring instead to remain at the farm, escaping into the woods whenever Jorn and Ildri had driven to the village. Kyreen now wondered about meeting other youth, maybe even finding friends. She had witnessed the camaraderie between Jorn and Havard on the latter's periodic visits to the farm. It was during those times that she daydreamed about finding a friend, someone with whom to share her thoughts and dreams. Kyreen missed her mother and her brother fiercely, and thought of them every single day. She was careful, however, never to mention them or the desire for friends to her foster parents for fear they may take her words as a sign of discontentment and thus become disappointed with their adopted daughter.

In addition to her own mix of emotions, Kyreen was trying to process the emotions flowing from Jorn. His anger in check, it felt as though the old man was more nervous than Kyreen about this visit to the village.

"That house there, with the red door," Jorn said gruffly, pointing with his good arm. The herb Kyreen had given him at the farm was beginning to wear off and his injuries were throbbing painfully. As he watched the girl maneuver the mule with ease, Jorn once more marveled at this child. The composure she had shown handling the serpent was remarkable behavior for a man, let alone a girl of only eleven seasons. But Kyreen also frightened Jorn. Despite his confident words to Ildri that snowy night so many Fallows ago, Jorn worried the men of the lodge would remember the strangers in black armor. Anything that the girl did to make herself stand out could only result in harm. Jorn's pride also worried someone would realize how much he, Jorn, relied upon Kyreen's help on the farm. That he was weak enough to need assistance was bad enough; receiving it from a female, an eleven-year-old girl, was the pinnacle of shame for any Hanorian man. He would be stripped of his spot on the Village Council, laughed out of the village, made an outcast in his own community.

A balding man appearing to be of middle years, his bushy beard a mass of bright auburn curls, stepped out of the house as Kyreen halted the wagon. Squinting up at them, he placed a pair of glass spectacles upon his face with sepia-stained hands.

"Jorn, by the Lords, what happened to ye?" he exclaimed, hurrying forward with extended hands to assist the older man from the wagon.

Kyreen, apparently unnoticed by the apothecary, waited until the pair disappeared into the building before stepping down from the wagon. Feeling foolish in the blue cap Ildri had insisted she wear,

Kyreen took off the headpiece and stuffed it under the wagon seat. The yellow apron covering her clothes she left on. Jorn may not notice the hat, but she was certain he would take note of a missing smock. She then fastened the mule to the post and glanced around the deserted square.

With Sowing well underway, most of the men were probably in the fields. Presumably all the women and girls were busy with baking or laundry or some other form of housework.

Unsure of what else to do, Kyreen entered the apothecary's shop in time to overhear the apothecary exclaim to Jorn, "...did a fantastic job. I never knew Ildri was so well versed with herbs."

"Aye," Jorn replied, his blue gaze observing the girl's silent entrance. "My wife has many talents. The knee is but a dull ache now."

Turning to mix some herbs, the apothecary took note of Kyreen. "Ah, ye must be Jorn's daughter. I am Yorick." He turned back to Jorn and began to apply the light green paste to the broken arm.

"Kyreen, sire. Well met and a pleasure," Kyreen replied, straining to recall the formal greeting Ildri had taught her many seasons prior. The girl bobbed a curtsey, feeling foolish with her pants and apron.

Yorick noticed the girl watching his hands as he began to wrap Jorn's arm. "Kyreen, well met. Are ye interested in apothecary, lass?"

"No!" Jorn's quick response echoed loudly through the small room. "She has no interest in such trivialities. Cooking is the lass's calling. Kyreen, go tend to the mule. Yorick does not need a youngster distracting him."

The sting of Jorn's harsh tone and the implication of both lies sent Kyreen reeling out the door. Unable to hold back the tears this time, she stood with her face pressed firmly against the mule's neck for many long moments. As the initial surge of emotion began to subside, sounds and emotions from nearby penetrated Kyreen's personal sorrow. Swiping the back of a hand across her eyes, she looked around, seeking the source of these new feelings. The narrow strip of road in front of the apothecary was empty. Voices, children's voices, carried across the wind from behind a row of tall shrubs lining the adjacent yard. Curious, Kyreen sneaked over.

"Engla is a baby!"

"Engla still plays with dollies!" "Does the baby want her dolly?"

Slipping to her knees, Kyreen crept under the bushes to peek out, absently nibbling at her bottom lip. Three boys and a girl, all blonde and blue-eyed, stood in the grassy clearing. The boys, much taller and obviously older, were positioned in a three-point circle around the little girl, tossing an object amongst them.

"Please, Markku! Do not hurt her!"

"Please, Markku! Do not hurt her!" The tallest boy mimicked. He stood with his back to Kyreen, tugging at the doll's arms, making as if to rip apart the toy. His intense delight at the small girl's misery washed over Kyreen, making her so nauseated that the hidden girl very nearly threw up.

The smallest of the boys, bearing a strong resemblance to the tormented girl, noticed Kyreen when she slipped out and stood up. In his surprise, he missed the tossed doll. Quick like a rabbit, the little girl darted forward, snatched up her doll and scampered across the clearing, away from her tormentors.

"Stian, you dolt! What is your problem?"

Seeing his cohorts staring behind him, Markku turned. A fresh sneer blossomed on his lip. "What… is… it?" he laughed.

Possessing an arrogance normally found in one much older, the boy strolled around the stranger, coming to a halt behind Kyreen, who had not moved a muscle or uttered a sound since standing. Though Kyreen gauged the boy to be a year or so older than herself, she stood slightly taller than he. Markku hooked a finger under Kyreen's braid, lifting up the plait scornfully. "Ye dress in trousers like a boy, yet ye have hair like a girl."

"And wears an apron," the third boy added tentatively. Kyreen took him to be Markku's younger brother, his emotions balancing precariously between anxiety to please and fear of reprisal.

Kyreen remained motionless, giving no visible sign that she had heard either of the boys' words. Markku dropped the plait, wiping his hand on his trousers. "It is too dumb to answer," he proclaimed. Bolstered by their leader's actions, the other two boys sauntered over, laughing.

Engla, watching from across the clearing, clutched the doll to her chest. Though she did not know who the stranger was, Engla was intensely grateful that the boys' attentions had been diverted. Under normal circumstances, Stian was a wonderful brother. When Markku and Kalle visited, however, her brother became a vile creature, just like his friends. Thank the Lords of Hayrik, the boys' visits were not frequent.

Engla had seen the strange girl's arrival through those same bushes just moments before, but had not recognized the old man that Poppa had helped into the shop. It had been this distraction that had allowed Markku and the others to sneak up on her. Now Engla stared at the exotic face, so exquisite yet so impassive, and thought she had never witnessed such beauty in all her ten years. It was then Engla knew she could not allow this girl to face the boys alone. She took two steps forward.

"Leave her alone, Markku!"

The stranger's green eyes which had been watching Markku, flicked towards Engla briefly before returning quickly to the boy. The younger girl thought the stranger's lips had lifted in a brief smile, but the gesture was so fleeting it may have been the fabrication of a little girl's overactive imagination.

"Kyreen!" Jorn's voice rang out from next door.

Instead of retreating the way she had arrived, Kyreen pivoted away from the group of boys and began to walk around the bushes. Seeing Markku stoop down, his hand closing around a rock, Engla's mouth opened to call out a warning. The words died unspoken upon her lips as the tall stranger sidestepped, plucking the stone from the space her head had just occupied.

Kyreen spun around, smoothly shooting the small projectile back towards an unsuspecting Markku. The girl's aim was true and Markku was not nearly so quick. The boy dropped to the ground, a red mark blossoming in the middle of his forehead. Kyreen stood ready, balanced on the balls of her feet, eyes moving between the two remaining boys, who, upon seeing their leader prone, scampered away.

Yorick emerged at the edge of the bushes in time to witness Stian and Kalle disappear around the corner of the building. The man looked between his daughter clutching her doll, Markku on the ground and Kyreen in battle stance. Given Markku's unsavory reputation, Yorick had no difficulty discerning the situation. He motioned the two girls to him and, with an arm around each, guided them back into his front yard where Jorn was already sitting up in the wagon, waiting for Kyreen.

"It appears Kyreen has made my daughter's acquaintance," he announced to Jorn. "Maybe Engla can travel with me next week to check on your recovery?"

"Oh, Poppa! That would be wonderful! Thank you!" Engla exclaimed, her blue eyes sparkling at the thought of spending time with this strange girl, so different from any other person she had ever met.

Kyreen climbed up into the wagon, feeling angst at her actions in the clearing and also feeling the disapproval from Jorn. Wordlessly, she gathered up the reins as Jorn made his farewells to Yorick.

"Jorn, since ye are in town anyway, ye should check out the

livestock sale," Yorick mentioned, gently patting the mule's haunches. "Your mule is looking a bit ragged."

Kyreen mentally flinched. Though she knew Yorick's comment had been innocent and good-natured, she worried about Jorn's reaction. To her surprise, the old man nodded. The sedative must still be working, she thought.

"Poppa, may I go, too?" Engla asked impulsively, then winced remembering her manners. She bobbed a curtsey towards Jorn to add, "With the good sir's permission?"

At Jorn's curt nod, Yorick lifted his youngest child up into the back of the wagon. He placed a kiss on her cheek with whispered warnings to be on her best behavior. As he watched the wagon roll away, Yorick remembered the fallen boy in the adjacent yard. When he walked around the corner of the shrubs, however, the clearing was empty.

Chapter 5

The sun was high in the cloudless sky when the travelers reached the fork. A wide well-traveled road continued south, while a smaller, less used trail turned east toward the desert provinces. Pulling up, Tyra allowed the twins a few minutes on the ground, urging them to scamper off to play in the shade of an ancient oak. She and Arvis dismounted and huddled in conference.

Kyreen stooped to pick up some pebbles, presumably joining her brother in throwing rocks into the bushes, but her attention and her mind were with the adults. While Mama's mind was still closed, the child sensed a deep sadness. A change was happening and it was not good.

After a quick embrace with Arvis, Tyra turned to her children, motioning them forward. Arvis quietly ruffled Kyreen's head with affection before remounting his steed. Tyra gathered her son into her arms and embraced him tightly, pressing a fierce kiss to his satin cheek before handing him up to Arvis. Once the lad was settled in front of him, Arvis gave the queen a final nod and wheeled the horse around, departing in a cloud of dust down the trail heading east. Tyra stood still, gazing after them long after they had disappeared and the sound of the horse's hooves had faded into the dappled shadows.

"Mama?" Kyreen asked tentatively. Tyra's grief washed over her, scaring the young child.

Despite her strong resolve, Tyra's face was wet when she looked down at her daughter. "Yes, my love. We must get started." Scooping the child up and settling her before her on the tall sorrel gelding, Tyra reined the horse around and spurred it on, heading down the wide road to the southern provinces.

The pair rode in silence, each lost in their thoughts. The woman thinking of her two golden loves, her deceased husband and their son, the boy she hoped would survive. She determined this plan had to work and he must live. Both her children would live; she would die for their survival.

The child leaning against Tyra concentrated fiercely, stretching her mind as it had never been stretched, aching to keep contact with her brother. The bond continued to fade bit by bit as the two groups moved steadily apart until finally, just as the last light faded from the dense woods, Kyreen lost her brother's thoughts. Never before in her young life had she felt so alone.

Always the two had been together, their connection even closer because of being twins. As the waning moon began its ascent, silent tears trailed down the girl's cheeks and the tall sorrel's tireless gait continued southbound, taking her farther and farther away from her brother.

Ildri absently stirred the stew, her thoughts not on the dinner she was preparing. Jorn and Kyreen had been gone so long the sun was beginning to set over the mountains. About the time the old woman had begun to wonder how she could make it to the village on foot in the dark, she heard the rumble of wagon wheels. Relieved beyond words, she hurried from the cottage and stopped short at the sight before her.

Behind the wagon trailed not one, not two, but three animals, a black ox, its horns trimmed to mere nubs, and two horses of a dusty chestnut color. The coats of all three were shaggy, ill-kept and dull in the evening light. From her position across the yard, Ildri saw that the animals were all underfed, ribs evident in the steer and the smaller of the two horses. The larger horse's belly was completely distended, causing its back to sway unmercifully and even one as unschooled in animals as Ildri could tell the mare was close to dropping a foal.

"…and I will fix up the back stalls," Ildri overheard Kyreen tell Jorn as the old woman walked over to the wagon. Ildri had never heard her daughter's voice so animated. Kyreen's fair skin was flushed pink and her eyes sparkled brightly as she hopped down from the wagon. The girl hugged Ildri and bade her a good evening before skipping into the barn.

Ildri instinctively reached up to assist Jorn from the wagon and was mildly surprised when he did not brush her hand away.

"By the Lords, Jorn, I had begun to worry. What are these?" she said with a glance to the unfamiliar animals. Up close they looked even more forlorn and ragged than before.

"An ox… to help with the Sowing."

Ildri glanced sharply at her husband. He had been stubbornly refusing to purchase new livestock for the past two Sowings. She wondered what had changed his mind and then, noticing the way he watched the doorway into which Kyreen had disappeared, Ildri thought maybe she should not ask.

Jorn attempted to maintain an appearance of nonchalance, but inwardly he still reeled from the day's events.

Upon arriving at the livestock sale with Kyreen and Engla, Jorn had agreed to consider purchasing an ox, if the price was not too steep. Allowing for his knee, which still ached, Jorn had stood at the head of the sale aisle and watched Kyreen peruse the stock available for purchase. With Engla trailing behind her, the girl had carefully made her way down the wide walkway, occasionally pausing before continuing, yet never conversing with the men, who paid the two girls no notice.

Watching Kyreen closely, Jorn noticed she did not even glance into certain stalls. Sometimes the stock was inferior, but not always. Gradually it dawned on Jorn that Kyreen was avoiding the sellers with less than desirable business reputations. The pens where the girl did pause offered quality stock sold by honest reliable men.

When Kyreen and Engla had traversed the entire length of the barn, they walked back to Jorn and Kyreen said quietly, "The second stall from the end. He offers good stock. It is thin and needs care, but is sound. It looks to have traveled long and hard. I believe you can purchase it for low dinars."

Indeed, Jorn did not recognize the tall lanky stranger with light brown hair and beard. His clothing was dusty and he had the same disheveled look as the beast he was selling.

"There are two horses in the adjacent stall," Kyreen continued in hushed tones, "The man, he is eager to go to the lodge. He might throw them in as well…if you were to ask."

Jorn looked at the miserable creature and then at his daughter. In her eyes, he saw again the strong proud woman from the clearing six years prior. Kyreen had her mother's looks, could she not also possess the same magic? Suppressing his anxiety at the thought, Jorn mentally prepared to negotiate.

"Aye, lass. Ye wait in the wagon whilst I barter."

The stranger's face stayed guarded as the old man hobbled towards him. All morning these Hanorian men had been walking past him and his small selection without a first glance, let alone a second. It looked to be another long day at the end of a long journey. Road bandits had hijacked his caravan a fortnight hence mid-way to Hanoria. The only reason he had his life was that he had been in the brush looking for these three miserable creatures when the bandits had struck.

"Hail and well met," Jorn greeted, leaning a shoulder against the stall post, his gaze fixed on the ox. "Long journey," he stated, not questioning.

"Aye," the man answered, not in the mood for small talk.

Jorn opened with a ridiculously low amount, as was tradition. For the next few minutes, the two exchanged words, adjusting the price up and down. As the deal looked to be nearing agreement, Jorn spared a glance into the adjacent stall.

"Your stock as well?" The merchant nodded. "For sale?"

"Aye. Another ten dinars?"

Jorn appeared to consider, his eyes drifting between the two stalls. He allowed his eyes to rest long upon the pair of horses, even more bedraggled than the ox. "I offer two more dinars."

"Eight?"

"Two."

"Six?"

"Two."

"Four?"

As Jorn pushed off the post to turn away, the merchant stepped forward. "Wait, good sir! Two dinars more. Yes. That is a fair price."

After signing the papers to authorize the money exchange and taking possession of his new stock, Jorn had stopped in at the lodge to visit Havard. Not only would it have been unseemly for Jorn to come to the village and leave without seeing his best friend, but the old man craved a quick tankard of ale before beginning the long trip back to the farm. He left Kyreen and Engla sitting in the back of the wagon.

"I nay had a chance to thank you," Engla began shyly after several long minutes of silence, "For getting my doll back from the boys."

Kyreen, unsure of the proper response, said, "I do not believe they would have truly harmed the doll."

Another uncomfortable silence fell for several moments between the girls. Engla shot a sidelong glance at the older girl. "Would ye mind if I came to the farm with Poppa when he visits your father?"

Again, unsure of what to say, Kyreen stated, "It is a long trip and the farm is not much to look at."

"Engla!"

Both girls jumped as Stian's head popped over the edge of the wagon. He grinned at his sister then glared at Kyreen, who looked over his shoulder for the boy's friends.

"I am alone," Stian said peevishly, climbing up into the wagon, making sure to keep his sister between himself and the strange girl. He fixed his blue gaze on Kyreen, trying to emulate Markku's sneer. The result was a pained expression.

"What are ye doing with… with…" In the absence of Markku and Kalle, Stian's true amicable demeanor surfaced and he visibly deflated. "Sorry," he mumbled, lowering his head to stare at the hands folded in his lap.

Kyreen felt no animosity within the boy and opened her mouth to say so, but stopped when Engla cuffed her brother on the back of the head.

"Why do ye have to be so daft, Stian?" his sister scolded.

Kyreen was shocked when the boy accepted the rebuff of his younger sister without any reaction, physical or emotional.

Engla continued her reprimand, "Every time Markku and his brother show up, ye transform into a fiend. I will tell Poppa this time, Stian. Truly I will. Markku could have hurt Kyreen with that stone."

Stian stole a look at the silent dark-haired girl before looking at Engla. "But he did nay hit her. She…" he pointed towards Kyreen with his chin, "…hurt him. She dropped him like a hunted stag. He could be dead, ye know."

"Who could be dead?"

All three children jumped hearing Jorn's voice. Kyreen's face flushed bright red, embarrassed to see the old man and his best friend Havard standing beside the wagon. Without being prompted, the two Hanorian children scrambled over the side and dropped to the ground.

"Who could be dead?" Jorn repeated his question.

"The squirrel Stian shot this morn whilst ye visited with Poppa," Engla interjected quickly before Stian, his mouth open, could reply.

She bobbed a curtsey to Jorn and Havard. "Fare thee well, good sirs. With your leave, my brother and I shall return home on foot."

With another quick curtsey towards Jorn, Engla added, "Thank you for bringing me to the sale."

Jorn, preoccupied with the task of climbing into the wagon, nodded briskly. "Ye are welcome, child. Tell your father we expect him in a fortnight. Ye are invited as well."

Engla turned her sparkling gaze to Kyreen, who had climbed into the front seat. "Well met, Kyreen. I shall see ye in a fortnight."

"Aye. Uhm…well met, Engla," Kyreen stammered.

After Havard and Jorn completed their farewells and the tavern keeper had disappeared back into his establishment, Engla and Stian stood side-by-side watching the wagon roll off, Engla clutching the doll to her chest and fiercely wishing the fortnight to pass quickly.

"And the horses?" Ildri's question jolted Jorn out of his thoughts.

"What?"

"The horses, Jorn," Ildri repeated. "What shall we do with them?"

"The lass thinks they be of quality stock and can make us a profit with some fattening."

Uninterested in the business of farming, Ildri turned back towards the house. "Very well then. Please hurry Kyreen along. Dinner is ready."

Jorn nodded absently, his gaze returning to the empty barn doorway. All the way home, an uncommonly animated Kyreen had talked endlessly about breeding horses, training horses, developing a herd, even pasture rotations. The plans the child had made in such a short time were extraordinarily complex, yet sound. Once again Jorn recalled how Kyreen had avoided shady merchants and found a decent man with good stock despite outwardly appearances. Even Havard had been impressed with Jorn's purchase, noticing the quality underneath the shabby coats and had congratulated Jorn on his shrewd business sense. Slipping a flask from his pocket, Jorn took a long drink of spirits before hobbling into the barn to fetch his daughter.

Chapter 6

It was almost morn before Tyra felt safe enough to rest. Hobbling the exhausted horse, she laid the blanket out and set the sleeping child upon it. Driven to near exhaustion herself, the queen was too wound up to sleep. Dutifully she chewed on some bread and cheese, resting against a tree trunk, her mind ever alert and working on plans for their survival. After some time, she dozed, for it was her child's soft hand, not the faint baying of hounds, which awakened her.

Kyreen, her toiletry executed, fresh water in the canteen from the nearby stream, held the horse by its reins. "They woke me just a bit ago," the child explained, nibbling her bottom lip tentatively. "I could not get the saddle on, Mama. I tried."

Relief and panic simultaneously assaulted the young queen. Their pursuers have taken her trail, not Arvis and Quillan's. Her son was safe. Now she must evade the men following her and take her daughter to safety.

"You did well, my child," Tyra said softly, rising to finish tacking the horse.

Within minutes the two are back on the trail, leading their pursuers ever southward.

"Hey, witch!"

"Sorceress!"

"Get back to the farm where ye were hatched, strangeling!"

Kyreen continued leading her horse down the street, ignoring taunts from the six youth trailing behind her. Technically they were young men, all around the same age as she, though Kyreen stood taller than them all. She kept her gaze down, watching the toes of her dusty boots, alert for thrown stones, just wanting to keep the gelding from harm. When Kyreen turned into the apothecary's yard, the group scattered after spying Yorick in the doorway.

"Kyreen, well met, child! Enter! Come, come!" Yorick greeted the girl, oblivious to the conflict just beyond his yard. Warm emotions flooded from the man as he guided Kyreen into his shop where Engla was working on a pile of mending.

As Yorick excused himself to the back where he was mixing herbs, Engla motioned Kyreen into a chair.

"Well met, Kyreen! Have they been at ye again?" she asked, seeing the grim set of her friend's jawline.

"Aye, Engla, but do not permit them to worry you," Kyreen answered. "As long as all they toss are words, no one is harmed."

"If only ye would permit me to tell Poppa. He would take care of them, especially Markku. That lad needs a lesson."

Kyreen shook her head. "They only follow the lead of the older men who treat me no better. At least the youth are upfront and open about their disdain."

Worry framed Engla's round face as she looked at her dear friend. It always amazed her how forgiving Kyreen could be. Engla knew the older girl had a temper, but Kyreen always kept control of her emotions. It was just one of the tall ebony-haired girl's many traits that Engla envied.

Despite the distance to Jorn's farm separating them, the friendship between the two girls had blossomed over the last eight years. Kyreen had continued to grow like a young sapling and was as tall as the tallest man in the Village. Her exotic looks and her quiet demeanor made her a prime target on her few ventures to town.

For Engla and her brother Stian, their acceptance into the Village had been easier. For, while the siblings had not been born in the Village and their father was an outsider, their mother was a native Hanorian. It also helped that the brother and sister physically resembled the other villagers with their blonde hair and blue eyes. Still, because of their father's profession, the villagers remained wary of the apothecary and his family. Yorick would never be offered a place on the Town Council, and both of the siblings remained unmarried without any marriage prospects. Hanoria had been without an apothecary for several years when the family returned to the province, yet the bulk of Yorick's business took place from his back door in the shadows of the night. Most Hanorians refused to cross his sill during the light of day, believing his potions to be sorcery.

"How is ye mother?" Engla inquired, continuing with her mending. Kyreen sighed. "Ever the same."

Four years prior, Kyreen had discovered Ildri collapsed on the floor one afternoon. When the old woman's eyes had opened once more, the light had disappeared. She could be hand fed and would walk compliantly wherever guided. Left to her own volition, however, Ildri would sit in one place all day, silently rocking back and forth. Despite Yorick's potions and

Kyreen's tender care, Ildri continued to be uncommunicative and listless. Kyreen, who had taken over running the farm due to Jorn's own failing health, had added the household chores to her other duties.

With Ildri ill, Kyreen had been forced to change the farm's main crop from wheat to alfalfa, much to Jorn's chagrin. Finally, after many years of barely breaking even, the wheat harvests following Jorn's purchase of that first ox had been extremely profitable, requiring even more extra help from the village. Jorn had even purchased an additional ox and double yoke plow.

While the wheat crops had done well, however, profits from the horse business were double those of the wheat income. The mare, her yearling stud colt and the foal dropped days after their arrival to the farm had all flourished under Kyreen's care. The yearling colt had grown into a fine stud, having sired many exceptional foals over the years. As Kyreen had planned, the farthest fields, never cleared for farming, had been developed into excellent grazing lands for the growing herd. Continuing to depend on Kyreen's good eye, Jorn had purchased more mares each Sowing season while a handful of quality yearlings were taken to sale.

Those few horses always brought in more dinars than an entire year's wheat harvest ever did. But once Ildri took ill, Kyreen had pointed out that she could not handle a bountiful wheat harvest so Jorn had relented.

After the switch to alfalfa, maintenance around the farm had drastically decreased and Jorn had begun spending more time in the Village at the lodge with Havard. Some nights he did not even bother returning home, choosing instead to sleep in town.

"Greetings, Kyreen! How are ye?" Stian burst through the door, his blonde hair disheveled. After planting a kiss on his sister's head, Stian dropped into a chair. "I did not expect ye until the morn. Jorn did nay say ye would be coming to town when I saw him."

Despite their thorny beginnings, Stian and Kyreen's friendship had also flourished over the years. With no desire to follow his father into apothecary, Stian spent many days at Jorn's farm with Kyreen. The two were always planning and talking about the farm. While Kyreen's heart was in the livestock, Stian's interest lay in the farm itself. He was extremely knowledgeable in rotation and planting schedules.

"Ildri needed herbs," Engla explained, using her teeth to cut the thread from a hole she had just repaired on a pair of Stian's trousers.

"Has she turned for the worse?" Stian's concern was two-fold.

Kyreen shook her head. "No. Rest easy, friend. The trip is still on. We leave for Orra at first dawn."

While that first livestock purchase had impressed the village men, many came to suspect in the subsequent seasons that, while Jorn made the physical purchase, it was his strange dark-haired daughter who actually chose the stock. Shortly after, the Village council passed an ordinance forbidding women to attend the sales, thus preventing Kyreen from going into the barn. To avoid this trifle of village politics, Kyreen and Stian made the trek to Orra's sales twice a year. This year, in addition to looking for new mares, Kyreen planned to take three yearlings colts to sell.

"Jorn did not return home last night. He did not know my plans," Kyreen answered, a slight frown creasing her brow. Stian did not normally frequent the lodge. "When did ye see him?"

"Last night," Engla answered. "He came visiting with Poppa."

"What for?"

The siblings shrugged in unison.

"Poppa did nay say," Engla answered, glancing towards the doorway leading to the shop located in the back of the house, "But he has been in a good mood all morning."

"I thought he seemed overly happy," Kyreen commented, her own gaze drifting towards the front door. "If you will excuse me, mayhap I should go speak with Yorick."

Before either of her friends could react, Kyreen disappeared into the back room. A heartbeat later, the front door burst open and a blond youth entered, his breath ragged from running.

"Kalle!" Engla exclaimed startled, once again wondering at Kyreen's remarkable ability to discern the future.

Kalle ignored the girl, his gaze finding and fixing upon Stian. "Why did ye not say anything this morn? Did ye think we would nay find out? Tis the talk of the lodge, Stian!"

Stian looked over at his sister, then back at Kalle, perplexed, "What is the talk? Ye make no sense, Kalle."

"Kyreen! You! To wed! How could ye do it? I know she tis ye friend, but as a wife? Ye must be daft, man!"

"Kyreen and Stian wed?" Engla set down her mending and rose to her feet. "Kalle, is this one of your dim-witted jokes? Tis nay funny if so."

"Engla, I kid about many things, but Kyreen and Stian wed tis nay funny. Tis disastrous! Tis…." Spying Kyreen in the doorway, Kalle's words trailed off. He immediately backed through the door, mumbling farewell to Stian and Engla.

Once Kalle was gone, Stian looked at Kyreen, red-faced. "I did nay know, Kyreen. I… I…"

Engla looked into her friend's face and realized Kyreen was not in shock like herself and Stian. No, Kyreen was struggling to control her temper. Engla walked across the room, reaching up to put an arm around Kyreen. "I am sure this is simply a rumor, started by that dreadful Markku. Let us have tea to calm your nerves."

"No," came the soft reply. "It is true. Your father just told me. If Stian agrees to marry me, Jorn shall give him control of the farm and the herd." Kyreen shook off Engla's arm and strode to the door.

"Kyreen! Please!" Engla called. "I do nay believe ye should see Jorn in this mood!"

The girl paused and glanced over her shoulder at Engla. "I have no plans on seeing that old man," she said, turning her gaze to Stian. "Is there any reason you cannot leave today?"

Stian shook his head. "No, none."

"I shall bring the yearlings back by midday. The moon is full. We shall ride into the night." Looking back at Engla, Kyreen added, "Your father has the list of herbs for Ildri. Will you ensure Jorn receives them?"

"Of course. Are ye sure this is best, Kyreen? Should ye leave?"

"You were correct, Engla. I should not see Jorn in this mood. I may not be able to control my actions if I were to see his face. His name may be upon the farm and the herd, but he does not own me. I am not chattel and shall not stay around to be sold as such."

Although Kyreen took care not to slam the front door, Engla still flinched at its closing. Though her own instincts were not at honed as her friends, the young Hanorian felt a storm brewing. Casting a final glance at her brother, who was still staring at the front door, Engla turned back to her mending, uttering a silent prayer to the ten Lords of Hayrik for her best friend, her brother and for their journey.

Chapter 7

Predawn gray filtered through the bushes, surrounding the two sleeping forms. Suddenly the small form moved, instantly awake. She heard something, something foreign, something close. She paused to listen, small teeth nibbling at her bottom lip. Mama was sleeping and Kyreen had felt her mother's exhaustion. The days have shortened and nights are much cooler. Kyreen would have liked to remain at the warm beaches and salt grass marshes where they had spent several restful weeks at the beginning of the summer solstices, but something spooked Mama and she had insisted they keep moving south. Then, with last full moon, they had turned eastward, towards the mountains. When Kyreen first spotted the mountains, they were just distant shadows and sometimes she could not see them at all.

Then last night, just before dusk, Mama had paused on top of a tall hill, looking back as always. Kyreen, unable to catch her breath, had gazed forward...and up. She could barely see the darkening sky peeking over the summit height. She wondered if Mama truly planned on climbing all the way up. She wondered too what they might find on the other side. Did it drop off into nothing or was there another slope going down into another valley? Maybe there was another vast ocean stretching out forever like the one at the beach in the west.

Mama, more distracted than usual, had not been in the mood for questions or even talking. Instead Tyra had handed Kyreen a stale chunk of bread, their last bit of food, and pushed the girl on until well after dark. The light of the rising half-full moon had radiated from behind the shadow of the mountains when the pair had finally stopped for the night.

Evening was the time of day Kyreen missed the horse most of all. Yes, it was hard to walk all day instead of riding, especially when Mama heard something which made her especially anxious and pushed Kyreen into a run. But the girl missed more than the transportation. Besides being another presence for the lonely child, the act of tacking and untacking, or brushing the shiny sorrel coat, feeding and watering, all soothed Kyreen. The normality of the caring for the horse was a familiar and comforting undertaking, something she would have done had she still been home, had they never had to flee Calan and... her brother.

Quillan entered Kyreen's thoughts many time during the day, but even more so at night. She tried not to be sad because Mama would feel it and Mama did not need a crybaby. Mama needed Kyreen to be a Big Girl and to be Strong. Still Kyreen missed her brother so much that her insides ached, not a sharp stick poking her in the stomach like when she was hungry but more of a deep ache that started way down inside and spread out from her center, engulfing her entire being.

Another noise drew Kyreen's attention back to the present. Definitely close and definitely not a forest creature Kyreen's instincts told her. Even as Kyreen debated with herself, wondering if this was Important or a false alarm, a form appeared overhead, just a dark outline, and Kyreen sensed the man for the first time. His intent was not congenial.

The girl realized this must be one of the men from whom they have been running for two years now and who her mother feared ... no, Kyreen thought, fear was not the right word... This man and his companions alarmed her mother. Kyreen was the one who was always afraid and Mama was the strong one. Even as Kyreen had these thoughts, the leaves above her began to rustle. The man was simply searching. He had inadvertently stumbled across their nest. Kyreen watched with increasing alarm as a hand, encased in black leather, appeared. The man's fingers curled around a branch and started to pull an opening.

Mama surely must be fatigued if Kyreen's internal panic had not yet jarred her awake. That same panic rendered the child immobile, unable to move or speak. Then, as the unsuspecting man began to bend forward, his features still obscured in shadows, Kyreen's hand found the dagger resting upon her mother's abdomen. The small hand wrapped around the hilt tightly and, without a sound, Kyreen thrust upward with all her strength. The razor-sharp weapon slid into the man's cheek. Rising to her feet, Kyreen forced the blade up, up, up, along the side of the man's face, until the blade slipped out at his scalp line.

With the first of the mercenary's scream Tyra was on her feet and instantly alert. The man dropped to his knees, hands covering his bloody face. In the commotion of the other men running to aid their leader, Tyra gathered the child into her arms and slipped unnoticed out of the thicket, giving thanks to the goddess for the initial confusion. Had the hound keeper thought to release the dogs, who were barking wildly, she and Kyreen surely would have been captured.

Tyra fled silently through the forest, slowed down by Kyreen's weight, but too spooked to stop until finally the child's weight became too much. Tyra set her daughter down, taking the bloodied dagger from the child's fist before pulling Kyreen close. For a long moment—too long for safety, too short for relief—they embraced.

A sennight after Jorn's attempt at a nuptial bargain, Kyreen and Stian returned to Hanoria. The trip into Orra had given the friends the time necessary to discuss the situation. Though Kyreen could understand the old man's motivation, she still had difficulty forgiving him for taking such actions without first consulting her. Now, on the way back to Hanoria, with her anger subsided, Kyreen resolved to work this out with Jorn upon her return to the farm. Primarily, Kyreen had been happy this episode had not affected her friendship with Stian.

As for the business trip, the yearlings had sold extremely well in Orra, but Kyreen had not found any mares to purchase even though she diligently attended the auction all four days, even lingering an extra day to inspect the livestock barns. More than once she had silently wondered if maybe Jorn's attempt at an arranged marriage had been too much of a distraction. As for Stian, every evening, once the business of the day was complete, he disappeared into the taverns as he had taken to doing on previous trips, leaving Kyreen to fill her evenings alone in her rented room, reading a novel borrowed from the innkeeper.

Their morning's journey from Orra began with a chill that quickly burned away with the rising of the sun. With Sowing Season well underway the road remained mostly empty, allowing the two to ride side by side and talk. Farmsteads here were situated well off the roadway, and trees were sparse; most of the forest in this area having been cleared generations ago to be used in houses and barns. Still the rolling hills obscure any long distance views. Both horses knew the road well and, realizing they were headed home, their pace quickened.

Even so the afternoon cast shadows upon the riders and their horses when they finally reached Hanoria proper. Kyreen adjusted the cloak about her shoulders and pulled up the hood, thankful for the calfskin gloves shielding her fingers from the biting wind.

"Before we return to the village," Stian said, his resolve hitting Kyreen in waves, "I must entreat you once more. Will ye reconsider Jorn's betrothal proposal?"

Although she did not wish to revisit this subject again, Kyreen heard the yearning in her friend's voice and suppressed the flare of anger in her breast before answering. "Stian, you know you are one of my dearest friends, second only to Engla…" she began.

"Then what be your objections?" Stian implored. "We work well together. We would make a good match. The farm would thrive under my management. You could continue working with the herd. I do not see any problems with the arrangement."

Kyreen exhaled softly, unsure how to explain her reasoning. "A marriage bond is sacred," she said, adding softly, "and intimate."

Stian's blue eyes widened, his cheeks reddening with embarrassment. "Are ye worried about the marriage bed? I would not expect that of ye! I am sure a sleeping arrangement could be made…" His voice trailed off, though it appeared there was more he wished to say.

Kyreen eyed her friend for a long moment before responding, her kind tone softening her words, "I believe that you believe what you say, Stian, but I am not sure I could be happy with anything less than a full marriage."

If possible, Stian's face turned even redder. The emotions he exuded were a mix of shame and anger, hurt and chagrin. His eyes shimmering, he mumbled, "Please keep your mind open until we speak with Jorn?"

Kyreen nodded and the two fell silent as their horses crested the final hill and the Village came into view. Thoughtfully she nibbled her bottom lip, pondering on the emotions swirling within her friend. She knew he was truthful about not wishing to bed her, for she had been sensing that emotion for years from the Hanorian men. While their voices shouted with hurtful words and their faces glared with anger, always beneath the surface Kyreen could sense the physical attraction men had for her. When she had first felt these emotions from the men, she had been frightened and confused. Over the years, however, she had learned to tune it out until it became something in the background. Yet never, not once, had she ever felt that emotion from Stian.

Before Kyreen could reflect further on this revelation, the pair pulled up in front of the apothecary's shop. Almost immediately Yorick and Engla stepped out, as though they had been waiting. All pondering faded from Kyreen's thoughts and she frowned.

"What is it?" she asked sharply, gazing down at the two from the back of her horse. "What has happened?"

Yorick placed a hand on Kyreen's leg and looked up at her, his blue eyes mournful behind his spectacles. "Tis ye mother, Kyreen. She has crossed over."

"How? When?"

"Two days after ye and Stian left," Engla replied, barely restraining her tears.

Kyreen looked down, her gaze moving between the two. "There is something else you are not telling me."

Yorick and Engla exchanged glances, neither desiring to speak first.

After a long moment, Yorick sighed. "Tis Jorn. He is mad with grief."

"You mean he is drunk," Kyreen said bluntly, long knowing her foster father's weakness for distilled spirits. "Tell me. Where was he when Ildri crossed? Did he even bother to go home and care for his wife after you told him I had gone to Orra? Was he lifting ales with the other men while his wife sat neglected at home? Should you say he is mad with guilt? Is that what you are not telling me?"

Yorick nodded slowly, "Aye, lass. Once more ye reveal what is unspoken in our hearts, what we had not the courage to tell ye."

"Where is he now?"

"Havard took him home last night, bringing back the wagon so Jorn could not return to the village."

Without another word, Kyreen reined her mount around and spurred the gelding towards the farm.

As Stian gathered up his reins to follow, Yorick held up a hand. "Nay, Stian. Tis a family matter and we are not family yet. We must not further involve ourselves."

When Kyreen sped into the clearing she immediately sensed something was wrong. This place she had called home for more than half her life felt foreign, something was not right. Dismounting, she headed first to the barn. The cow and goat were both there, bleating loudly. Despite the lateness of the day, neither animal had been fed or milked. Kyreen tossed a flake of hay to each animal. Milking would have to wait.

She headed out the back door, looking past the garden, just sprouting, towards the far pasture as she exited the barn and stopped short. Empty. The pasture was empty. Where there should have been a dozen mares in varying shades of sorrel and chestnut, there was nothing. Where there should have been a dozen gangly foals shadowing their mothers, there was nothing. Where there should have been that colt Kyreen had picked out eight years ago, now a proud stallion watching over his herd, his dark chestnut coat sparkling in the sunlight, there was nothing.

Enraged, Kyreen ran to the cottage, banging open the door. Jorn, bleary eyed, sat at the table, a half-empty bottle set before him. At the noise, he focused a bloodshot gaze towards his daughter.

"'Bout time ye returned, eh?"

"Do not turn your blames to me, old man," Kyreen spat, emphasizing every syllable. She walked across the room, keeping the table between them. "Where are they?"

Jorn waved a shaky hand. "Gone. Everyone, everything is gone. Ildri. Gone. Those blasted horses. Gone. Even the wagon and mule. Gone, gone, gone."

Kyreen grabbed the bottle from in front of the old man, throwing it into the fireplace. For as long as Kyreen had lived in the cottage, and probably the forty odd years before that, flames had burned in that hearth. Now glass shattered amongst gray ashes.

Once started, Kyreen could not control her anger. She strode to the wood box and withdrew a partially emptied bottle, which joined the first in the cold fireplace. The girl continued to root out the hidden bottles Jorn had strewn throughout the small house. While it did not allay her anger, the action did take her focus off of Jorn for a few minutes. As she found the last bottle, she finally paused, turning to look at Jorn to voice the question burning in her heart.

"Who?" She asked, knowing the price had been too low and knowing it was only for coinage to buy drinks.

Kyreen was not stupid. She had a fair idea who had bought the herd. Truly there was only one person in the province with the resources to venture into horse breeding with a fully formed herd. She prayed to the goddess she was mistaken, but deep inside, she knew the answer before Jorn spoke.

"Soren."

Tears sprang to the girl's eyes, shimmering unshed, her heart breaking. Soren, the wealthiest man in Hanoria, father to Markku and Kalle. Her herd was now his property. The mares she had found and nurtured; the foals she had brought into this world with loving hands; the stallion she had nursed to health and adulthood, all gone. Gone to a man even more heartless and ruthless and mean-spirited than the two sons he had spawned.

Kyreen walked out into the yard, the bright sunlight relieving none of the shadows in her heart. The bottle hung forgotten in her hand as she lowered herself onto the stump. Despite everything that had happened over the years, this moment was her most hopeless. Never since losing contact with her brother on that evening of their third birthday had Kyreen ever felt so alone. Even then, though, she had had her mother. When her mother had gone away, Ildri had been there to comfort Kyreen. The work with the herd had sustained Kyreen throughout Ildri's illness. Now, at this moment, the young woman felt completely and utterly alone.

Once the tears subsided, she looked around the empty clearing. The cottage sat squat and forlorn. Weeds choked the new sprouts in the untended garden. Truly Kyreen was a stranger in this land. She did not belong here, at this homestead, in Hanoria, in this region. She could not, she would not stay a moment longer. Her decision made Kyreen set the bottle upon the stump and returned to the cottage where Jorn still sat at the table immersed in his own half-drunken stupor.

A few minutes later, heart still racing, Kyreen had her possessions packed. Aside from a meager stack of clothing, there was not much she wanted to take with her... a small sandalwood box that had been given to her by Ildri and the leather-bound journal in which she chronicled the farm records. Kyreen paused at the top of the ladder and glanced around the cramped loft that had been hers for so many years. Without Ildri's smile it was just a dreary room. Truth be told, the entire house had barely limped along after Ildri had fallen into that waking-sleep. Now it was in mourning. Kyreen could not bear to remain within its walls one more moment.

Jorn did not look up as she descended the ladder. If not for the bulky burlap sack resting in the middle of the table, it would have appeared that he had not moved since Kyreen's outburst. Having no more patience for the old man, Kyreen made to brush past without speaking. His hand rose silently, stopping her.

"Please. Sit," his voice was quiet, emotionless.

Kyreen paused; habit directing her obedience while her simmering temper pulled at her to leave.

Taking advantage of the girl's indecision, Jorn's hand lowered slowly to rest upon the sack. Curiosity sided with obedience and Kyreen stepped towards the table. Whatever rested beneath the coarse fabric was slender and as long as the table was wide. Half-forgotten memories, long suppressed, identified the silhouette even as Jorn spoke again.

"He arrived early at Sowing right after the thaws in your fifth year with us. Ye and Ildri were gone. I nay know if he planned it that way or if the Lords granted me fortune this one time. If he had come one day earlier or one day later, your path, my path, even Ildri's path, would have been... changed."

Kyreen felt the anger stirring in her breast anew. "Who came?" She shuddered at the sound of her voice, cold and brittle as icicles of Fallow.

"He was... different. He tried to disguise himself, but I saw... When the mule brayed he turned his head and I saw his ears." Jorn's eyes roamed around the room, never settling in one place, searching.

Watching him, Kyreen first thought he was avoiding her gaze. Then she realized he was trying to find a bottle. Impatience flooded and her hand slammed the wooden tabletop.

"Enough! I will leave you the last one after you tell your tale." Her voice lowered and the glittering green eyes narrowed. "But, old man, if you continue to stall I will break the damned bottle and allow the earth to claim your precious liquid."

The threat worked and words flew from Jorn's mouth. Kyreen could almost imagine it was a snowy Fallow evening, the three of them again cozied up in the small house, listening to one of Jorn's many wonderful stories. She had nearly forgotten those warmly pleasant years when they had first become a family. Jorn closed his eyes, his voice quiet, yet audible.

It had been early spring, an unusually warm day for the time of year. Kyreen had persuaded Ildri to visit the beehives and harvest some early honey. Jorn had taken advantage of the time alone to enjoy his pipe while preparing the plow for planting.

The stranger had appeared silently, his soft greeting startling Jorn so badly the Hanorian had dropped his pipe to the ground. Cheeks flaming, Jorn took extra time picking it up, inspecting the bowl for damage.

The stranger had waited patiently, standing on the edge of the woods. He was a little taller than Jorn, just about as tall as Kyreen had grown over the long winter. While most Hanorians had blonde hair, this man's was much paler, actually milk-white, completely straight, hanging down his back. Separately his features were ordinary, but in their arrangement created an exotic look. His pale skin was unshaved, accented with a long, narrow nose and glinting violet eyes. The clothing on his slender form was well made in earth greens and browns, ideal for a woodsman's camouflage. Although the farm was an hour from town by mule, the man had not looked as though he had been traipsing through the dense forest.

"Might I be of service?" Jorn had finally said, having regained his composure.

The formal greeting did not appear to perturb the stranger. He inclined his pale head as he replied, "Most gracious offer, Jorn of Hanoria, one which I most gratefully accept."

The sound of his own name from the lips of this unknown man with his foreign accent surprised Jorn. In that moment, he remembered his last encounter with a stranger who spoke his name and knew why the man was here.

"I seek the little one you have in your protection, Kyreen. It is time for her to return home."

"No!" Panicked, Jorn took a step forward. The man never flinched nor made any move to acknowledge Jorn's outburst. "This be Kyreen's home. How do I know ye are who ye say ye are? There were people who wished harm to the w... child."

To this day, so many years later, Jorn could not say if the word upon his lips was 'woman' or 'witch.'

The stranger did not seem surprised by Jorn's words. Instead he produced a burlap sack, the same that now sat on Jorn's table all these years later, saying, "This is Kyreen's birthright. Show it to her. Tell her Arvis waits for her at the tavern in Orra this next fortnight. If she chooses to stay here, we will leave without her."

Kyreen bit her lip, welcoming the bitter taste of blood. Nine years? Calan? Arvis? Memories flooded forth, unleashing a torrent of emotions.

Arvis had been here? At the farm? What about her brother? Arvis had said "We." Had her twin been this close, in Orra, awaiting her arrival? What could he have thought when she did not show? Had they returned to Calan without her? The questions swirled through her mind.

His tale told, Jorn finally risked a look at his foster daughter. As usual, nothing registered on her face, that beautiful face which could have been carved from granite, sharp and unmoving white stone, just like her mother's. And just like her mother, it was the glittering emerald eyes which spoke volumes of emotions. Now, thankfully, Kyreen's eyes had drifted shut, sparing him the additional shame of seeing how deeply his betrayal had hurt her.

Eventually, her eyes opened and she looked directly at the defeated old man, not sure she truly wanted to hear the answer, but nevertheless compelled to ask, "Why?"

Jorn hesitated, unsure of what to say. How could he make her understand that he loved her? As much as if she had been born of his blood? That he was afraid of losing her? At first, he had simply put the package away in order to contemplate the stranger's words. Days had stretched on and he had never even told Ildri about the visit. After the deadline had passed Jorn had reasoned there was no cause to share the visit with Kyreen. After a while it was easy to pretend that the strange white-haired man had never appeared, that this was Kyreen's home, that she had chosen to stay here.

Jorn's life had been so much better since Kyreen's arrival to their empty lives and empty farm. Ildri's final years had been her happiest ever and Kyreen was the sole reason. Not for the first time, Jorn cursed his selfishness and silently begged forgiveness from the ten Lords of Hayrik, although he knew there was no way he could ever make this right. As the silence grew between them, Jorn once again lost his nerve to speak and then he lost Kyreen, too. She gathered up the sack, leaving the cottage for the last time without a backward glance.

Kyreen's one regret was leaving the cow and goat. She would stop in town and ask Stian to care for them until… Kyreen realized she had no clear idea where she was going, but she knew she would not be returning. In the barn, she secured the burlap sack to the back of her saddle, hearing Jorn's approach, but refusing to acknowledge his presence at the barn door.

"Please stay," Jorn's voice came softly from the barn door. "I will call off the betrothal. Stian can have the farm. He will do right by ye. I will not be any trouble."

Kyreen tried to quell the bitterness, but her voice still shook with anger when, leading the gelding out of the barn, she finally spoke, "You say that now, old man. Tomorrow, halfway through a fresh bottle, you may change your mind."

Jorn thrust a parchment into her hand before shuffling back towards the house. Kyreen read the document, her skepticism quickly shifting into amazement. In crude hand printed lettering Jorn had deeded the farm and all possessions to Stian. No provisions. No clauses. No tricks. That Jorn would be willing to give up the one thing he had spent his life holding onto almost made Kyreen return to the house. Almost. Instead she carefully placed the document inside the leather-bound journal which she then put back into her saddlebags before swinging up into the saddle.

From the shadow of the front door, Jorn watched his daughter turn her mount towards town and disappear down the lane. It took all his will power to wait even that short amount of time.

Humiliation welling, he hurried to the barn as fast as his arthritic joints would permit. Just as Kyreen had promised, the bottle stood waiting for him on the feed barrel. Taking care not to spill a precious drop, Jorn drained the half-full bottle with one drink, the welcomed numbness softening his pains.

Chapter 8

The two elderly men emerged from the tavern, pausing on the porch—the tall sinewy man to empty the ashes from his pipe, the other to fasten the clasp of his cloak. Even had they not been engrossed in their conversation, it was doubtful either would have noticed the stranger observing them from the shadows of the nearby tree-line for Tyra was well-trained in the art of camouflage. From her vantage point, she could sense the mood and tone of their conversation. She could not, however, hear their words.

The relationship between the two men was deep-rooted, perceptibly long-lived and favorable. The Calanian had spent the last several hours outside this tavern, collecting information, searching for the right situation. In this time, much had been learned about the short red-faced rotund man. His name was Havard and he owned the village tavern. He was a good man with a generous heart, and by all appearances an ideal choice for Tyra's plan. His tavern, however, situated in the middle of this small village on the south-eastern edge of this southernmost province, was not ideal. Tyra's plan relied on seclusion. Leaving Kyreen in a populated area, even for as short a time span as a fortnight, was not an option. Though the tavern keeper had accompanied many men to the covered stoop, this was the first time he had donned a cloak and descended the steps, so Tyra focused her attention on Havard's weather-worn companion, a farmer she concluded from his practical, sturdy wardrobe. The man moved stiffly with stooped shoulders as though every step caused him pain, both physical and emotional. Within this man, Tyra also sensed many of the desirable qualities she has felt in tavern-keeper. The rapport between the men was a good omen. The tavern-keeper was much more relaxed and at ease with the tall stranger than with anyone else Tyra had observed. This type of connection was built upon a lifetime of friendship. That the tavern-keeper trusted this stranger reassured Tyra greatly.

She did, however, sense a deep anger within the tall man. Not a spiteful or vengeful anger rooted in selfishness or greed. No, this anger was a slow-burning fire, born of seasons of loss, of frustrations, of broken dreams. It burned internally, eating a man's soul from within, and could drive a good person to vengeful, spiteful, even self-destructive behavior.

'Could,' Tyra emphasized silently. If the plan went accordingly

Kyreen would be with this man less than two days. While Tyra preferred to not think about failure, she knew if she were to miss the three year rendezvous next spring, then Arvis would track their movements and have Kyreen by mid-summer's bloom.

The concealed woman watched with growing hope as the men crossed the abandoned courtyard and disappeared into the barn. Feeling extremely exposed, Tyra edged towards the side of the barn, desperate to hear their conversation.

"Jorn, my friend, as always your visit is too short."

"Much work to get done before the Snows," came the taller man's response. Though the words and tone are carefully guarded, Tyra sensed resentment beneath the surface. Yes, this man, Jorn, harbored anger, but struggled to contain it within himself. As the men came out into the afternoon sun, Jorn leading a gray mule, Tyra moved undetected back into the shadows. For two years Tyra had managed to keep her

and Kyreen's pursuers at a safe distance. Although Kyreen thought her mother fearless, Tyra did fear these men pursuing them and not just for her children's futures, but for also her people's wellbeing. She had heard nothing about Calan since their flight began. She hoped that the Galorian threat had been crushed and that her people have returned to their lives.

She worried, too, about her son, but was confident Quillan was beyond the mercenaries' reach. Arvis would have taken her son across the desert and deep into the elf lands, where no human could find them without elven assistance. Right now, however, she must do something to ensure Kyreen's safety. The incident in the clearing a fortnight prior, when Tyra had been so deeply asleep, when Kyreen had injured the mercenary, when they had fled amidst the confusion, had been a warning. Running was no longer a viable option. Somehow, someway, Kyreen, too, must be placed beyond the reach of Galor and its hired mercenaries. Though Tyra had never met this man who had pursued her and her daughter these many seasons, Tyra knew his kind. Pursuit for money had its limits and Tyra had been counting on the mercenary to abandon the quest, especially here in the mountains with the winter storms approaching. Now, however, Tyra knew this man would renew the vigilance of his pursuit. For with one fortuitous slice of the dagger, her young daughter had inadvertently changed this hunt from business to something much, much more personal.

The queen returned her attention to the two men in the clearing making their final farewells. After much creaking of leather and his joints, Jorn was in the saddle. He looked down at his friend with a smile, but even across the distance Tyra again felt the resentment. Jorn's voice reflected none of this when he answered the question Tyra had missed Havard asking. "It will be a while. Even if the first snows are still in the future, I must gather wood before its arrival."

"Jorn, I do wish ye would allow Darvin or Klan to help ye."

Another wave of anger assaulted the concealed woman, which again Jorn hid from his friend. "Havard, ye sons are busy enough trying to keep ye from drinking all the profits without adding another old man's care into the mix."

Now strong emotions—concern and frustration—radiated from the tavern-keeper, but wisely Havard held his tongue. From her position in the shadows Tyra sensed this was an old on-going argument between the two longtime friends.

"Give Ildri my greetings and well wishes, old friend," Havard replied, patting the mule's gray haunches. "The Ten Lords of Hayrick surely blessed ye upon the day ye wed that woman."

Jorn chuckled and nodded his farewell, urging the mule forward. Tyra felt a change in emotions as the old man rode away. This time Jorn's thoughts were tinged with sadness, disappointment, even failure, but the queen smiled softly because under all of this was love. The man's love for his wife grounded him. It was this love that made up her mind and Tyra moved away from the tavern to follow the old man riding the mule.

As Havard turned to head back into the tavern, a motion from the corner of his eye caused him to pause on the porch and turn. The woods were quiet and empty, but the tavern-keeper felt a chill run down his spine. After a long moment, he shrugged the feeling off as an old man's imagination and headed back inside, anxious for the warmth of hearth and ale.

Yorick had just begun the evening chores and was feeding the chickens when Kyreen's horse trotted into view. Even from the distance of the wooden bridge, he recognized the stiff anger in her posture.

'So, the old fool has finally done it,' was his first thought, quickly followed by concern for the young woman. Despite her steely exterior, Yorick could still perceive the timid child hiding beneath the surface.

Growing up an outsider in Hanoria was no easy task as Yorick's own children had discovered. At least Stian and Engla physically resembled the other children of the village. For Kyreen, so different in every way, growing up here had been a terrible hardship. Yet, instead of reacting to the villagers, Kyreen had managed to repel the fear and hatred of her adopted family's people, at least until today. Today it appeared as if Kyreen was about to explode.

"Greetings, young one," he called out once Kyreen was within hearing.

The intensity of Yorick's pity slapped Kyreen so hard her body spasmed as though physically assaulted. Biting back the bitter tears, she merely nodded in response and pulled her horse to a halt before him.

"Good eve, Yorick," she responded. "Are Stian and Engla home? I have come to bade them farewell."

Leaning against a fence post Yorick stared up at Kyreen, his spectacled eyes looming large behind his lens. He sighed, realizing his daughter's best friend had once again smothered her emotions.

"I am sorry, Kyreen," he answered truthfully. "Engla is out on an errand and Stian accompanied the lass. Please stay the eve with us and wait until morn to leave. Ye know ye are always welcomed within our walls."

Even as he made the request, the apothecary knew the girl's answer. Just a short while ago, Yorick had learned from his son about the sale of Kyreen's herd to Soren after Stian had spoken with Kalle. Engla, upon hearing the news, had become even more animated than usual and had decided to seek out Soren at the tavern to convince him to return the herd. Although Yorick and Stian both knew her argument would fall upon deaf ears, neither had been able to convince Engla otherwise, so Yorick sent Stian along to ensure Engla's safety. While the apothecary did not believe Soren or any of the other men would physically harm his daughter, especially with Havard there, Engla was not a typical passive Hanorian woman. She was apt to go too far with her words and Yorick trusted Stian's cool head to keep Engla from getting too far into trouble.

"No, I must leave tonight," Kyreen's voice was hard when she finally answered Yorick's invitation.

"Tonight? Why not in the…" An emphatic shake of the ebony curls stopped Yorick's protestations. He sighed once more, feeling even more dwarfed than usual gazing up at Kyreen on the tall sorrel horse.

"Very well, ye are grown, Kyreen, and, though my fellow villagers disagree, I believe ye are more than capable to make ye own decisions. At least stay for evening meal," he tried, framing the appeal carefully.

Kyreen glanced around the empty clearing, knowing several pairs of eyes watched this interaction from the shadows of the neighboring houses. Even Yorick's own wife Fjola stood listening at the door, carefully hidden from sight, but emotions running high. Fjola had never warmed to her children's friend, always managing to avoid Kyreen during the girl's infrequent visits.

With a quiet sigh and to Yorick's great surprise, Kyreen swung off the gelding. But instead of tying the horse, she opened up one of the saddlebags and pulled out the journal, from which she withdrew the parchment Jorn had so recently signed.

Folding the paper in quarters, Kyreen turned to face Yorick, gazing fondly upon the apothecary. He and Havard had been the only Hanorian adults besides her foster parents to treat her decently and without disdain.

"Thank you for your kind offer," she finally said, green eyes glittering apologetically. "I have spent the bulk of my life as an unwelcome stranger amongst people I only wished to befriend. No more. By your leave, Yorick, I shall finally make the village content and depart upon this eve.

"Please give this document and journal to Stian upon his return. The livestock which remain at the farm require care."

As Yorick took the items and made to unfold the parchment, Kyreen shook her head. "My apologies, dear sir, but the paper is for Stian's eyes. Be assured, your son will reveal its contents upon reading. May I request your discretion until then?"

Yorick, intrigued by Kyreen's formality, nodded and slipped the paper back into the journal's pages.

"By your leave, Kyreen, ye have my word that Stian's shall be the first eyes to see this document," he said and Kyreen knew that the document would be safe. Only Stian's death would cause Yorick to break his word.

Swinging back into the saddle, Kyreen looked around the clearing once more and then rested her gaze upon the father of her two best friends. "If you would permit of me one final request, Yorick? Please pass my fondest farewell wishes to Engla and Stian. They have been dear friends to me these many years. I shall miss them greatly."

Yorick nodded, knowing there was nothing left holding the girl in Hanoria. He realized he did not know anything about her origins or her own people. He only knew there was no way this tall ebony-haired child was related to either Ildri or Jorn, no matter the story they had concocted many years ago.

"Where shall ye go, lass?" he asked as she turned her gelding towards the road to Orra.

Pausing to look back at Yorick, Kyreen's hand fell to rest upon the burlap sack secured to her saddle. She flashed the apothecary one final sad smile in the fading light. "I believe I shall go home."

PART II

Chapter 9

To the east, wisps of clouds wove through beams of moonlight. A solitary wolf raised a mournful howl, which was answered seconds later by a bark from the opposite mountainside. On the valley floor, the horse's ears flickered, instinctively knowing he and his rider were not the object of the canines' song. Fragrant aromas of spring grass tickled the horse's nostrils, enticing him, but he remained true to his training and ignored the temptation. Steadily he plodded on as the exhausted girl in the saddle slumbered, her troubled dreams sprinkled with fleeting images of a golden- haired toddler, violet eyes and sorrel foals. Within the trees bordering the lane, forest animals continued their nocturnal activities, none giving notice to the traveling pair.

A few hours later, as the half-moon reached the axis of its nightly journey, Kyreen jerked awake simultaneously refreshed and irritated. How could she be napping in the saddle like a babe upon her mother's bosom? This thought brought Tyra to mind, returning Kyreen's attention to the package hurriedly strapped to the back of her saddle. She yearned to gaze upon the ancient weapon, but more urgent is the desire to put additional distance between her and her forlorn homestead. Kyreen urged the gelding into a lope and the horse's long gait swallowed another two hours of road before Kyreen finally stopped in a small clearing, more for the horse's sake than for her own. Moments later the hobbled gelding, freshly brushed and watered, munched contentedly on tender clover.

Kyreen settled down upon a flat rock before a small fire lit more for light than warmth or protection. Placing the burlap sack on the ground before her, she stared at it for several long moments, her peaceful exterior hiding the torrent of emotions stirring within. Though a decade and a half had passed since she had laid eyes on the sack's contents, Kyreen well remembered what lay beneath the coarse fabric. Her birthright, those had been Arvis's words to Jorn.

For a brief moment, her mind strayed and her lips curled in a fond smile of memory. Arvis. He had been her father's best friend and also her mother's closest advisor, godfather to Kyreen and Quillan. The twins had learned early the sacrifice of being the queen's children, as Tyra's attention was many times distracted with the day-to-day running of her small country. So, it was to this man that Kyreen and her brother would run when seeking comfort whether it was a skinned knee or hurt feelings. Though the details of his pale face had faded over the years, Kyreen recalled fondly the warmth of his hugs, the animation of his storytelling and the sparkle of his lavender eyes.

Knowing she was avoiding the inevitable, Kyreen returned her attentions to the burlap sack. Taking a deep breath, tentative fingers untied the twine and reached inside the rough fabric. Carefully she withdrew the heavy weapon, the sheath's dark leather soft and supple in her hands. The sword's hilt glinted in the dim firelight. The tapered hilt—brass, silver and copper braided together—rested between a silver rose pommel and brass scrolled guard. Taking a deep breath, Kyreen pulled the sword out, revealing two straight parallel edges which narrowed to a pointed end. Her mother's sword. Remarkable Calanian workmanship balanced the weapon so well that Kyreen raised the blade above her head with one hand and little effort. Firelight glinted off ancient runes etched along the long narrow steel blade. This razor-sharp weapon, capable of cutting off limbs in one stroke, had been handed down through the ages to the rulers of Calan.

Kyreen's eyes closed in order to better recall the memory from that spring afternoon so long ago when her mother had given this weapon to Arvis. She swallowed the lump growing in her throat, but not before a single ragged sob escaped. She carefully re-sheathed the sword, hot tears staining the leather scabbard. After kicking dirt over the fire, she took a final look around the clearing to check that she and the horse were invisible from the road. With the saddle as her hard pillow, she wrapped a blanket about her shoulders, settling beneath a sheltering bush with the sword resting close by. Once again the clearing, bathed only in moonlight fell silent, save for the gelding's teeth crunching grass and muffled sobs from under the girl's blanket.

Chapter 10

Bright sunshine flooded the clearing as a lone cart rumbled down the road, the dusty mule laboring in its harness. From the back, a little boy popped up between the man and woman in the front seat.

"Papa, please! May we stop?" the child inquired tentatively.

Papa, under normal circumstances, had infinite patience. But these were not normal circumstances. The journey from the family's small homestead deep within the province of Flueren had been wrought with mishaps. First, the boy's sister Hanne had fallen ill with fever. Then the wagon axel had broken. Now the mule had injured its back leg and was barely able to pull the wagon. The jostling slow progress of the wagon served only to aggravate the condition of the child's near bursting bladder.

"Please, Papa?" the boy repeated quietly.

Kare sighed with a glance to his wife Sonja and pulled back on the reins. "Very well, Sven," he said. "Just enough time for a quick stop before we are moving once more. We need to make Orra by eve."

Not waiting for the wagon to roll to a full stop, the small child darted over the side and sped towards the nearby trees, oblivious to everything around him. A few moments later, much relieved, he emerged from the shade of the trees, very surprised to see a tall chestnut horse peacefully grazing just yards from him. A horse! A real horse! Not a mule like the gray creature pulling their cart and not one of those huge clumsy beasts that worked his grandfather's fields. Murmuring quietly, a hand extended in friendship, Sven slowly moved towards the grazing animal who, without apparent notice, managed to shuffle away, always positioned just beyond Sven's reach.

"That one has always been cunning. He enjoys his grazing."

The voice so surprised Sven that his hand jerked towards his mouth. He spun around towards the source of the voice, just an outline of a form squatting in the shadows of a nearby shrub.

Rising, the figure moved into the sunlight. Clad in fawn skin trousers and a linen tunic, the stranger flashed Sven a smile that never quite reached the hard green eyes beneath the leather hat.

"Hail and well met, young one. It is nice to see you are empty of fear beside a horse as large as this one here," the stranger said, extending a hand towards the boy in greeting. "My name is Kyre...Ky."

"Sven! Sven, hurry up! Papa says you had better..." the little girl stopped short upon seeing this strange person reaching to grab her baby brother. A split second later, her piercing scream filled the clearing, startling the gelding.

Instinctively, Kyreen leapt for the gelding, pressing calm thoughts towards the frightened animal. Luck and lightning reflexes combined so that her fingers closed around the halter before the animal could trample the boy. With her other hand, Kyreen drew off her hat to cover the animal's eyes.

All this happened so quickly that by the time Kare rounded the stand of bushes all he saw was a tall slender young man with a mop of dark wild curls steadying a skittish chestnut horse and his youngest child rooted in place, mouth hanging open in awe.

"Hush your hollering, Hanne," the man said quietly, dropping a heavy hand onto his daughter's shoulder, his eyes never leaving the stranger's face. "Ye shall be driving your mother into labor."

At that moment, Kare's wife, her normally petite form enlarged in the last stages of pregnancy, walked up.

"Who is going into labor?" she asked, her bright gaze quickly taking in the same scene.

Hanne looked up between her parents, hazel eyes shimmering with unshed tears. "I thought he was going to hurt Sven," she explained, nervous hands twisting at her skirt.

"Sven, get over here," Karl commanded, though not unkindly, stepping forward.

Kyreen watched the husky man crossing towards her. Nervously she placed the hat back on her head covering freshly shorn curls. She had just finished sawing off her long locks mere moments before the boy had appeared. Had Sven not been so intent upon his toilet, he surely would have noticed her in the bushes amongst the piles of ebony curls.

With the minutes granted her, Kyreen had hurriedly shoved the locks deep within the bush, cursing the events leading to this moment. With Calan so many leagues away, travelling as a woman, especially a solitary woman, might have proven problematic. So, after waking late this morning, Kyreen had decided to disguise herself and this chore had taken much longer than expected. Now Kyreen was about to learn if indeed she could pass for a young man.

"Hail and well met, young one," the man said, proffering a beefy calloused hand. "Kare of Flueren."

Her own slim hand enveloped by Kare's hand, Kyreen managed to avoid stumbling over the introduction this time. "Hail and well met, Kare of Flueren. I am Ky of Labeck," she said, naming a central province bordering Hanoria.

Kyreen, picking up a glimmer of doubt in addition to the flicker that crossed the man's steady gaze, added, "I have been living with relatives in Hanoria for the past four seasons. Now I am sent to Myrddin to begin a blacksmithing apprenticeship with my uncle."

Kyreen felt Kare relax his thoughts as they shook hands. Once the rest of the introductions and formalities had been dispatched, Kyreen stoked the fire from last night to brew tea for the midday meal. She also used leaves from the tea to prepare a poultice for the mule's injured leg.

While the family had welcomed her with grace and seemed at ease with each other, Kyreen sensed an underlying tension between husband and wife. At first she thought to attribute it to the unborn child, especially after the pregnant woman alluded to troubles with previous miscarriages, but Kyreen's intuition told her different. Both Sonja and Kare radiated only hope and happiness when talking about the upcoming birth. A girl, Kyreen thought.

Though she did not know how she knew, every spring when foaling, Kyreen could always predict ahead of time whether to expect a filly or a colt. She also knew this babe was healthy with a strong will for life. The thought made Kyreen smile.

"What are ye thinking?" the little girl asked shyly, clutching a rag doll to her chest with one hand and a hunk of cheese in her other hand.

"Hanne!" her mother reproached. "Let the… Ky eat in peace."

Kyreen noted the flash in Sonja's eyes when she spoke and wondered if the short curls and trousers may not have been enough to fool the woman. Kyreen had caught Sonja staring at her several times earlier with a melancholy expression. As soon as Sonja saw Kyreen's returning gaze, she would quickly avert her eyes. Sadness and regret accompanied these glances.

The children ate quickly and full of energy headed immediately off to play amongst the trees. Kare, after a look from his wife, took his tea and followed the sounds of laughter into the woods.

Alone with Sonja, Kyreen sipped her own tea pensively. After a long moment, she rested her gaze upon the woman.

"Forgive my forwardness, lady," she said. "But you gaze upon me with some emotion. Have I offended you in some way?"

A sad smile spread across Sonja's face. "Nay. It is the pregnancy. Impending motherhood brings out the emotions, making even the most impassive woman into a weepy lass. Ye remind me of me eldest son Leif. Ye are about the same age as he."

Kyreen, though well practiced at hiding her emotions, allowed a questioning, and hopefully encouraging, look to dawn upon her face.

Shifting to find a more comfortable position, almost impossible with the bulk of pregnancy, Sonja sipped her tea before explaining, "Kare is nay my first husband. Me first husband, me..." Sonja's blue eyes flicked toward the trees from whence the sounds of merriment wafted, before turning back to stare at the fire, "...me love, is... was Dyre, Kare's older brother. Leif was, is our only child. Dyre was badly injured in an accident during the Sowing when Leif was just a babe. His health never recovered. When Leif was in his eighth season, my husband crossed over. As the next son in line, Kare took over the family's farm. He had been so helpful during Dyre's illness, with the farm, with Leif, with everything. He is such a hard worker, Kare never had time to pursue love, so was logical we would wed once the mourning was over. Kare needed a wife. I needed a husband. Leif needed a father." Sonja paused for a pensive sip of her lukewarm tea before softly adding, "He never forgave me though."

Kyreen pondered the woman's last statement as they sat in silence, both staring into the dying fire. Who never forgave Sonja? Leif, because of the loss of his father and resenting Kare's new position? Kare, because his wife still loved and longed for his deceased brother? Or the spirit of Sonja's dead crippled husband because Sonja wed too soon after his death? Perhaps the answer was all three. As she did so often with the mares birthing in spring, Kyreen continued to sip her tea and wait patiently. Storytelling as Jorn had often reminded Kyreen could not be rushed any more than birthing.

Eventually, Sonja sighed and returned her gaze to the stranger sitting across the fire. "Despite the differences, ye remind me so much of Leif. He is not so tall nor his hair as dark or curly. Ye both, however, have a restless soul, the kind that cannot be corralled. That restlessness stirred within Leif until Flueren could no longer contain him and he had to flee. He left early in the Sowing, even before the fields were prepared. Kare was nay happy at his timing, but it would not have been good to restrain the lad. Though it has only been two moon cycles, there has been no word and I worry. One reason I insisted on this birthing journey was to mayhap discover word about Leif." Abruptly, Sonja's expression rearranged from wistful to motherly business.

Kyreen glanced over her shoulder to see Kare and the children emerging from the forest. Both of the children's clothes were soaked and muddy. Kyreen shook her head and chuckled. "I see the little ones discovered the creek." Rising, she stepped over the smoldering fire to offer assistance to Sonja.

Once to her feet, Sonja placed her mouth close to Kyreen's ear. "Men," she whispered, "Do not make tea when women are present. Not ever. Not even around one as pregnant as I."

Icy fear gripped Kyreen's heart as she glanced again over her shoulder. "Does Kare know?" she whispered.

Sonja shook her head and patted the girl's arm reassuringly. "Nay. Kare accepts the world as it is presented."

Chapter 11

Kyreen rode the gelding with Sven perched behind the saddle and Kare trailed behind with Sonja and Hanne in the wagon. Traffic along this stretch of road was light as most citizens traveled the river barges.

So excited to be riding such a grand animal, Sven had peppered Kyreen with question after question about horses until his mother threatened to make him ride in the wagon. Immediately the young boy had clamped both hands over his mouth, eyes wide as he concentrated on keeping silent.

As a hush descended upon the forest, Hanoria far behind her, Kyreen felt her soul relax. The mountain that she and the gelding had descended just the previous night was just an inky shadow against the horizon behind them. The pine forest of the village and homestead where she had spent the bulk of her childhood had receded into an old forest of hardwoods. The oaks and maples here rose tall, proudly displaying the tender green leaves of the spring growth. Off to her left sunlight glinted off the slow-moving river. To her right the undergrowth grew thick for a few yards before the ground rose up, gently at first, then into a steep incline that disappeared into the tree line. This road would lead her to Myrddin and from there she would head north. How far she was not sure, but north was where Calan lay.

Kyreen wondered what might have happened to the province in the dozen years since her family's pre-dawn flight. Had Quillan returned and taken the throne? Was Arvis his second-in-command? Had someone else stepped up before Quillan's return? Would Kyreen be expected to take her place on the throne?

The peace Kyreen had just felt quickly dissolved and uncertainty flowed into its place. Why was she heading to Calan? Just because she did not belong in Hanoria did not necessarily mean she belonged in Calan. These memories of her home were shadowy wisps. What would she do when she arrived? The small amount of gold in her pouch would not be enough to buy a farm or livestock or begin any venture. How would she support herself?

Despite the warmth of this family with whom she travelled Kyreen once again felt alone and isolated. Suppressing a shiver, Kyreen pulled up the gelding, falling back so as to engage Kare in conversation about his farm. The man's features, so similar to his son's, lit up, his animated discussion quickly chasing the shadows to the back of Kyreen's mind.

It was very late afternoon, almost twilight, with the sky just beginning to purple when Kyreen and the family made the final turn into Orra. Knowing the family planned to take the morning barge, Kyreen pulled up the gelding and turned in her saddle to speak with Kare.

"I believe this is where we part ways, Kare," she said. "I thank you for your company. I shall continue on through the town and rest on the other side."

Sven stifled a yawn as his small arms hugged Kyreen's waist. Today had been the best day of his young life and, though he teetered on the brink of exhaustion, he was reluctant to see his ride end. Kare, more comfortable now that the bulk of the journey was over and this day's journey had been made without mishap, chuckled softly as he lifted his son from the gelding's back.

"Well met and fair journeys, Ky," he said, placing Sven in the back of the wagon beside the slumbering Hanne. He motioned towards the mule, "and many thanks for the poultice. The animal should be able to easily make tomorrow's short journey from the dock to Sonja's sister's farm."

"Let us pray that I can say the same," Sonja joked from her seat in the wagon, fondly patting her enlarged stomach.

Immediately the smile faded from Kare's face and his brow furrowed. "Are ye... Is the babe...?" he stopped as Sonja held up a hand.

"I jest, husband," she said. "The babe will not be born tonight."

As Kyreen watched the woman reassure her husband, Sonja glanced her way and the young woman sensed the message left unspoken. The babe may not arrive this eve but she would surely be born within the next day or two. Kyreen smiled and inclined her head towards the woman.

"Fare thee well, Sonja," she said. "Best wishes to you and your babe. May she be a blessing upon your home."

Immediately Kyreen felt the error of her words reflected in the questioning gazes of Kare and Sonja. With a wave of her hand she turned the gelding and hurried away from the wagon. Such was her intent to avoid questioning, that Kyreen almost missed the ragged horse tied to a post outside the town's largest inn.

Had her gelding not snorted and whinnied in the direction of the horse tethered there, Kyreen would not have glanced over. Though the road dirt caked the horse's sweaty hide, the girl immediately recognized the line of its withers and curve of its neck. The animal's mane and tail were dusty and frayed, but still familiar. Kyreen pulled up to the hitching post, praying to be mistaken. Heart breaking, she looked down on the abused animal, a mere shadow of the stud colt she had already once coaxed to health, the stallion she had left in the pasture just a fortnight before, the horse Jorn had sold for drinking money. His mouth bloodied from the bit and eyelashes caked with sweat and dirt framing his dark eyes, the stallion recognized both his former mistress and the horse upon which she rode. The reins were wound so tightly around the post that he could not lower or turn his head, but he managed to whinny softly and shift his weight so as to press a shoulder against the gelding.

Her eyes shimmering with unshed tears, Kyreen spared a wondering glance towards the inn's front door. Who had ridden this animal so hard from Hanoria? Who had callously left the stud tied here? Who was inside the inn right now? It had to be Markku. Although it had been Markku's father to make the transaction, Soren rarely left the province and Kyreen was sure even he would not treat his horse with such disdain. Soren took pride in his properties and kept his possessions well maintained. Markku, on the other hand, only coveted and had no desire to maintain his father's belongings.

Hearing the door open, Kyreen reined away from the stallion and moved down the street, a plan forming in her mind. This presented yet another delay, but she reminded herself that for once she was not on a schedule. Calan would still be there when she arrived and there was no way she was leaving Orra without her horse.

Chapter 12

A few hours later, the deserted streets blanketed in shadows, Kyreen approached the inn on foot. After securing the gelding in a clearing outside of Orra, she had hiked back through the woods. During those hours, her anger had not dissipated at all. If anything, Kyreen was angrier now than she had been when confronting Jorn in the cabin. What Jorn had done to her had been wrong, but not dangerous. What had been done to the stallion was wicked. No animal deserved such treatment.

Kyreen's anger bubbled afresh when she slipped around the corner of the building and saw the stallion still tied to the hitching post. From inside the inn, she could hear the sounds of men drinking and laughing.

The girl eased to a window and peered inside, the bright lantern light temporarily blinding her after the dark of the forest. Just as she had guessed, Markku sat at a table, surrounded by men eagerly listening to his tales and drinking his coinage. Kyreen inhaled deeply, fighting the urge to confront Markku openly. Nothing good could come from that. Although Orra sat a long distance from Hanoria, Soren did have business contacts in this town and all over the neighboring provinces. Plus, his money could buy him— and his son— plenty of support. Finally regaining control of her emotions, Kyreen moved away from the window and approached the horse.

With quiet murmurings, she carefully unfastened the bridle, wincing as the metal bit tore from the tender skin, causing the stallion's mouth to bleed anew. After placing the soft rope halter around his head, Kyreen quickly uncinched the saddle, setting everything on the ground before leading the stallion away. Let Markku have his tack. Kyreen was here for her property, nothing more.

Although nobody roamed the streets, Kyreen felt exposed walking out of town. With every step, she fought the urge to run. When finally, they were outside of town, she moved away from the road, traversing the deer trail she had used earlier. Still she kept the pace slow, more for the horse than herself. The poor creature had been ridden so hard even the act of walking was painful.

Once back in the clearing, Kyreen spent a long time cleaning up the stallion. The gelding grazed nearby, but never wandered too far away. It was as though he, too, was worried about the stallion and wanted to keep close. When finally every clump of mud had been combed from the flaxen mane and tail, and all the dirt brushed from the sorrel coat, Kyreen hobbled the stallion and turned him out to graze. Watching the gelding and stallion grazing side-by-side, their flaxen manes and tails reflecting silver in the waning moonlight, Kyreen felt immense relief. She also felt a tingle of apprehension, wondering what might be happening back in town.

Surely Markku would eventually remember his horse and make arrangements for its care. Had she been rash leaving the tack there on the street? What would happen when Markku saw his saddle and bridle? Would he know Kyreen had taken the horse? Most likely yes, and most assuredly Markku would involve local authorities, using all of his father's influence and money to search for the stallion. She wondered exactly how far Markku would look for the stallion. Did anyone notice her in town earlier? She knew that if she could make it to Myrddin and then head north, she could escape. Nobody in Hanoria knew her origins.

Stifling a yawn, the girl knew that, despite the urgency of leaving this area, she could not resume the journey tonight. Not only did she need rest, but so did both of the horses. Stretching out on her pallet, wrapping a blanket around her body, Kyreen's mind finally quieted down and she drifted into an uneasy sleep.

Chapter 13

No one gave a second glance at the lone rider entering Wentworth at mid-morning. People milled the streets and the merchants in the bazaar conducted their business beneath colorful tents. The overnight barge from Orra had just arrived. Goods and passengers were being off-loaded while goods and passengers bound for the large city of Myrddin waited to be loaded. Kyreen slouched in the saddle, mentally willing herself invisible to passerbys. She could not, however, quell her nervousness, which travelled down the reins, causing both animals, even the normally calm gelding, to prance. Inhaling deeply, the girl reached out mentally, calming the animals. The stud colt, already a high-strung creature, shied from the pedestrians, gazing white-eyed at carts rumbling pass. Reluctantly, Kyreen dismounted and took a lead in each hand, keeping the brim of her dusty hat low.

She glanced back at the stud, his sorrel coat a dull brown. In the bright sunshine, her hasty dye job on the beautiful shiny coat looked shockingly unnatural. Maybe if she walked in the shade, she thought angling towards the edge of the street.

"Ky! Ky! Look, Papa! It's Ky!" a child's voice drifted over the turmoil.

Heart sinking, Kyreen paused and turned towards the voice. Sven and his father were leading the mule and cart off the wharf and onto the city's cobblestones. Trailing, slowly, Sonja made her way down the gangway, Hanne's hand in hers. Even from this distance, Kyreen could feel the woman's discomfort. Labor had begun. The baby would be coming soon.

"Ky, what fortune. We did not expect to see ye again on our journey," Kare said, stretching a large calloused hand towards the youth.

Kyreen took the man's hand self-consciously, and relieved. Sonja must not have told her husband.

Sven, petting the gelding's nose, looked over at the stud colt. "When did ye get another horse? Is he broke? He sure is dirty. Where are ye headed? We are heading west? Are you heading west? Will ye travel with us? Can I ride one of the horses?"

The rapid-fire questions surely would have continued had Kare not placed a beefy hand upon his son's head.

Sven looked up at his father, chastened. "Sorry, Papa."

He looked to Kyreen. "Sorry, Ky. I talk too much. Least wise that is what Momma and Papa tell me. I really do not, ye know. Hanne talks much more than I do. She is always…."

"Sven," Sonja interrupted her youngest son, having caught up to the men. Laughter danced in her eyes and voice, covering her discomfort. "Let Ky alone and help your mother up into the wagon," she paused, her gaze turning to Kyreen. "Hail and well met once more, Ky. Please forgive me," she continued, clambering awkwardly up into the wagon," this baby is in a hurry. We need to make my sister's stead by dark or I fear I shall be giving birth on the side of the road."

"Of course," Kyreen replied, relieved and knowing once again the other woman had graciously relieved an awkward situation. She looked to mule, still favoring his hock and made an impulsive decision. "Which way are you headed? Sven said west?"

"Aye. For a bit, then we turn south," Kare replied. "We should easily make Eileen's farm by dark."

"As it happens, I, too, am heading west to Myrddin. I do not care to take the barge with my horses. Might I travel with you? The children are welcome to ride the gelding. It is not much, but may help lighten the mule's load."

"So it shall be! Let us not dawdle," Kare answered, clapping a hand to Kyreen's shoulder. He glanced up at his wife, silently listening to the exchange. "I do not desire my child be born on the road nor do I wish to play midwife." He winked at Sonja, who managed to smile through the contraction she hid from everyone except Kyreen.

Feeling a little less conspicuous in a group, Kyreen placed the children upon the gelding, Sven in front, his small hands on the reins, Hanne in back, clutching an arm around her brother, the other hand tightly holding her doll. Kare made sure Sonja was comfortable as could be in the back of the wagon then took the mule's reins in hand. Kyreen fell in step beside him, the reins of her horses held loosely in one hand.

As they exited the town and the clamor of the dock of the bazaar fell behind them, Kare glanced at the stud colt. "A nice enough horse, Ky. Not much strength there though," he said, looking at the animal as a farmer looking for a workhorse, not as an aficionado of horse flesh.

"Aye. Thank you," Kyreen replied cautiously.

"Back in Orra, we had some commotion yester eve. We were loaded and ready to leave at midnight. Before the barge left, however, men came and searched the vessel. They never said what it was they were looking for, but words flow easily on the river. Seems a horse went missing from outside the inn. A find specimen. A stud," Kare paused, his eyes looking over the dull brown coat before moving to Kyreen's face, "Of course, it was a sorrel, as red as a forge fire with flaxen mane and tail. Very different from this horse here."

Kyreen's heart thumped rapidly and she was sure Kare could see through her. Outwardly, however, she managed to nod. "Yes, different. I passed a traveler on the road late yesterday. Road bandits had struck and he had this colt along with another, a mare in foal, almost ready to drop. I haven't time for a newborn, but I liked the look of this here horse. The man was down on his luck so I made an offer. Thanks be to the Lords, he took it. Otherwise I'd never have afforded a horse such as this."

Kare nodded slowly, returning his eyes to the dusty road ahead. "Very fortunate indeed, especially considering the wounds about the mouth. No telling what this horse might have suffered had you not happened upon his owner," Kare glanced at the sky, allowing his words to hang before adding, "I suppose we should move quickly since I smell rain on the clouds and I would imagine ye wish to be as far from Wentworth as possible if caught in a downpour."

Again, Kyreen nodded, her cheeks flaming in the shadow of her hat brim. The meaning buried in Kare's words struck her twofold. First, Kare knew the colt was camouflaged. A good rain would rinse the muddy brown from the colt's golden coat. Second, Kare acknowledged Kyreen to be a horse thief, a fugitive from the law of Orra, yet he recognized the stallion had been abused.

Worried, she nibbled her bottom lip as the town of Wentworth fell behind them. Markku's family may not have much influence outside of Hanoria, but the family was rich and able to afford a search. Markku's pride would never allow the theft to go unnoticed and would deal harshly with anyone involved. With luck Kyreen would leave Kare and his family soon and would not put them in danger.

Chapter 14

Kyreen glanced nervously over her shoulder at the wagon. Wentworth was well behind the travelers with the family's destination still a distance away, and, although Sonja never uttered a sound, her labor pains were increasing both in intensity and shortened intervals. Kyreen nibbled on her bottom lip anew, wondering how much longer the other woman could hide the labor from her family. What would they do if indeed the babe decided to arrive here on the road? Even as these thoughts milled through the girl's head, Sonja called out to her husband.

Immediately, Kare was by his wife's side. "Sonja? What is wrong?"

Kyreen, not wanting the children to become alarmed, moved the horses towards a grassy patch along the side of the road, within the shade of the forest. Hanne eagerly took Kyreen's arms, grateful to be off the gelding's back. Sven, however, groaned when Kyreen pulled him from the saddle.

"Go take care of your needs," Kyreen said quietly. "I know not how long we rest here."

After both children had scampered off into the trees, Kyreen secured the horses loosely to a low-hanging branch before walking back towards the wagon. Kare and Sonja were in conversation as Kyreen approached.

"Please forgive the intrusion," the young woman said quietly.

Sonja smiled wanly through another contraction. "Ky, it appears our child will not wait for a more convenient time to be born."

Kare ran a hand over his face, visibly troubled. "We need a midwife. Oh, by the Lords, why did I agree to this trip?"

Kyreen looked at Sonja. When the other woman nodded, Kyreen said, "Kare, I can help. I am not a midwife, but I have birthed dozens of foals."

Kare grabbed Kyreen by the arm and jerked her away from the wagon. "If ye think I would allow a man to deliver my child, then you are daft," he hissed. "It is not proper! If any man must deliver this child, then it should be me!"

Kyreen winced as the man's fingers dug into her arm. "Kare," she tried to explain only to be cut off by a moan from Sonja.

"Kare," the laboring woman called, her teeth clenched tightly. "Please. There is no time to explain. The babe comes but I feel something is wrong. I need Ky's help."

Kare looked at his wife in the back of the wagon and back at Kyreen. When his grip loosened, Kyreen exhaled the breath she'd been holding and slipped from his grasp. Clambering into the back of the wagon, the girl took a quick inventory of the situation.

"You have something," she asked quietly, "To wrap the babe in?"

Sonja nodded and pointed to a knapsack in the corner of the wagon.

Kyreen rustled through, pulling out various bits of fabric, a light blanket and some cloth squares, then looked over at Kare, still standing where she had left him.

"Help Sonja over to the clearing. I will move the wagon off the road. Then I need you to make a fire and heat some water," Kyreen commanded, taking a large cloth and handing it to Sonja she struggled to sit up. "Take this and get comfortable," she said, quietly adding, "Kare needs to know now, not after."

Sonja nodded, not trusting herself to speak as she maneuvered out of the back of the wagon. Kyreen took the mule's bridle and followed the couple. She could not hear Sonja's words, but felt Kare's shock and saw his body stiffen as his wife spoke. They disappeared from sight around the bushes and Kyreen turned her attention to the animals. By the time Kare returned, both horses and the mule were tethered to the wagon and grazing.

"Sonja asked for you," he mumbled, avoiding Kyreen's gaze and dumping the armful of wood onto the ground.

"Thank you," Kyreen murmured, hurrying over to Sonja's side.

As soon as she felt the woman's pain, all other thoughts left Kyreen's brain. Gone were thoughts of Jorn and Ildri, Markku and the stallion, Kare and his pride, her brother and Calan. For the next couple of hours, she concentrated on the task before her.

With gentle tones and soft hands, Kyreen guided the babe into the world. As she had told Kare, Kyreen had never delivered a child, but she did have experience with horses and approached the birth similarly. Just as Kyreen had predicted, the baby was a girl. Her cry echoed in the clearing as Kyreen wiped the newborn clean and swaddled her in a clean cloth.

Kare's face, lined with worry, appeared around a bush. "All is well?" he inquired, his concern overriding his pride.

Kyreen stood and walked over to the man, handing him the child. "Aye," she said. "All is well. You have a daughter."

Even as she spoke pain radiated from Sonja, so startling Kyreen that she almost missed handing the child to Kare.

Steering him away from the birthing spot, back towards his older children, Kyreen whispered, "I shall take care of this and get Sonja ready to see the other children, right?"

"Aye," replied Kare, unaware of Kyreen's concern, his gaze never leaving the face of his newest daughter, her cries dropping to a soft whimper.

Kyreen hurried to Sonja's side, trying to calm the anxiety rising within her. Though a hard labor, the birth had been fairly routine with the baby presenting properly, but still Sonja was exhausted.

Kyreen pressed on the abdomen slightly, a frown creasing her forehead. Another baby? How did she miss this? How had she not sensed two babies? This unborn child's life force was much weaker than the other babe's. That must be it, Kyreen told herself.

"Sonja?" she spoke softly. "Looks like you have a surprise here for Kare."

"What do ye mean, Ky?" Sonja's voice barely reached the girl's ears. "I am so very tired. Might I take a nap now?"

"Soon, but not yet," Kyreen replied, keeping her voice calm, willing Sonja to relax and getting ready for the baby to be born. From within the womb, Kyreen felt the unborn child's struggles weakening. Quelling her own anxiety, the girl quietly urged the laboring woman through this next delivery.

In the clearing, Hanne sat quietly on the ground, a triumphant smile upon her face. The baby was a girl! That would shut Sven up for sure, she thought. Holding her arms out, she said, "I am ready to hold the baby, Papa."

Kare leaned over to let his eldest daughter hold her new sister when Sonja cried out in pain. Startled the man jerked upright, pulling the baby close to his body. A heartbeat later another cry carried into the clearing. Not his wife this time, but another babe. Kare glanced down at the daughter in his arms, who had awakened when Kare stood up. Although startled, the newborn remained quiet. Another babe? Even as he stared at the child in his arms, Kare realized all sounds from the other side of the bushes had ceased. He bent down to Hanne, her arms still held out for her sister.

"Hold her head," he commanded quietly. "And do not move. I shall be right back."

Hanne nodded, her eyes locked on her baby sister. A sister! After two brothers, Hanne was ecstatic. This was better than a doll any day. As the babe drifted back to sleep, Hanne started talking softly to the newborn, quietly explaining all the fun things they will do together.

Needing to act, but unsure of what to do, Kare moved towards the bushes. Child birthing was part of the women's world, upon which he had no desire to intrude. Still, his wife was there with a stranger, a woman he had thought to be a man. Steeling himself, Kare walked around the bush and stopped short at the sight of his wife lying in a pool of bloody grass. Just to the side, Kyreen stooped over a tiny motionless form, no bigger than Hanne's rag doll and just as lifeless, his skin a deep blue against the white cloth upon which he lay.

"Breathe," the girl whispered over and over, two fingers vigorously rubbing the baby's chest. The listless body twitched and a sputtering cry erupted from the tiny form. Even as the weak cry grew in volume and strength, Kyreen wrapped the babe in a clean cloth and stood, carrying the bundle to Kare, her smile bright.

Without a hat shading her face, Kare fully saw the girl's face for the first time. Unshed tears glittered in her green eyes, her alabaster skin radiated in the sunlight, her facial features chiseled beauty. He thought, how could I have ever thought this woman to be a man?

As he took the child, she said, "A boy. Twins. How I missed it, I know not."

"Ky?" Sonja called feebly. "All is well?"

"Go. Take care of the little ones while I care for your wife," Kyreen said not unkindly, motioning Kare away before moving back to kneel beside Sonja.

Wiping the woman's brow, Kyreen replied, "Aye. All is well. You have two beautiful babes, a boy and a girl."

Sonja chuckled weakly. "Hanne and Sven both got their wish."

"Rest now while I clean everything up then you can meet your children proper," Kyreen whispered.

A short time later, Kyreen led a shaky Sonja to the fire where Kare had water boiling. As Kyreen prepared a cup of tea for the other woman, she glanced over at the large man, holding both sleeping babes in his arms. Hanne stared at Kyreen with an adoring smile while Sven looked very disgruntled.

Squatting beside Sonja, proffering the tea to the exhausted woman, Kyreen said, "Drink up and then we should be on the road. You and the babes need rest, real rest, not out here in the woods."

Sonja nodded, grateful for the drink's warmth spreading through her chilled body. Kyreen poured herself some tea and settled beside Kare. The silence between them grew, heavy and uncomfortable.

Finally, Kyreen said quietly, "Kare, please forgive the deception. It was not my wish to..."

Kare interrupted, his voice also hushed, careful not to wake the sleeping newborns, "Do not say another word, Ky. The Lords were watching out for me and my family when they set our paths to cross."

He paused to look down at the children, then his wife across the fire before adding, "Twins are an omen, either of great blessing or of great misfortune. Without your aid, I could easily be digging three holes in the ground rather than worrying about making Eileen's farm by nightfall. For these blessings I hold, I am eternally grateful to ye."

The sincerity of Kare's emotions surprised Kyreen, who had expected the discovery of her ruse to be met with anger or antagonism. Tears shimmered anew in her eyes as she took a sip of her tea. From the corner of her eye, she saw Sven cross his arms and heard his snort of annoyance. As she was deciding how to address the young boy's obvious disapproval of her gender, another movement caught her eye and she sprung to her feet, the mug falling to the ground.

Chapter 15

Two men had approached unnoticed from the road. One was short with tousled dirty blond hair and a paunch around the middle. Kyreen heard Jorn's words in her head. "Evidence of too much time in a tavern and too little time at honest labor," he would have said with a snort.

The man's companion was tall and extremely thin, his facial features sunken and emaciated, scraggly dark hair covering his chin and poking out from under his dingy hat. Their clothes were dirty and threadbare, and both men carried clubs, heavy wooden weapons, awkward yet dangerous. Kyreen's eyes narrowed and her hand went for the knife at her belt.

"Not so fast there, youngster," said the shorter of the two, taking a position behind Sonja. "Slowly take that blade out and gently toss it this way."

He looked at Kare and nodded. "Ye stay there, good sir, and mind the babes. Good lad," he continued, when Kyreen did as instructed.

Using the thick end of his club, he prodded Sonja in the back and said, "Will ye be so kind as to join ye men o'er there, m'lady?"

The tall dark-haired bandit grabbed Sven and Hanne by the shoulder, shoving them towards Sonja, who gathered the children in her arms as she settled down beside Kare.

Kyreen silently breathed a sigh of relief. Now that the family was huddled together the bandits no longer had a shield. Patience, she reminded herself, wait for the moment. She raised her hands in the universal symbol of yielding.

Kare, imposing even as he sat upon the log, glared up at the two men. "We have not much. A few coins," he said.

"Now that is a mistake, good sir," the short man retorted, pointing with his club. "Ye have a fine mule and wagon there, and two riding horses over yonder."

Kyreen kept her gaze fixed on the talkative bandit, tracking the other from the corner of her eye. He was moving away from the group, towards the animals his partner had just denoted.

Kare's voice raised in anger. "Ye cannot take the mule. My wife has just given birth. She cannot walk!"

The bandit shrugged indifferently, glancing over at his partner, "Ingo, quit ye dawdling. Make haste. Get those animals."

When the bandit turned his head to address his partner, Kyreen pounced, leaping across the fire to grapple the man to the ground. While she had a few inches of height on the man, he carried more weight which she used to her advantage, letting the force of her attack slam his head back into the ground, stunning him.

Kyreen sprung to her feet, and, in three quick bounds, was in front of the other bandit, the one called Ingo. Caught unaware Ingo did not even react as the girl slammed an open palm to his chest, knocking the breath from his lungs. A sweeping kick knocked the man's legs out from under him, slamming him to the ground, but before she could finish the move, strong arms grabbed Kyreen from behind. A third bandit had appeared from some hiding place. Kyreen twisted in vain, unable to shake her foe's grasp. As she struggled to no avail, Kyreen caught sight of Kare standing over the first bandit, one huge boot planted on the man's chest, still holding a babe in each arm. Had the circumstances not been so intense, she would have smiled.

Then she noticed another bandit, a fourth man, tall and much better dressed than the others, standing to the side of, and just behind, Kare, a bow in hand, calmly knocking an arrow. As Kyreen made to call a warning, the bandit holding her wrapped a beefy arm around her neck, cutting off the girl's air supply.

Ingo was rising unsteadily to his feet. "Hold him steady, Skule," he rasped, his breathing ragged and his eyes burning for revenge.

At this moment, all conscious thought was pushed aside and almost-forgotten lessons from long ago took over. Kyreen forced her body limp, so surprising her attacker that she slid to her knees and out from Skule's grasp. Uncoiling from her knees, Kyreen slammed the side of her hand into Ingo's neck, causing more pain than harm, but disabling him so she could twist around to face the bandit who had been choking her. Her eyes widened and she craned her neck up. The man called Skule was huge, towering over Kyreen and easily double, probably even triple her weight.

As the huge man reached for her with his beefy hands, Kyreen was reminded of a bear she and Engla had encountered in the forest many seasons prior. Since climbing a tree and waiting for the beast to pass was not an option at this occasion, Kyreen swept a kick to his outer thigh and the big man collapsed to the ground, howling in pain. The girl returned her attention back to Ingo who was clutching his throat, hoarsely emitting squawking sounds, his discarded club lying on the ground at his feet.

Scooping up the weapon, Kyreen jammed the fat end into Ingo's stomach, and watched him drop once again to his knees, then crumple prone into the fetal position. An instant later, an arrow whizzed harmlessly over the space where the tall dark bandit's head had just been and past Kyreen, falling harmlessly into the bushes, redirecting Kyreen's attention to the bandit standing behind Kare and his family. The archer was pulling another arrow from his quiver, and as he knocked it in place, they locked eyes.

Grasping the club in both hands, Kyreen spun twice, flinging the weapon across the clearing with both great accuracy and tremendous velocity. With superb reflexes, the surprised man managed to twist away, spinning so the brunt of the weapon's force slammed into the quiver strapped to his back. As he staggered, struggling to keep his balance, Kyreen closed the distance between them with lightning speed. Even as quick as she arrived, the archer managed to recover as she struck out. Kyreen's blow deflected off his forearm with enough force to drive the man down to one knee. She struck once, twice and a third time.

The archer, unable to stand, still managed to keep his arm up, her blows glancing off the arm-guard strapped to his forearm. In the back of her head, Kyreen noticed that no matter where she struck the archer managed to shield his body and protect the bow in his other hand. He cared for his weapon and she planned to use that distraction. Even as Kyreen spun around, maneuvering to strike the bow from the archer's hand, Kare's voice penetrated the fury clouding her thoughts.

"Ky!" The desperation of his tone pulled the girl up short and she risked a look over her shoulder.

Kare stood directly behind her, having handed the twins to Sonja, but the large farmer had the good sense not to approach Kyreen in her rage. As soon as she glanced his way, he stepped forward, placing a hand upon her shoulder. His other hand held Kyreen's hat, dislodged in the scuffle.

"He is not with them, lad," Kare said, emphasizing the last word and handing Kyreen her hat. "He was helping us."

Kyreen crammed the hat back on her curls, her fury draining as quickly as it had risen. When she looked back at the archer, who had taken that reprieve to move out of reach, he held his hands up, nodding vigorously. She appraised him, her eyes narrow with suspicion.

Usually Kyreen could get an immediate read upon meeting a person, but this time nothing clear came through. She would need to keep a close eye on him. A quick survey of the clearing showed the other bandits had fled during the distraction of her scuffle with the archer.

Kare took Kyreen's hesitation as a positive sign and stepped forward, his hand proffered. "Kare of Flueren. Thanks be to the Lords for your arrival, man."

The archer took Kare's hand. "Collin, sir. Collin of Myrddin," he replied, his eyes drifting to Kyreen. "Ye pack a fairly vicious punch there." He held a hand out to the girl.

With reluctance, Kyreen stepped forward and grasped the man's hand. Boy, actually, she thought silently. Not much older than she, Collin was just a tad taller yet much broader of shoulder than Kyreen, with a mop of shaggy dark hair, tawny skin and golden hazel eyes. The grasp of his hand was firm, but not too hard. He was not trying to overpower or challenge Kyreen. Still there was something in his demeanor that annoyed her. He was definitely hiding something. Again, Kyreen resolved to keep a close watch on this one.

"This is Ky of..." Kare filled the silence, covering Kyreen's social gaffe.

"Labeck," she finished the introduction and felt the stranger tense. She pulled back her hand. He knew this to be a lie and she heard herself ask, "How?"

"How what?" Both Kare and Collin asked in unison.

"How...did you happen upon us?" Kyreen recovered quickly.

She felt a brief flash of discomfort before the newcomer smiled. "I am heading to the city. My business in Wentworth finished up and I decided to take the road home. The river barge is always so crowded," he replied, his gaze never leaving Kyreen's face.

"And your horse?"

"Tethered beyond the copse. I heard the scuffle and tied him there before investigating."

Kyreen's brow creased. Collin's gaze never wavered. He knew she knew his words to be a lie yet he had no concern. This man lied as effortlessly as he had handled the bow.

Before she could respond, Kare clapped both of them on the back, exclaiming, "How fortunate! Ky here is headed that way. Now ye shall have company once we part ways, Ky. Wonderful news, indeed!"

Kare paused, glancing to the skies. White thunderheads had rolled in during the scuffle and shadows now covered the forest floor. "We should be on the road soon. The turn-off for the homestead is but a short distance away."

Kyreen nodded and spun away, striding towards her horses. A companion! Of course, Kare would think a companion to be grand now that he knew her to be a woman. She fumed quietly as she readjusted the gelding's saddle. Pulling the cinch tight, Kyreen risked a glance back towards the fire. Collin stood where she had left him, his eyes fixed upon her, Sven by his side.

Even from here Kyreen could hear the boy's voice peppering the newcomer with questions about his bow and the city. Their gazes locked, and Kyreen resolved to hold it all afternoon if necessary. Eventually the stranger turned away, flashing a charming smile upon Sven and answered the boy's most recent question. Slowly Kyreen exhaled her pent-up breath and returned attention to her own chore. The ride into Myrddin would be interesting indeed.

Chapter 16

After saying good-bye to Kare and family without further incident, Kyreen and Collin continued down the deserted road towards Myrddin. The clouds overhead had continued to darken with the threat of rain. The river, long ago faded from sight and hearing, would continue its windy trek north around the mountain range while the road veered nearly straight west ward, directly into the heart of the mountains. Distance-wise the river covered more miles, but was the preferred method into Myrddin as the road had to climb up and over the mountain corridor. Kyreen urged the gelding into a gentle trot, wishing to cover as much as possible before the rain began.

She cast an appraising eye at her companion, who had urged his own mount faster to match the gelding's pace. Collin had surprised her twice already. First, he was not the chatty companion that Kyreen had expected. Since leaving the family Collin had not uttered a word. Second, his horse, while not as fine a specimen as either of Kyreen's horses, had turned out to be of decent stock. The gelding was a leggy dapple gray with black mane and tail. His chest was a bit narrow for Kyreen's taste, but he held a fine carriage, pranced without nervousness, and his eyes flashed with spirit. Though Collin appeared to sit easy in the saddle, Kyreen could sense horsemanship was not natural to him, but more a learned skill. He never relaxed or gave the gray a slack rein.

Still, she reminded herself, he was hiding something, but then again so was she. Hiding did not mean conspiracy or treason. All in all, she finally conceded, the situation could be worse. At least he thought her to be a man and traveling with a companion would be safer and the ride to Myrddin was only two days.

She cast another fleeting look at Collin. Something stirred deep inside, a thrilling emotion, causing butterflies to erupt within her stomach. The strength of this reaction staggered Kyreen as she struggled to identify the unfamiliar pang. With a shake of her head, she pushed these thoughts and feelings aside. This was no time for distractions. Setting her jaw, she urged the gelding into a slightly faster pace, determined to concentrate on the road ahead. The sooner they arrived in Myrddin, the sooner she would part ways with Collin.

When the rains finally arrived in the late afternoon, Kyreen pulled off the road at a small clearing. Dismounting, she aimed her gaze to the skies.

Although less than an hour of daylight still remained, she was reluctant to stop and only her duty to their mounts kept her from pressing forward. With the gray clouds overhead, visibility was dimming. The clearing here was suitable, so why take the chance of injuring one of the horses or not finding a suitable campsite?

Collin pulled his horse up next to her. "Time for camp already?" he asked.

Although these were his first words since they had parted from the family, his tone grated Kyreen. She shrugged and began caring for the horses, letting the thunder answer for her. She had just finished placing an oilcloth over the leather tack when the skies opened in torrential downpours, decreasing the fading daylight even more.

Kyreen used the rain showers to wash the stallion's coat clean. Thank the goddess the spring temperatures here were more temperate than in Hanoria. Once all the horses, including Collin's grey, were groomed, she tethered the three to a line between two trees, feeding them some of the grain from her pack before joining Collin at the small fire he had going in the shelter of an ancient hardwood tree, its overhead tangle of branches so thick that no rain penetrated. Inside a small pan resting on a stone at the edge of the flames, water had just begun to bubble.

"A tent?" Kyreen blurted without thought, having caught sight of the tent erected at the edge of their small refuge. She settled on the ground while Collin ignored her, continuing to wipe down his bow with a rag.

After a long moment, she shrugged, realizing he was not about to respond. Rummaging through her bag Kyreen pulled out a bag of tea, some dried meat and two of the yellow apples Sonja had pressed upon them at their farewells. Kyreen held up one of the apples for Collin, quirking an eyebrow inquisitively. Even as he nodded she tossed it to him, surprised anew when he managed to snatch it from the air. He crunched the fruit and fixed his gaze upon Kyreen.

"Did I pass?" Collin asked, firelight reflecting merrily in his hazel eyes. He leaned back on one elbow, legs stretched out towards the fire.

Now it was Kyreen's turn to disregard Collin. Leaning forward she passed a piece of dried meat to him before leaning back to bite into her own apple. Quickly finishing the light meal, Kyreen glanced at the burlap sack she had set next to her knapsack. As much as Kyreen had wanted to spend time with the blade during her evening, she was reluctant to pull it out in front of this man, still such a stranger.

Collin's presence annoyed her to no end, but she could not pinpoint exactly what about the man upset her. Usually she could gauge a person within minutes of meeting, but Collin, no. She had ridden beside him for hours today which had only muddled her insights. He had done nothing to warrant the suspicions that tickled her, but then again, she did not know about what he was keeping secret. She looked over at Collin to find his gaze still fixed on her face, the flickering light from the fire turning his tawny skin a deep golden bronze. That unfamiliar pang flared once more in the pit of her stomach and she angrily pushed it back. This physical reaction to him must be what was clouding her readings. She began to assemble the evening tea, welcoming the distraction.

As Collin finished his apple he tossed the core out of the firelight into the rain. Kyreen's gaze followed the trash's trajectory before looking back at Collin, her expression disdainful over the rim of her mug. He shrugged, "What?"

Kyreen contemplated him in silence, ignoring the flutter in her stomach, instead allowing her mind to drift to an early memory. One of the first lessons taught to the Calanian youth was to never leave evidence. Everything one carried into the forest was to be carried out or buried without leaving a trace. For two years on the run with her mother, this lesson had saved the pair countless times, exasperating their followers over and over. The habit had become so instilled within Kyreen that for all the years she resided with Jorn and Ildri, she had secured her belongings out of sight in the small loft. Had anyone ever come upon the cottage in her absence, they would never know the couple had a child living with them.

"What's in the rag?" he asked, his expression challenging her to deny her interest in the package beside her. When Kyreen did not answer, he prodded a little further. "Looks like... a blade? Too much weapon for you, laddie?"

Kyreen grinned. While she may be inexperienced and struggling with this new sensation, this physical attraction that Collin evoked inside her, she was practiced handling verbal jabs. If Collin held some interest in the burlap sack it might be good to ignore the blade for tonight.

"Tis none of your concern," she said with her own smile, adding almost as an afterthought, "...laddie."

Without another word, she rose, gathered her belongings and moved to the base of the old tree. Wrapping a blanket about her shoulders and setting her head upon her knapsack, she settled down on her side, back to the fire, the burlap sack securely setting in front of her. Silently she ran through her daily recitations, calming both her mind and emotions. Still it was a while before she drifted to sleep, acutely aware of Collin's gaze upon her.

And gaze upon her, he did. This girl, this Calanian—yes, he knew of her charade and her origins—was nothing like Collin had expected.

Everything Collin had learned about the girl and her mother had not prepared him to find her boldly walking down the street of a busy town. The assignment in Wentworth had been a way for Collin to escape Myrddin for a few days, hoist some tankards at the village tavern and flirt with local girls. His task there had been fairly straight forward, mundane and, in most people's opinions including his, futile. No one had expected the Calanian to show up there, or anywhere for that matter. Never was he ever to have engaged her and now he was not only travelling with the fugitive, but actually escorting her into Myrddin.

Collin wondered where the mercenary was now. Had he gone back to Galor? Collin did not know for sure. He only hoped that they would not meet up with the scarred man whose exit from the city a fortnight ago had coincided with Collin's own departure.

Admittedly it had been a fluke of chance that Collin had even spotted the girl. If not for Collin hearing Sven calling out to the girl, Collin never would have paid attention to the tall youth leading two horses through the township. Everything in her demeanor had puzzled him until he had finally realized the girl's worries revolved around the stallion, the stolen horse. For the first time, but definitely not the last, Collin wondered if this girl, if Kyreen—yes, he also knew her true name—had any idea of what awaited her in Myrddin and beyond. She did not behave like a fugitive or a refuge. Today's interactions had definitely blurred the edges of his judgment. Though she gave an impression of strength and invincibility, Collin had spied the naivety and vulnerability beneath her stony surface.

The girl's handling of the bandits had shown her trained, prepared, and even willing to inflict damage when pressed. That she was so incredibly beautiful did not help either. Did she truly believe she was fooling anyone with her farce?

So many times today Collin had had to catch himself before flashing

Kyreen a wink or making a flirtatious comment. As long as she thought he thought she was a man, Kyreen would be comfortable travelling with him. If Collin kept his mouth shut and head down, he might be able to continue with this silly charade until they made Myrddin. Then he would turn this Calanian over to Dwyn, the guild master. Collin's job would be done and he would receive his portion of the reward.

The reward. It promised to be quite a sum of gold. It was upon that which he should concentrate his thoughts. The reward. He need not worry about this girl, her vulnerability and those bewitching green eyes. The reward. He would continue telling himself that. Focus on the reward.

Kicking dirt over the dying fire, Collin retired into his small tent, directing his thoughts toward the reward. Still, when the Myrddinian did finally drift into a fitful sleep, green, not gold, was the color which monopolized his dreams.

Chapter 17

After giving the gelding's cinch one last tug, Kyreen glanced over the clearing a final time. Light from the sun rising into clear blue skies trickled orange throughout the grove. Earlier she had retrieved Collin's stray apple core from the bushes to be buried with the rest of their refuse. Satisfied all traces of their camp had been erased, she swung into the saddle and addressed Collin for the first time that morning.

"Be there any towns twixt here and Myrddin?" she asked.

"Just two on the other side of the mountains. The first on the river is the barge's last stop before Myrddin and the last is half-day between the two," Collin answered, already on the gray's back.

After his many close calls yesterday and a restless night's sleep leaving him drowsy, Collin had resolved not to address Kyreen unless she directly asked him a question. Too many questions would be raised if he accidently slipped and revealed the depth of his knowledge.

Kyreen nodded and turned the gelding towards the road, the stallion's lead loose in her hand. As she calculated the grain and gold remaining in her bags, she absently chewed her lower lip. Lost in her thoughts, Kyreen did not notice Collin watching her.

Was she planning on entering the town instead of skirting it? Were her thoughts solely on the stud's owner pursuing her? Did she have any clue that a man much more dangerous than the stallion's owner awaited her in Myrddin? If she did, would she change her plans? Collin doubted it.

She seemed like one who approached problems straight on, unskilled and unfamiliar in the fine art of deception. Collin could certainly help her there.

Help her? By the Lords, what was he thinking? The unexpected thought startled Collin so that he pulled the gray up short.

"What is it?" Kyreen's voice broke through Collin's musings.

Sensing his distress, she had pulled her horse up even with him, her gaze sweeping across the forest flanking the road.

Collin shook his head. "Nothing," he replied, urging the horse back into motion.

Kyreen studied Collin's back for a long moment before once again spurring her mount forward. Though he was still hiding something from her, his feelings had changed. This morning he harbored more emotion towards his conflict. Kyreen kept her attention sharp on the forest, wondering not for the first time if she had been wise to continue to travel with this stranger.

As the road began its ascent, the travelers emerged from the tree line around mid-morning. After the forest's intimate embrace, Kyreen felt exposed and open to the elements. Here the road was nothing more than a narrow pathway weaving through a grassy field border by rolling hills, themselves flanked by majestic snow-topped mountains. Without the woods' insulation and with the increased altitude, the drop in temperature was readily felt by the trekkers. Kyreen cast a worried glance at the mist swirling above.

After her many years in Hanoria, she had learned well the signs of impending snowstorms. By her calculations, they only had a few hours to get someplace sheltered. This looked to be a fast-moving system, not a major storm. Still it would slow down their progress.

Thick heavy snowflakes began to fall shortly after midday cutting visibility to practically nothing. The pathway of hard packed dirt quickly became slick and, although anxious to continue, Kyreen dare not risk any of the horses slipping. Once she finally relented that they must halt, it became apparent there would be no easily-accessible sheltering trees to protect the animals. Her two horses still had relatively thick winter coats from the cold season in Hanoria. Collin's grey, however, was not accustomed to snows. Thank the goddess there was very little wind, so it should have no trouble overnight if she tethered it between the other two. Kyreen resolved to monitor the horses throughout the evening.

While Kyreen cared for the horses, Collin took to setting up the tent and gathering wood. What little he found was already too damp to light for a fire. Giving up on the warmth of a fire, Collin stood eyeing the tent as Kyreen finished caring for the horses and pondered his next words to the girl.

If he invited Kyreen into the tent, she would unceremoniously and staunchly reject the notion. Pleading would never work, neither would mockery. Ignoring her freezing in the snow would backfire as well. Never would she invite herself into the tent. Frowning, he brooded in silent frustration at this woman's stubbornness. No matter how he approached the subject, Kyreen would resist any suggestions of sharing the tent with him.

"You assemble this structure then stand in the snow like a clodpate?"

With a start, Collin realized Kyreen, having finished caring for the horses, had moved to stand in front of him. A heartbeat later he also realized that for the first very time her tone was not derisive, but that she was actually joking. From under the hat brim, now piled with snow, Kyreen's eyes twinkled merrily.

When he failed to respond, she asked, "Is the tent for show or can we possibly use it as shelter from this snowfall?"

Feeling simultaneously embarrassed and delighted, Collin held back the flap to the tent and mumbled, "Shelter."

A short time later, having shed their soaked outer garments and boots, the pair found themselves seated in tight quarters. The outside world faded away as the muffled sound of snowfall blocked all exterior noises.

Collin looked over at Kyreen's face in the muted light and realized the mistake of being in such close proximity. How could he possible continue this charade? Even as he opened his mouth to speak, Kyreen pulled the scabbard from the burlap sack, giving Collin a welcomed diversion.

"Ready to tell me about your little blade?"

"No," Kyreen stated, surprising them both with her directness, "But if it will keep you quiet...."

She drew the sword from the sheath and Collin whistled softly. Kyreen held her hands out, palms up, so that the tri-colored hilt rested in one hand and the steel blade in the other. Even in the dimness, Collin recognized master workmanship. The sword was neither the biggest nor the most intricately decorated he had ever beheld, but breathtaking nonetheless. His fingers ached to run along the runes etched along the blade and wrap around the hilt, but he resisted the urge. Tearing his gaze from the sword, he glanced at Kyreen, who was also staring at the weapon resting in her palms. For once the girl's expression was unguarded, a combination of grief and joy swirling across Kyreen's face with the memories.

Mama wielding the blade during morning ritual...The painting of Mama's parents, the sword painted hanging from King Rolf's side... The scabbard resting upon a bedside table whilst the twins jumped upon Mama's mattress...Mama allowing Kyreen to carry the sheathed sword back to the castle one sunny afternoon after a training session...Mama handing the blade to Arvis in the shade of ancient oak trees. Except for training sessions and rituals practiced by her mother so long ago, Kyreen had never seen the sword unsheathed, had never truly examined the blade.

'By the goddess, you were scarcely three when last you saw the blade,' she silently chastised herself, realizing belatedly that Collin was watching her, waiting for her to speak.

"This blade," she said, pausing to swallow the lump in her throat, "belonged to my mother…mother's family."

Collin nods, returning his gaze to the blade. Though questions were tugging at his tongue, he remained quiet. Kyreen was skittish. Any words he spoke would most likely stay her tongue, so he continued waiting until she was ready.

"I…It…," Kyreen stumbled, not knowing how much to reveal, but feeling the need to share Jorn's betrayal. "The blade was lost when I was but a child and although it was returned several years back I only received it a few days past."

Fighting with every fiber of his being, Collin resolved to remain silent. His expression however asked the silent question.

"My foster father," Kyreen answered. "He chose to keep the blade from me for fear I would leave as soon as I took possession, which actually I did. Of course, I was leaving Hanoria for other reasons." She paused again, unaware she had spilled a secret. She closed her eyes, pressing back the tears.

"Jorn is not a bad man, just weak," she continued, hating that she was making excuses for him. Although his actions still burned at her heart, she could not forget her first years at the homestead. When her mother had disappeared, when Kyreen finally accepted Tyra would not—no—could not return, the Hanorian couple had sheltered her and did their best to be her family. For that Kyreen owed Jorn some respect.

Collin watched the struggle reflected within Kyreen's eyes, his mind whirling. Hanoria. That explained why the girl had not been seen for years. Remote and isolationist, Hanoria would have be an ideal hiding place. He wondered how the Calanian queen had found a Hanorian willing to protect her daughter. Quite an accomplishment. It also explained much of Kyreen's behavior. Collin doubted news of Calan had ever reached the out-of-the-way Hanorian village. Kyreen must not know of Calan's misfortune, he reasoned. Even more reason for him to continue with her. She would need help.

Collin became aware of Kyreen's gaze upon him, her face closed up again. Her eyes searched his questioningly and he wondered at the rumors about Calanian mind readers.

Brusquely, he tore his gaze away and reached out as to grab the blade. His feint distracted Kyreen as he had hoped and she pulled the weapon out of his reach.

"Are ye daft, man?" she asked, disdain once again present in her tone.

Obviously, taken aback by his actions, she sheathed the sword and placed it back into the burlap sack, making a show of knotting the twine. Casting him one final derisive glance, she moved to pull on her boots. "I am going to check the horses. Can I trust you alone with my belongings or must I slog outside with my pack?"

"I shall not molest your precious cargo, m...my word," Collin stumbled, almost calling Kyreen 'M'lady.' Inwardly he cringed, berating himself silently. One of these times he would truly blunder and then he would be in trouble. Collin did not wish to incur this girl's wrath in the best of times, let alone here, on this desolate mountain.

Kyreen narrowed her eyes at him, obviously not convinced. In the end, she left her property in the tent.

Collin feigned sleep upon Kyreen's return, not wishing any more close calls, but she was not fooled.

"The snows appear to be letting up. We have another couple of hours of daylight."

Collin waited a few heartbeats, hoping she would give up.

"If we press on, we can most likely clear the summit before dark settles," Kyreen continued. He heard rustling, as though she were assembling her belongings. He sighed and sat up.

"Nice nap?" Kyreen asked, flashing him a smile as warm as the weather outside.

"Have ye a death wish?" he asked, ignoring her question. "Do ye know for sure how far be the summit?"

Though Kyreen paused, he could see she was still unconvinced. He knew her weakness and pressed on, "What about the horses? Seems folly to continue with limited visibility. Especially that stallion of yours. He needs to rest, not stumble around on an icy road."

"Fine!" Kyreen's voice rang sharp in the close quarters. "We stay. Just promise me you will be quiet. Better yet," she gathered her pack and the burlap sack, "I shall find shelter outside."

Collin grabbed her arm. "Wait," he pleaded, "Please do not leave."

Kyreen froze at his touch, her gaze locked on the fingers upon her arm. Feeling her trembling beneath his hand, Collin made a rash decision without fully thinking through the consequences. Rising to his knees, he leaned forward, sliding his hand up behind Kyreen's head. Closing his eyes, Collin drew Kyreen's face closer to his and the darkness behind his eyelids exploded into searing hot pain from the girl's forehead slamming into the bridge of his nose. Despite the close quarters, Kyreen still managed to follow the head-butt with a gut-wrenching jab to Collin's abdomen, expelling the air from his lungs. Before Collin had a chance to recover, she had fled the tent.

Groaning as much from regret as pain, Collin rolled onto his back. He knew he had to go after her, lest she slip away, but he found the thought of moving unmanageable.

Belatedly he felt a warm liquid trickling down his cheek and realized his nose must be bleeding. Thrusting a hand out in search of a rag to staunch the flow, his fingers encountered the rough fabric encasing Kyreen's sword. She would never leave without the blade. Silently giving thanks to the Lords, Collin continued fumbling blindly, located his own pack, retrieved a square bit of cloth for his face, then permitted darkness to pull him into a deep and, mercifully, dreamless sleep.

Chapter 18

"Keep close," Collin warned, "Keep quiet. Do not look directly at anyone."

Kyreen nodded, her gaze fixed on the massive front gates of Myrddin. Nothing in her life had prepared her for the bedlam that was the entrance of the realm's largest city. The cacophony of noise was nothing compared to the wave of emotions that smashed into her conscious. People, animals, and carts milled around in apparent disarray as city guard did nothing to direct traffic. Collin, however, knew the process and confidently nudged his mount through the crowd to the appropriate line. Kyreen struggled to suppress her physical reactions to the sensations assaulting her senses and to keep up with Collin, but the undercurrent of the crowd kept catching the stallion and pulling the horse away from her. She finally pulled the animal in to grasp the stud's halter so as to keep him close in the turmoil. When she turned her attention back to Collin, however, he had already traversed the throng and was looking back towards her expectantly.

Once he saw Kyreen heading his way, Collin swung off the gray's back and addressed the guard. Too far away to hear their conversation, Kyreen nonetheless observed the amity between the two men. The set of Collin's shoulders had relaxed and he laughed at a comment from the soldier. The change in his demeanor was more than physical. Kyreen felt in Collin a liberation and comfort. Myrddin truly was his home and this guard was one of Collin's people. How different this Collin was from the silent stoic individual with whom she had spent the last few days on the road.

The morning after the snowstorm, neither Collin nor Kyreen had discussed what had, or rather had not happened in the tent. Collin had completely withdrawn, speaking less than a dozen words to Kyreen during their last two days on the road, and then only in answer to a direct question. Through Collin's silence, however, Kyreen had felt the conflicts raging within him. As much as her attraction to him annoyed Kyreen, she could not imagine the turmoil he must be feeling having tried to kiss another man. Now as she watched him conclude his business with the guard, it was nearly enough to make Kyreen feel sorry for Collin and a shadow of a smile lifted the corners of her mouth as she finally covered the distance between them.

Seeing the smile, Collin just raised an eyebrow and, remounting the gray, headed through the pedestrian gate. For, although Kyreen sensed the correct emotions—guilt, embarrassment, disgrace and mortification—she was after all mistaken at the underlying reason. All the more reason Collin was grateful to have this journey completed and returning to the familiarity of his city. Pausing in the center of the entrance square, he closed his eyes and inhaled deeply. This was home. He glanced at Kyreen.

"Keep close," he said, "The stables are near."

Kyreen stiffened. "Stables? I never agreed to…"

Collin cut her off in mid-sentence. "Yes, stables. Where else in the city would ye keep your horses?"

As Kyreen opened her mouth to protest, he shook his head emphatically. "No arguments. I know the stable master. Your animals shall be well kept."

A short time later, Kyreen followed Collin away from the large wooden structure. She glanced over her shoulder, catching a final glimpse of sorrel as her horses were led into the shadows. The sense of loss was deeper than she had expected and tears sprung to her eyes. Blinking, she turned her attention to Collin who was speeding away from her, his gait lengthening with every stride.

"Collin," she called out, her words swept away in the chaos of the street. From her right, she heard horns and shouts. A second later the crowd surged, sweeping her towards the sounds.

She struggled to keep her path, barely able to see Collin's head bobbing down a side street, but in a moment, that was gone and she was carried away.

After what could have been five seconds or five minutes, the surge receded and Kyreen was able to disengage herself from the crowd. Pressing back against a hard wooden wall, she glanced around. This appeared to be the town center, a few ancient trees scattered amongst green grass framed by cobblestone streets. On the far side of the square, opposite Kyreen's position, set a large ugly contraption. A feeling of trepidation spread as she gazed upon the wooden structure, so grossly out of place in these otherwise idyllic surroundings.

A shout rose among the crowd gathered around the construction. The people parted for an approaching party. When she saw the guards and five prisoners, hands secured behind their backs, Kyreen realized she had been staring at gallows, the faded gray scaffold with wooden crossbeams wide enough for hanging seven at one time. When Kyreen finally grasped the contraptions purpose and the deadly situation she was witnessing, the crowd's exhilaration nauseated her. The prisoners had been marched up the steps and now balanced atop five of the seven barrels.

Desperate to escape, Kyreen stood on tiptoe and cast a glance around. In the short time, she had stood in one place, the entire square had filled with bodies. That was when Kyreen spotted her, a dark-haired woman, dressed in trousers, the forest green cloak draped about her tall lanky frame. The woman was also glancing around the square, her countenance facing Kyreen's direction, but her eyes were averted down the street. It had been a decade and a half since Kyreen had seen her mother, but the alabaster skin, the chiseled features, the errant ebony curls were unmistakable.

Stepping away from the wall, Kyreen inadvertently brushed against a vendor, his pots clanking noisily as he stumbled from the contact.

"Watch it there, laddie," the peddler growled, eyeing Kyreen suspiciously. Just the week before two lads not much younger than this upstart had pinched a couple of his best wares in a similar bump-and-run con. "I got me eyes on ye, jackanapes."

Kyreen backed away, apologizing even as she turned back towards the woman, who had begun to move towards the gallows. Without taking her eyes from the cloaked woman, Kyreen began weaving through the crowd. Everyone's attention was riveted on the gallows, on the people about to be hanged, in morbid fascination. Kyreen fought to shield her mind from the nauseating emotions rolling from the people.

A roar went through the crowd, drawing the girl's attention back to the gallows. It was then Kyreen truly noticed the prisoners, hoods being drawn over their faces. Just before the executioner hooded the one on the very end, Kyreen saw this prisoner, by far the smallest, was a child, a girl mayhap ten summers of age with alabaster skin and dark curls.

The executioner reached to pull the noose around the child's neck, and Kyreen looked back to where the cloaked woman had been. The woman had disappeared. Cursing herself, Kyreen cast her gaze all around, but could not locate the mysterious woman.

As the first prisoner's barrel was kicked out from beneath him, Kyreen worked her way towards the gallows, trying to shield the overwhelming emotions that threatened to suffocate her. Though a few disgruntled protests were uttered, Kyreen's progress was easy with everyone's attention held by the death show.

By the time the third prisoner's fate was sealed with the kick of a barrel, Kyreen was close enough to the gallows to hear the child's soft voice, murmuring what seemed to be a prayer. Although Kyreen could not make out the individual words, the rhythm was familiar. With a jolt, she realized the child was reciting the same mantra Kyreen herself said twice a day.

At that moment, the fourth prisoner dropped and Kyreen heard the unmistakable hiss of an arrow being loosed from the bow. An instant later the executioner fell to his knees, clutching his shoulder. Kyreen followed the trajectory back and spotted the cloaked woman, standing at the foot of the stairway. A tall dark-haired man behind her knocked another arrow into his bow even as the woman started up the stairs. The second arrow struck the lone guard at the top of the stairs, another shoulder shot, non-fatal, a fact Kyreen registered dimly.

"She's gonna fall," voices cried out all around and Kyreen looked back up at the child. Before the arrow had struck his shoulder, the executioner had placed his boot to the barrel under the child, and, on his way to his knees, had jarred the barrel upon which the child stood.

Horrified, Kyreen watched the child totter, fighting to balance as the barrel threatened to tip over. Just as the barrel gave way, the cloaked woman swooped in, gathering the child in one arm and slicing the rope in the other.

"Outta my way," commanded a gruff voice from beside Kyreen even as she was roughly pushed aside. A guard made his way towards the gallows, his hands reaching towards the platform so as to leap up. Without giving thought to her actions, Kyreen shifted her weight so as to knock the man beside her into the guard, causing both men to fall to the ground. Smoothly, Kyreen slipped through the chaotic crowd, a few paces away from the guard before looking up at the gallows. Kyreen pressed up onto her toes, straining to see. The woman, the man and the child had vanished. Just then a heavy hand dropped down upon Kyreen's shoulder.

Chapter 19

"There ye are," a voice whispered in Kyreen's ear and she registered Collin's voice just in time to stop slamming her elbow into his stomach.

His face displayed anger, but Kyreen registered concern, almost panic, in the emotions rolling from the man. She fought the urge to look again for the woman and child, not wanting to explain to Collin. There was something odd in his behavior, something she could not pinpoint, but she did not yet trust him.

"Sorry," she said, falling in step beside him as the people began to dissipate, "I am not used to the crowds. I was swept away from you."

Evidently the escape did not concern the common folks, only the guards remained agitated. Kyreen noted how Collin turned his body, shielding his face as a group of soldiers trotted pass. There was definitely more to this boy, this man, than he was letting on to her.

This time, taking no chances, Collin kept a firm grip on Kyreen's elbow as they wove through the streets. Adept at navigating dense forests, Kyreen found the winding, crowded streets disorienting. Unable to firmly pinpoint the sun's positioning, she once again found herself lost in the city's maze of streets. There was no way she would ever find the city gates, let alone her horses. She couldn't approach the authorities. What if Markku had sent word about the stolen horse? No, she was alone and completely dependent on Collin. Anxiety clenched at her heart and she broke out in a sweat.

"Here we are," Collin stopped before a worn door with peeling blue paint. He looked into Kyreen's face. "Are ye alright? You look a little flush."

Kyreen pulled her arm from his grip and shook her head. "Fine. I just do not like this city. It is too closed in. I cannot breathe."

Collin gave her a long silent look before shrugging. "It is not that bad," was all he said before opening the door, rapping loudly with his knuckles as he did so.

"Hallo? Glain? Ye decent, lass?"

A squeal vibrated through the dimness and Kyreen heard footsteps from somewhere above head. As the two travelers stepped completely into the house and Collin shut the door behind them, a tiny shadow erupted from the stairway and wrapped around Collin.

"Oh, laddie! Where have ye been?" the high-pitched voice inquired even as the auburn-haired woman, a girl really, not much older than Kyreen, plastered kisses on both of Collin's cheeks before firmly pressing a kiss to his lips. Her greeting complete, the woman stepped back, beaming up at Collin before noticing Kyreen's presence. "Oh, company? Ye brought a friend home, eh? Lucky I always makes up extra stew."

Kyreen remained silent, happy to let Collin initiate the introductions. Pretending to be a man had proved tougher than she had originally thought. Better to do nothing and be thought of as a lout than reveal too much.

The situation did not ruffle Collin. He nodded, waving between the two women, "Glain, Ky. Ky, Glain. We're only here for the night. Is the top room open for Ky?"

Glain nodded to Kyreen, "Well met, Ky. My Collin was never much for talking or manners, but…" she glanced towards Collin, "The room at the top of the stairs, third floor, is always available, ye know that, Collin. Let me fetch the linens."

As Glain turned to go, Collin reached out and slapped her rear, meriting a delighted squeal and a half-hearted swat as the woman headed towards the back of the house.

Once she was gone, Collin turned towards Ky. "I have an errand to run. Glain will get you set up in the room and if you're hungry she'll get you something to eat. Do not leave the house. I'll be back before dark."

Before Kyreen could protest, Collin was out the door and she was alone in the semi-darkness. A moment later, Glain returned, laden with freshly laundered linens. She glanced around unconcernedly.

"Collin headed out, I suppose," she said more as a statement than question, shrugging before Kyreen could answer, "This way, luv."

Kyreen followed Glain up the main stairway to the second floor. At the end of the wide hallway, Glain opened a door and disappeared into the dimness. Kyreen followed, stubbing her toe on the first step of a steep, narrow stairwell. Climbing the stairway and disoriented by the dark closing around her, Kyreen nearly stumbled into Glain, who had stopped at the top of the stairs, fumbling with a ring of keys hanging from her belt.

"Never use this room except when Collin shows his face," Glain commented, almost as if to herself, "He is pretty particular about his things and always locks the door afore he leaves. Kinnae say why. Taint nothing worth stealing up here. Ah, here we go! Pardon me, laddie."

After jingling the key in the lock, Glain took a step down to allow the door, having no space inside the room, to open outward the cramped landing. Glain dumped the linens on one of the two narrow beds, which lined either wall. Standing in the narrow span between the beds, she extended her arms wide to pat either wall.

"Close and cozy, but he loves his room. I will leave ye be, lad," the woman said, squeezing past Kyreen and closing the door before descending the stairs.

Kyreen stood still, listening to hear the door closing at the bottom of the stairs, her eyes taking in the room, although there was not much to take in. The ceiling was not as low, but other than that, Collin's room reminded Kyreen of the loft she grew up in at Jorn and Ildri's cottage.

Kyreen moved between the narrow beds, the head of each pressed to the wall flanking the room's only window. This room was situated in a spire which rose high and through the clear glass of the tall narrow window one could look down upon the neighboring rooftops. Sitting on one of the beds, her knapsack resting in her lap, Kyreen leaned to the side, placing a cheek against the cool glass, and looked down. Even up here, viewing all the buildings wedged so tightly together, she felt claustrophobic. Far over the ragged clay rooftops, however, her gaze caught sight of the ocean, just a tiny sliver shining in the afternoon light.

A vague memory tickled the back of her mind, and then skittered away before solidifying. At one time, she and her mother must have travelled through Myrddin. All the roads from all the provinces began, ended or ran through this city. Kyreen wondered if she had seen this very sea with her mother. Had either of them noticed? How old had she been then? Had they stayed in the city? Kyreen doubted it. Tyra never would have felt safe with all these people or these tall structures which obstructed the sun.

A squeak startled Kyreen back to the present. Its jump falling short, a tiny black and white kitten clung desperately to the bed cover. As it scrambled to gain leverage and haul itself bodily up, Kyreen reached over to boost the creature up, a shadow of a smile gracing her lips. After thoroughly sniffing the battered knapsack, the kitten crawled into the girl's lap, burrowing down into the crook of a bent knee and curled up contentedly, emitting a purr so loud it vibrated through the small room. Kyreen rested her cheek against the pane once more, absently stroking the kitten's soft fur. Although the spring air still held a chill, the sun streaming through the tall window warmed this room. Lazy dust motes floated on sun beams and the girl's eyes began to close. Very shortly both girl and kitten were fast asleep.

Chapter 20

When Collin opened the door a short while later, neither Kyreen nor the kitten stirred. The greeting fell quiet upon his lips as he paused. The late afternoon sun softened the sharpness of the girl's face as did sleep. She looked younger than her nineteen summers, the weight of her worries lifted away.

Collin felt an unfamiliar pang. He felt protective of this woman, masquerading as a man. For an instant he wondered if he could convince her to ride south with him, although he knew that would not solve anything. If Collin had been able to find her so quickly after all these years, it would only be a matter of time before the mercenary Falk caught up with them. It would be better to continue with her to the north. Collin was fairly sure Kyreen had no idea what waited for her there. He doubted she even knew where exactly she was headed, let alone what had happened to the people of Calan. She would need his help, his support.

It had taken some maneuvering to convince Dwyn to not come take Kyreen right now. Only the incident in the city square this afternoon had given Collin the ammunition needed when he had reported to the guild master. Absently stroking the guild mark embossed on his bracer, Collin thought back to the meeting from which he had just departed.

Dwyn had sat eating his mid-day meal in the back room of the tavern which fronted the guild hall, while Collin had stood before the table. With his shaggy brown hair and clothes still dusty from the road, hat in hand, Collin had not been invited to join in the meal nor occupy either of the empty seats flanking the table. Dwyn broke a chunk of bread and sopped at his stew, eyeing Collin warily. Neither Collin nor his older brother Urian had ever been a friend to the guild master, even before Dwyn had mysteriously maneuvered up through the ranks and taken over the guild's leadership last year. As is common with those who gained power through deceit and fear, Dwyn suspected everyone, imagining plots within every shadow or gesture. Once Dwyn confirmed to Collin that the child in the gallows had been Calanian, Collin proposed they allow Kyreen to leave the city with him in hopes of finding the Calanian refugee camp.

"What be in this for you, runt?" Dwyn asked, his words muffled by the bread he had just shoved into his mouth.

Instincts warned Collin to tread carefully. He glanced away from the disgusting spectacle that was Dwyn's midday meal, needing to concentrate. Collin's gaze found Rhun, the guild's sergeant of arms, looming behind Dwyn's chair. Unlike Dwyn, Rhun had been close friends with Collin's brother, spending so much time at their home growing up that Collin considered him family. Now, however, Collin found no alliance in the big man's stoic face. Rhun's lack of reaction reinforced Collin's apprehension. Dwyn must be handled carefully. The power this guild leader held not only affected Collin, but also those close to him, especially Glain and the boarding house.

"I merely wish to serve the guild, Dwyn," Collin replied, his tone meek, shoulders dropped, "Ky...this girl... she may know where the Calanian camp is. If she takes me there, we, you will have all of the Calan people for Falk, instead of one minor pawn."

Collin paused, wanting to continue, but Rhun's gaze had flicked his way very briefly, reminding him to watch his words. Collin kept his head bowed and gaze averted, surreptitiously watching the guild leader from the corner of his eyes.

Dwyn wanted to concentrate on his midday meal. He wanted to ignore the drudge standing before him. He also wanted to successfully conclude his business contract with the one-eyed man called Falk, the one searching for the Calanian girl. That the mercenary scared Dwyn more than anything or anyone else he had met merely served to elevate Falk's status in the guild leader's mind. Fear equaled power and Dwyn craved power more than anything.

Pensively Dwyn chewed and weighed his options. One puny girl or the entire rebel camp. Greed glinted in his eyes as he wiped the back of a hand across his mouth. If Guild Brodyr Llafur were able to deliver the girl in addition to all the rebels, not only would Falk obviously pay generously, but also mayhap the emperor of Galor would be inclined to declare an alliance with the guild. With a Galorian trade agreement in place, that contract with the Myrddin docks would not be such a big issue.

Dwyn drained his cup, making up his mind even as he slammed it back to the table. "Aye, Collin. Get the girl to take ye to the camp," he paused, apprising the man standing before him.

Although Collin did not physically resemble his brother, something about the young man—the tilt of his head, the glint in his eyes, the set of his shoulders—rankled Dwyn, who had joined Brodyr Llafur around the same time as Collin's older brother Urian. While the two had never openly conflicted, they had never been friends. Urian had never fully trusted Dwyn, and Dwyn had always harbored jealousy over Urian's deep-seated relationship with the guild. Urian's death—an unfortunate dock accident nearly three years prior—had secretly pleased Dwyn. Then this youngster Collin had come of age, joined Brodyr Llafur, and had immediately been ingrained within the tight brotherhood, not only because of his father and brother, but also the large man currently looming behind Dwyn, his second-in-command, Rhun, yet another long-standing problem for the guild leader. Sitting back in his chair, Dwyn resolutely pushed aside these unsavory contemplations, waving a hand at his ruined meal, summarily dismissing the young man before him.

"Keep Rhun updated," Dwyn ordered. "Falk arrives within a fortnight and I will take him to the Calanian pass myself. Do not fail me."

As he now watched Kyreen slumber, Collin wondered how long he could keep her safe. As soon as Falk arrived in the city, Dwyn would tell him of her presence here. Falk would not care to wait for the rebel camp. His desire for this particular Calan was fierce and personal. He would not be happy she had not been apprehended immediately. Collin would have to take her north at morning's first light.

Without realizing he had moved, Collin found himself standing inside the room, gazing down upon the sleeping girl. His fingers tingled, desiring to touch the cap of ebon curls, feel their softness, but he resisted the urge. Kyreen had yet to reveal her true nature to him. Their relationship was complex enough without voluntarily adding further complications.

Instead he dropped a hand lightly to her shoulder with a soft, "Ky?"

Instantly Kyreen jerked awake, her movement dislodging the kitten who mewed in protest. Her panicked gaze found Collin's face and she outwardly relaxed. Inwardly she cringed, appalled that she had been sleeping so soundly that he had not only been able to approach her, but had also ascended the narrow stairway without Kyreen detecting him.

"My apologies," she stuttered, picking the kitten up even as she stood.

The tiny room was even smaller with the both of them standing there. Unaccustomed to such close proximity, Kyreen marveled at the experience of looking up to see Collin's face. The afternoon sunlight illuminated his hazel eyes and tawny skin. Even in the warmth of the cramped space, she felt the heat radiating off his body. Involuntarily she felt her own body swaying forward, closing the space between them.

Collin gingerly took the kitten from her arms and stepped back, announcing, "Glain has a bath ready for you in the kitchen, if you care to bathe."

Kyreen hesitated, torn. What was happening to her? Taking midday naps. Practically throwing herself at a man, while she was pretending to be a man?

"Mayhap not now," she sighed and shrugged, knowing to disrobe in front of Glain was not possible.

"She has gone to market for supplies. The kitchen is empty save for a huge pot of hot water and an empty tub," Collin replied, heading down the stairs without waiting for Kyreen's answer.

Kyreen grabbed her sack and hurried down. By the time she maneuvered the stairs to the bottom level, Collin had disappeared. Tentatively she took a right through the dimly lit parlor, her nose following the delicious smell of something simmering in a kettle in the fireplace.

Collin, having taken the lid off for a sniff, turned in time to see Kyreen inhale deeply, eyes closed. He smiled.

"Fish chowder, one of Glain's best dishes," he explained, replacing the lid. He nodded towards the empty tub and the covered vat setting beside it.

Kyreen looked at the tub, then at Collin and back at the tub.

Seemingly oblivious, Collin took an apple from a bowl, seated himself on a stool and began to eat. Kyreen shifted her weight nervously. After a couple of bites, Collin looked over at her and made a decision. Placing the half- eaten apple on the counter, he crossed the kitchen and stood before Kyreen.

Perplexed she watched as he took the knapsack from her hands, set it down, then took her face between his hands, drawing his face close to hers, his hazel eyes locked on her green eyes.

"I know," he whispered before gently pressing his lips to hers.

A cacophony of emotions roiled within Kyreen before she relented, the sensation of his lips upon hers driving away the questions scurrying around her skull. Closing her eyes, she surrendered to the feeling, her arms sliding around his waist, her lips melding to his, relishing the lingering sweet taste of apple.

After a few long moments, Collin pulled back, sliding his hands to her shoulders.

"I will leave you to your bath, m'lady," he whispered huskily.

Chapter 21

Kyreen's eyes flew open. There it was again. She sat up, one hand automatically drawing the dirk from the pack she kept by her side. She paused, poised to spring, her vision adjusting to the dark.

After dinner Kyreen had excused herself to the room. Sharing a meal with six strangers had taxed her energies beyond belief. Deception was not one of her strongest suits and posing as a man, a feat she had once thought easy to assume, had proved more difficult than ever. After dutifully performing her evening exercises in the tiny room, Kyreen had lain in the dark, expecting sleep to elude her after the afternoon nap, but with the sounds of the house and its inhabitants far removed from this little tower room, she had quite easily slipped into sleep's embrace. Kyreen's internal clock estimated the time to be early morning, just before dawn. Unbidden the question arose in her mind—where had Collin spent the night?

Another creak, this from the doorway forced Kyreen to shake away both the thought and accompanying image. Was it a person? Was it someone sneaking up or down? Silently Kyreen swung her legs around, having never undressed, her booted feet resting lightly upon the wood floor. Kneecaps brushing Collin's unoccupied bed in the narrow space, she quietly rose to her feet, then sidestepped towards the door, easing the door open to step onto the top of the landing. A soft body brushed up against her ankle, as the tiny kitten entered the darkened room and scrambled up onto Kyreen's recently vacated bed. Relieved, Kyreen turned to lie back down, but another sound came from the stairwell. This time she recognized the tread as human steps. She pressed into the shadows along the wall to wait, the dirk ready in her hand. The footsteps ascend at a pace more hurried than stealthy. When the door swung open, Kyreen prepared to spring.

"Ky?" whispered Collin quietly, as he moved into the room.

The tension drained from Kyreen and she answered, "Here."

"Ye are awake. Good," he grasped her arm. "We must leave now. They are on their way."

Adrenaline began to flow anew, but Kyreen could not say whether it was from his hand against her skin or the worry in his voice. As his words register, she felt a familiar, yet long absent, focus descended upon her being. Deftly she slipped from his grasp to grab her pack, disgruntling the tiny feline.

Swinging the bag upon her back, she turned to face him once more, commenting, not asking, "You have a way out."

"Aye," he replied, turning away to lead the way down the narrow stairs.

As they descended in silence, Kyreen's mind raced with unvoiced questions. The biggest—who was on their way? — would certainly lead to more questions from Collin, questions for which they did not have the time to answer. Kyreen supposed it must be Markku. Surely he had followed her trail to Myrddin. Most of the roads in the province ended here. Did he have guards with him? Would he have her arrested or take his own justice? Had he found the stable and recovered the stallion?

As the pair reached the ground floor and rounded the corner to the kitchen, Kyreen saw a man standing with Glain. The woman was fully awake and still dressed in her street clothes. The stranger was very tall, almost a head taller than Collin, broad shouldered with dark coarse hair cropped close to his skull, his ebony skin shining in the low firelight, a shadow of bristly stubble covering his chin, his demeanor that of authority. In the instant it took Kyreen to absorb all this, she also noted the heavy broadsword hanging from the man's belt and the well-tended, well-worn armor covering his torso. Though the stranger's only reaction to their entry was to shift in his dark gaze in their direction, Kyreen felt herself being similarly appraised. Otherwise the kitchen was empty. Unbidden another question arose in her mind—How did this person know to seek out Collin?

Glancing at Kyreen over his shoulder, Collin said, "This is Rhun. They will be here within minutes, if not sooner."

Collin turned toward Rhun, and the two men clasped hands then embraced. Words were exchanged between them that Kyreen did not hear. Collin then enfolded Glain in a bear hug.

"Thank ye, Glain," he said, planting a firm kiss upon her forehead.

"Send word when ye can, love," Glain replied, her voice reflecting the tears shimmering in her eyes. Sparing a farewell nod to Kyreen, Glain then pressed a small cloth bundle into Collin's hand, adding softly, "Provisions for the road."

Collin hugged her once more, nodded at Rhun and turned to Kyreen.

"Through here," he said indicating the unused fireplace, ushering Kyreen ahead of him into the shadowed stairwell concealed behind the brick wall.

As the door behind them slid in to place, Kyreen suppressed a wave of panic. The pair descended in silence. Shortly, Collin's hand squeezed slightly on her shoulder, timed just as her boot touched dirt floor. She paused, allowing him to move around her, his hand slipping into hers as he guided her through the dark and found the door. As the cool night breeze rushed in, Kyreen silently released the breath she had been holding, relishing the breeze as it caressed her face and ruffled through her short curls. She inhaled, the tang of salt tickling her nostrils. After the dark cellar, the moonlit alley seemed overly bright. They each looked both ways up and down the alley, finding the passage narrow and deserted.

Muffled hoof beats and voices carried over the rooftops and the two froze, listening. As she realized just how close their escape had been, another long absent emotion flooded through Kyreen, this time a feeling of relief. Collin dropped her hand and began moving down the alleyway, choosing the passage to their left. Bathed in silver moonlight, Kyreen's disorientation intensified and she realized she must continue to trust Collin for now.

"Careful," Collin warned, over his shoulder, quickly returning his attention front as he picked his way through the clutter. Kyreen pushed aside the myriad of questions assaulting her brain to concentrate on following precisely in his footsteps.

By the time the two reached the stable, the sky had lightened to a bruised purple. To Kyreen's surprise, the stable master met them outside the corral gate, reins to all three horses in hand. Collin held up a hand to Kyreen in order to approach the man alone. Once again Collin's conversation was muffled, but this time less cordial than it had been with Rhun. Collin took the reins and pressed a coin into the other man's hand, dismissing the man's weak protest.

Turning towards Kyreen, Collin motioned her forward, transferring control of her two horses before he swung up into the gray's saddle. He looked down at the stable master.

"Ifor, you and I have never been friends, but you have my gratitude for your help this morn," Collin said, reaching down to clasp the man's forearm, "Favor and fortune."

"And to you," came the gruff reply.

Collin led Kyreen down the opposite road from their arrival, towards the merchant gates, which always opened two hours before dawn. Already merchants and traders were backed up as the three gate guards checked wares and collected gate fees. Much to Kyreen's relief, no one cast a glance towards the fugitives as the horses strolled through the gates. The guards were there to monitor who and what came into Myrddin, not who or what exited. Evidently whoever had arrived at Glain's house had not alerted the guards.

As Myrddin disappeared behind a curve in the road, Kyreen breathed a quiet sigh of relief. Immediately Collin urged his mount into a fast lope, and questions clouded her thoughts anew. Was he worried about pursuit or merely making conversation impossible? What did he know about their pursuers? What did he know of Kyreen's history? Kyreen decided now was neither the time nor the place for such a confrontation. Collin had helped her as a friend and she would have to be content with that for now.

Chapter 22

At midday Collin reined in his horse, pulling to a stop in a small clearing shadowed by ancient trees. They had met no one on the road in the hours since they left Myrddin. Kyreen glanced back over her shoulder at the deserted road, then around the clearing before dismounting. Immediately she loosened the saddle, lifting it and the wet blanket from the gelding's back and carried them to a resting spot beneath a tree.

"Do not," Collin said, looking down at her from his perch on the gray. "We are not stopping long."

"You may go on," Kyreen replied, pulling a halter and rope from her saddlebags before walking back to her horses. "These animals need water, rest and food in that order. I will not be treating them the same as Markku just to keep him from catching me."

Collin watched her in silence, processing that last sentence. There was that name again. Who was Markku? As he watched her care for the horses, realization dawned on Collin. The horses! Of course! Markku must be the stud's owner. Kyreen had no idea what happened in Calan, no idea of the heavy price upon her head, no idea how dangerous this road had become for them.

Deep in thought, he swung off his own mount and began to remove the tack. Vaguely he heard a quiet gurgling of running water. The river, which paralleled the road down to Myrddin, flowed just beyond a copse of bushes. Here it was not much more than a large creek, easily traversed, barely up to the horses' knees. By the time this water traveled to Myrddin, it and several other tributaries would have joined together, swelling in size and breadth. Here where they rested, however, appeared to be very close to the beginning. Collin knew of one more village on this road, one he himself had never been to, but had heard Rhun discuss. After that was the unknown, but Collin doubted that very much lie between that village and Kyreen's homeland, especially after hearing the mercenary's tale.

"Do ye know where ye are headed?" he finally asked as he fell into step with her heading towards the water with the horses.

"Home," came the terse answer.

"I know. Ye have said that before," pressed Collin, grabbing her arm, "But, by the gods, woman, what do ye expect to find when ye arrive 'home'?"

To Collin's surprise, Kyreen did not resist the contact and stopped walking. Her gelding and stud, smelling the water just yards away, continued toward the river, their leads slipping from Kyreen's hand. Collin allowed his gray to continue as well.

With a gentle touch to her shoulder, he turned Kyreen so that they faced each other. Lords above, she was beautiful! If he avoided looking straight at her face, Collin could usually ignore it, but this close, he could not. Those fathomless emerald eyes gazing up at him, shone with doubt and uncertainty. Her skin, so pale, so white, so flawless, contrasted greatly with the ebon curls framing her face. Collin resisted the urge to wrap his arms around her by breaking his gaze away and glancing towards the horses, now contentedly drinking from the river. A motion on the far bank caught his attention an instant too late.

"Do not stop on our account. For I, too, am curious. What do you expect to find if you continue down this road?" A female voice drifted to the pair from the road even as unseen persons grabbed Collin and Kyreen from behind, pressing daggers to each of their throats.

The woman swung down from her horse, as did the three riders accompanying her. One of the men took the reins from the woman and she moved closer to the pair. A slender hand pushed back the cloak's hood, revealing a pair of emerald eyes and pale features framed by errant curls escaping from the ebony hair pulled back into a braid.

Recognizing the woman from the square in Myrddin, the one who had saved the child, Kyreen glanced about for the child and spied her emerging from the bushes across the river accompanied by another woman. As they crossed the river, the girl gathered up the reins to Kyreen and Collin's horses.

Collin remained still, intrigued to see Kyreen's reaction as she stared at the gathering, a mix of men and women. Their physical similarities to Kyreen, especially this one woman obviously in charge, were eerie. All were tall; every man and even a couple of the women taller than Collin. They were dressed in forest colors, varying shades of browns and greens, cloaks over simple tunics and breeches with dusty boots. Their horses were tall, striking specimens, all chestnuts or sorrels, well-muscled and well-conditioned, built very similar to Kyreen's pair.

But it was the faces of the men and women in the clearing that tore at Kyreen's heart… features were sharp and angular as though carved from granite and alabaster pale. She observed a couple pairs of deep blue eyes staring at her, but the majority were emerald green. All had dark hair, brunette or black. The men kept their hair shorn short, close to the skull, while braids hung down the backs of each woman, the escaping wisps curling tightly around their faces. The resemblance to her mother caused a lump to grow in Kyreen's throat. This strange, proud woman, if not Tyra's sister, must then be a very close relative. Kyreen's heart leapt in her chest and the woman recoiled.

"By the goddess, have ye no control? Or manners for that matter?" she snapped, slapping Kyreen across the face.

Emotion drained from Kyreen, her cheek stinging but not nearly as much as her pride. Lessons from her childhood flooded back to her. For years Kyreen had excelled at shielding her inner thoughts from the outer world. Now she must work on clamping all emotions.

"And," Kyreen's mother's voice rang in her head, "never, under any circumstances, are you to ever invade another's thoughts without permission."

The woman stepped back, lowering her hand. "That's better. Not great, mind you, but at least I can think without being assaulted."

Collin watched in silent fascination. When the woman had, from Collin's perspective, slapped Kyreen without provocation, a wave of tension had rippled through the clearing. Collin had tensed for a fight although none of the woman's companions had moved. An instant later, the woman backed off and the friction was gone.

Glancing around the clearing with everyone intent on the two women, Collin realized something was happening about which he had no idea. He also realized that, even though everyone appeared to be completely focused on the two women, he had no chance of escape. These were not misfit road bandits like the ones he had hired in Wentworth. These were soldiers; even the child had an aura of battle seasoning, a hardness in the eyes, a tensing of the jaw, the ease with which all had a hand upon their weapon, ready to draw without hesitation.

"Forgive me. I interrupted your conversation. Please do continue," The leader gestured between the two companions, a bemused smile playing about her lips. "I believe you were discussing your destination. That would be...?"

Tensing, Collin opened his mouth to reply. The man standing beside him pressed a hefty hand to Collin's chest as if to hold him back. Their eyes met and the other man slowly almost imperceptibly shook his head negative.

Kyreen's gaze never left the leader's face, but, from the corner of her eye, she caught the exchange with Collin and picked up on his tension. Something was wrong. She was missing some pertinent information, something everyone in the clearing knew, including Collin. Again, the questions arose—Who is he? What does he have to do with her and her homeland? The fluttering of possible responses flew through her mind mimicking the flurries in her stomach. Stubbornly she pushed both away.

"I am heading towards the land of my birth," she finally answered, fighting to keep her tone and emotions level.

The other woman's jaw clenched and she stepped up to Kyreen. Collin watched as these women, virtually mirror images, stared at each other. When he first met Kyreen, Collin had been amazed at her fighting skills and poise. Now he realized her skills were a pale shadow compared to the older woman. Had he encountered this stranger, any one of her band, again including the child, the outcome would have been very swift and very decisive. Collin very much doubted he would have been left alive. Mercy did not appear to be something these people dispensed nor, if even half of the stories of Calan were true, had been shown.

Doubt rose anew inside Kyreen as she gazed into the steely eyes. She knew, though, that while she had not moved a muscle, everyone in the clearing save Collin could easily feel the turmoil within her. They all thought her to be weak and they were correct. She was weak! She had to get control of herself. Her jaw clenched as she bit down upon her tongue, the taste of blood flooding her mouth. Her chin lifted slightly, her shoulders squared and she found her body shifting so that she balanced on the balls of her feet.

The other woman lifted an eyebrow. "Still waiting for an answer. It's a simple question, girl. Quit with the cryptic answers. Where... is... home?"

Judging there to be no correct answer, Kyreen blurted, "Calan."

The woman's hand moved so swiftly that Collin never saw the initial strike. All he witnessed was Kyreen's rebuttal, her own hand moving swiftly in defense, both preventing the blow and surprising the woman.

Before the sound had faded from the clearing and before he could react, Collin found a sword at his side as the man beside him had drawn his weapon and poised its tip to rest against Collin's vest, where it could quite readily be slid between two ribs. The rest of group had not physically moved, yet all stood ready, silent and deadly.

"Mayhap I underestimated the whelp," the woman commented, flexing the sting from her thwarted hand as she gazed thoughtfully at Kyreen.

Watching the woman begin to move around her, Kyreen felt the shift in both herself and the woman. Never again would Kyreen be able to so easily block this woman's attack, but also Kyreen was entering familiar territory. She had spent her childhood defending against bullies. Granted none were as skilled and lethal as this woman here, but Kyreen had confidence in her defensive abilities.

This time the attack came from behind, faster and harder than the previous. Kyreen sidestepped and pirouetted away, discovering she could feel the tensing of her opponent without having to probe into her mind. After the third strike, Kyreen realized the woman had ceased fighting and was now testing Kyreen, probing the younger woman's abilities. The blows came just as hard and just as fast, yet the venom had dissipated.

From Collin's perspective, however, the fight continued to be brutal. Every blow looked and sounded deadly. The grace of both women astounded him. If not for the fierceness in their expressions and the audible slap of flesh-on-flesh, the pair could have been dancing. Aware now of Kyreen's past, Collin wondered how she had learned such moves alone in the vast wilderness with an aging Hanorian couple.

After an agonizing ten minutes Collin was slightly surprised when the woman stepped away from Kyreen, nodding her head in silent praise. While Kyreen did not appear visibly winded, a slight sheen of perspiration coated the girl's upper lip. She dropped her defensive position and lowered her own head towards the woman. In a flash, the woman was upon Kyreen, a silent blur hurdling forward. Kyreen lowered a shoulder, widened her stance, and allowed the woman's momentum to carry her up, over and then down on her back in the clearing. Kyreen spun and issued her first offensive attack, slamming the heel of her hand towards the woman's face, a blow that of course the woman easily blocked. Collin noticed that although their leader was on the ground none of the others moved or visibly reacted.

Raised in the rowdy backrooms and rough docks of Myrddin where numbers were the key decider, this behavior fascinated him. Would they have let their leader die? Did they not have allegiance and loyalty to their leader? Had Kyreen been on the ground, he would have at least considered stepping up to assist.

Then, looking at the woman resting on her back, peering up at Kyreen, Collin realized belatedly that though this strange woman appeared to be in a vulnerable position, she remained in control of the situation. She and Kyreen gazed at each other another long moment before the younger straightened and stepped back. When the woman extended an arm, Kyreen extended her own forearm to give unneeded aid.

"Not bad for an outsider," the woman acknowledged, keeping hold of Kyreen's arm. "I am Aren. This," she gestured to the man standing beside Collin, "is Viggo."

Before Kyreen could respond, others began to step forward, grasping her forearm and introducing themselves. Collin watched the ritual in silence, curious what would happen when Kyreen revealed her own name. He did not have long to wait for his answer before the youngest stepped forward, her right hand extended, the horses' reins wrapped around her left.

"Gunda," she said and, unlike the adults around her, added, "First daughter of Aren and Viggo."

Kyreen took the girl's forearm, marveling at the firmness of the child's grip and the steadiness of her gaze directly into Kyreen's eyes. In Hanoria children were not included in introductions unless their parents chose to name them to the group. Never would one shake hands with an adult. Not for the first time, Kyreen realized she has many adjustments to life outside of Jorn's small farm.

As the girl stepped back, Kyreen turned towards Aren. "I am Kyreen and this is Collin," she announced, gesturing towards her traveling companion. With her gaze turned towards Collin, Kyreen appeared to miss the group's reaction, but he did not. To a person, each flinched at the sound of her name, their gaze shifting towards their leader. Gunda's mouth opened as if to speak, but the woman standing beside Gunda swiftly placed a hand upon her shoulder and the girl shut her mouth without a sound. Aren shook her head imperceptibly, her own eyes never leaving Kyreen, and the group's tension left as fast as it had appeared. The name had been recognized but Aren did not wish to make an issue of it—yet.

Collin turned his gaze to Kyreen. Did she know who she was? Did she know what had happened after her mother left their homeland? Now more than ever he wondered exactly what Kyreen was expecting to find upon her return.

"Kyreen and Collin, well met," Aren's voice betrayed no emotion as she stepped between the two, placing a casual arm around their shoulders. "Our destination is a day and half ride to the north. It is on your way. May I invite you to ride with us?"

This last sentence had been worded as a question, but was not truly a request. Kyreen did pick up on this. She looked over at Collin, who shrugged.

"The company would be appreciated," he replied to Aren.

When Gunda offered him the gray's reins, Collin winked at the girl, who, despite her grown-up façade, blushed and giggled. "Thank you, m'lady."

"The horses need food before we continue," Kyreen stated, leading her horses over to the tree under which her saddle and bags rested. "We have been on the road since before dawn and they have yet to eat today."

"Yes, we know," Aren replied, trailing a hand along the stud's withers yet gazing at Kyreen, her expression unreadable. "We were breaking camp ourselves when Niel on lookout saw you two canter past."

Uncomfortable under the other woman's gaze, Kyreen measured out a small portion of oats for all three horses. Her supply, originally meant for one, was running low. She had hoped to buy more once reaching Calan, but now she was unsure. When she straightened and turned around, Kyreen saw Aren still gazing at her thoughtfully.

"My apologies if I let my guard down," Kyreen stated.

"It was not that," Aren replied, still obviously thinking. "I must speak with my people before we leave."

Kyreen nodded and resisted the urge to touch the other woman's thoughts as she moved towards her band. Old habits that must be broken, Kyreen thought, walking toward Collin and the horses.

In due time, the group was back on the road, heading north. Kyreen and Collin found themselves in the middle of the group. Aren led the way, while Viggo positioned his mount to the rear. Gunda and the other woman, an extremely tall slender woman each held onto a string of four horses.

Even as Collin wondered about the spare mounts, yet another woman rode away well before the rest of the group, her own spare mount in tow. Collin handed Kyreen an apple from the bundle Glain had packed for them.

"Are ye sure about this?" he inquired, taking a bite of the sweet fruit, a bit of juice dribbling down his chin.

Kyreen nodded. "It was our only true choice. When we get to their camp tonight, there will be time for talk."

"Camp? You think we will make their base by dusk?"

This time the ebony curls shook negative. "No, but they appear to travel this road frequently and covertly. Obviously, there is someplace safe to spend the night."

Collin took another bite, his gaze thoughtful and admiring. "True. Maybe a cave removed from the road. It makes sense."

"Not a cave. We sleep in the forest." Kyreen turned her attention back to the road, visibly dismissing Collin and ending the conversation.

Collin took another bite of the apple. By the gods she was infuriating. How could she say things with such authority? She had not been in Calan for more than fifteen years. Still she had been impressive in the clearing with the rebel leader. For now, the best thing he could do, Collin figured, was keep his mouth shut and his eyes open. Finishing the apple, he tossed the core into the bushes which earned him an irritated glance from not only Kyreen but a few of the other Calanians. Collin pointedly fixed his gaze on the road and ignored them all.

PART III

Aren set a pace Kyreen admired, one that ate up the miles without taxing the animals. The group left the road only twice. About an hour into their journey, the woman rider who had ridden ahead met the group. She was riding the spare mount hard and the mount she had been riding when she left the clearing earlier was not to be seen. After a short conversation with Aren, the group was motioned off the road where they waited in silence; everyone dismounted, holding the horses' muzzles lightly.

Collin followed Kyreen's lead, watching her with fascination as she did this smoothly, silently, and without verbal direction. The wait was not long before a group of soldiers from Myrddin loped past their hiding place. As soon as they were out of sight, the scout took off once again, on yet a third horse, a fresh horse. Then, an hour later, the group left the road a second time to skirt the small village of Gladys.

The sun had disappeared behind trees when Aren pulled her horse to a stop. From Collin's perspective, this was just a stretch of road, no different than any other portion they had been travelling all day, dusty, abandoned with dense forest closing in on either side. No sign of a clearing. No sound of water. Then one of the men dismounted and moving to the side of the road pulled away branches from a well-concealed path. Aren dismounted and disappeared into the shadow of the forest, leading her horse. After the last person entered the forest, the branches were replaced to again conceal the pathway. After a few minutes' walk along the narrow path, just wide enough for a horse, the group emerged into a small clearing, a rock-lined fire pit dominating the center.

Collin was impressed on two levels. First that Kyreen would know that there would be a hidden camp not in a cave, and second that this group was secretive enough to have a permanent camp undetected by the soldiers. Members of Brodyr Llafur, Collin's guild, also eschewed contact with the authorities and felt a kinship with others who did the same.

Within minutes the horses were relieved of their tack. Gunda shyly approached Collin and asked to tend to his gray for him. Collin looked to Kyreen for guidance. She was busy at her saddlebags, but nodded slightly, undetected by the young girl. He flashed Gunda a bright smile, which made color flood her pale features.

Once she recovered, the girl turned to Kyreen, asking with cool politeness, "And, may I care for your two steeds as well?"

Kyreen swung the saddlebags over her shoulder and handed the reins to Gunda. "Many thanks," she replied.

Her calm exterior belied the emotions roiling inside. For years her herd had been her focus, her escape, her salvation, her life. Although Kyreen knew the care given by this girl or any other Calanian would be exceptional, relinquishing control of their care to others was difficult.

Collin gathered his own knapsack and followed Kyreen towards the fire pit, where the advance woman had started a small, almost smokeless fire. Within minutes all had gathered about the circle, except for Gunda and the horsewoman who were caring for all the animals.

As soon as the last person dropped to one of the several log seats surrounding the fire pit, Aren stood herself and turned towards Kyreen. "It is time for sharing. This is a space of speaking, a space of safety, a space of truth. Tell me now, Kyreen. Who are you?"

As Aren resettled on a log beside her mate, all eyes turned to Kyreen, who smoothly rose to her feet. Her heart was racing in her chest and nervousness flooded her veins. Inhaling deeply, she began to move around the fire. Slowly and silently, she made one full circuit before coming to a halt before Aren, addressing her comments to the leader of this group. The ritual of Knowing, the one her mother had taught her so many years before, the one that Kyreen had practiced twice daily without fail all these years, was calming and familiar. Apprehension and unease fled; a warming tranquility settled in the void. When Kyreen began to speak, her voice was soft yet audible to all within the circle. Her words came slowly, almost in meditation.

"I am Kyreen, first daughter of Tyra, only child of Rolf, middle son of Arvid, youngest daughter of Ebba, first daughter of Nanna, middle daughter of Rasmus, first son of Eero, only child of Malin, first daughter of Yngwie, father of all, created by Liv, Mother of Life who's blood courses through all within the boundaries of this land, our home, Calan, which holds her people safe through storm and squall, assault and aggression," she paused, bending slightly at the waist, then straightening, her gaze never leaving Aren's as the ritual continued, "It is to these ancestors I bow, for without them I would not be here. It is to these ancestors I pledge to do my best so that one day I may join them in the great hall in the fifth world to sip from the chalice of Hereafter and raise my toasts—a toast first to those who once walked this fertile ground before me, a toast twice to those who still walk these verdant meadows and a toast thrice to those who will someday walk this fruitful land."

Even as Kyreen spoke the last word, Aren was rising to her feet, shooting up and delivering a vicious slap to Kyreen's face.

"How. Dare. You." she hissed, raising her hand to preparing another blow.

Kyreen, immersed in the ritual, had been caught unaware with the initial strike. Now, she stood firm, eye-to-eye with Aren, refusing to react or respond. When Aren's hand began to move again, Viggo, who had also risen to his feet unnoticed by either woman, stepped in, his hand wrapping vise-like around Aren's wrist.

"Aren," he reprimanded quietly, his voice tight and full of emotion. "We are not barbarians. Do not permit them to make us such, my love. This child means no disrespect. Perhaps she simply does not know."

The tension around the fire was evident in the stillness with which the group sat, staring at the two women. For his part, Collin's hand had moved to the sword resting on the ground beside him, but he had frozen without drawing the weapon, wanting to see where this interaction was headed. Within a second, however, whether it was from Viggo's tone or words or even the pressure of his grip, the emotion flooded from Aren's visage. She relaxed her body and looked at her husband, nodding.

"You are correct," she acquiesced, inclining her head to Kyreen, her green eyes glittering with unshed tears. "My apologies."

Kyreen exhaled, relieved, her cheek stinging and flushed bright red. She inclined her head towards Aren, pirouetted and moved back to sit beside Collin. Only then did she allow her own tensions to subside. Viggo, too, returned to his place, just right of Aren's vacant spot. Collin silently released the breath he had not been aware of holding.

Aren, her composure regained, began to walk the circle, traveling in the opposite direction of Kyreen, in front of whom she stopped after completing a full circuit. From this close perspective, Collin could see the trembling of her hands and the hard set of her jaw. Aren, he realized, was barely containing her emotions, held in place only by protocol.

When Aren began to speak, however, her voice betrayed none of this emotion. Like Kyreen, her tone was calm yet audible and the rhythm meditative. "I am Aren, first daughter of Andren, youngest son of Arvid, youngest daughter of Ebba, first daughter of Nanna, middle daughter of Rasmus, first son of Eero, only child of Malin, first daughter of Yngwie, father of all, created by Liv, Mother of Life who's blood courses through all."

As Aren's voice faded, two realizations came to Collin almost simultaneously. First, except for the first two names, Aren's list of ancestors matched Kyreen's exactly. They were related. Second, Aren had stopped speaking when all present expected something more to complete the ritual.

Aren glanced around the circle, her gaze contrite. "My apologies, friends," she announced, "I have failed. I cannot continue."

She returned her gaze to Kyreen. "You never answered me, cousin. Do you know what to expect upon your return to Calan?" The question was asked softly, almost tenderly. Gone were the accusations and anger.

This change filled Kyreen with dread. She felt the strength drain from her limbs as she shook her head. She fought, and almost succeeded to keep her voice steady. "No, Aren. My answer is no, I do not know what to expect."

Aren nodded and returned to her seat next to Viggo. "Which story shall we hear first, my people?" She looked around the circle at the silent faces.

"Shall we hear Kyreen's tale?" Viggo suggested. "For all, or almost all, present know the story of Calan." He reached over and gently squeezed Aren's hand, returning his attention to the newcomers.

In this moment, Kyreen fully appreciated her mother's wisdom and mourned anew her loss. The Calanian queen must have realized early into their flight that she would never return to her homeland, but had held hope for her daughter. Those seasons they were on the run, Tyra had spent valuable time preparing Kyreen for these moments, these tests. How could Tyra have known it would be almost two decades before her daughter found her way home? She could not have, but she prepared Kyreen nonetheless. The daily combat forms, the ancestry recitation, their tale of flight, these rituals that Tyra had drilled into Kyreen and made the girl promise to repeat twice a day, were all intended to allow Kyreen to return to her people. Taking a deep breath, she prepared herself.

Chapter 24

"We fled the castle on the morn of my third birthday," Kyreen began.

Collin listened enthralled as the words flowed and the story was told. When Kyreen reached the part where Tyra left her in the clearing with Jorn, she paused momentarily, unprepared to continue the story without her mother. At first shakily, then with more conviction, Kyreen continued. She spoke of Jorn and Ildri, the farm and the animals she tended, the first horse she had purchased and the ones that followed. She talked about Ildri's stroke and her duty as a daughter. She avoided speaking of Markku and her run-ins with him, the shunning of the village, Jorn's drinking and deception. She paused after telling of Ildri's crossing in her absence and making the decision to find her home.

"I met Collin on the road and he has journeyed with me here," she concluded.

As the sound of her voice faded, Kyreen looked around the quiet circle, uncertain of how to continue. Night had fallen during her tale.

Gunda and the other woman had completed the evening chores and joined the circle unnoticed. Overhead in the clear sky, stars twinkled brightly and the moon, barely a sliver, was just peaking over the treetops as it began its journey across the sky. Collin reached over and took her hand in his in silent support.

Aren's eyes shimmered anew in the dim firelight with unshed tears. Although Tyra had been a few years older than herself, the two had been extremely close. Both girls had been only children and had each lost a parent at a very young age—Tyra's mother dying at Tyra's birth and Aren's father falling in battle when she was just an infant.

Aren swallowed the lump growing in her throat. "Do you..." she started and faltered. "Do you know what happened to your mother?"

Kyreen sighed. "Jorn only told me, many years afterwards, that she was captured and killed by the men he saw in the tavern the night she left me with him. He and Ildri felt it best to not speak of such things for fear of displeasing the Lords of Hayrik. We never spoke of my mother and I pretended to be the orphaned child of a distant relative."

Kyreen pulled out the burlap sack, untied the twine and withdrew the scabbard. Though no sound was made, Collin felt the air leave the clearing as though every person has inhaled as one. Kyreen fought back the tears, as she moved over to extend the sword to Aren.

"This was…I only received this recently although Arvis brought it to Hanoria years ago," she said.

Aren took the sword quietly, exchanging glances with Viggo. Collin wondered, not for the first time, about these people and their communications. Rumors abounded about the magical properties of the Calanian people. Rumors he and his brother had always questioned as superstition, but now, here with this group, Collin realized there was some special power amongst them.

Viggo stood up and looked around the circle. "It is time for us to disperse. Eat your dinners and prepare your sleeping spots. Aren and Kyreen have much to discuss alone."

Even Collin understood this dismissal. He moved away from the fire pit and found a level spot on which he began to erect his small tent. Gunda, her duties with the horses complete, moved towards him, but her father called her away to eat. Collin smiled in the dark, both at the young girl's obvious crush and her father's even more obvious attempt to divert her attentions from Collin.

From behind him, Collin could hear the hushed tones of Aren as she began to speak. Kyreen was silent, except for a muffled exclamation twice. Collin flinched, instinctively knowing which parts of Aren's story would elicit such reactions. Although she made no other sound, Collin knew Kyreen would be crying and devastated. He finished preparing the tent for the evening and lay down on the grass outside of it, his sack as a pillow, to gaze at the stars.

After many long minutes, he sensed more than heard the women rise and move away from the fire, Aren towards her family and Kyreen towards Collin. He rose and waited silently for her approach. They stood in the dark, face to face for a long silent moment.

"My mother," she finally said, her voice so low he had to strain to hear her. "They…"

"I know," he responded just as quietly, gathering her hands within his own.

Vividly Collin recalled the guild meeting attended by Falk. Even then Collin had been struck by the lack of remorse in the man as Falk had told of the capture, torture and eventual death of the Calanian queen, his one good eye glinting in the firelight. It had been this same guild meeting that had granted Collin's greatest wish—to leave Myrddin, to travel beyond the cramped city, to have an adventure—and which had so deeply changed Collin's destiny. A hatred, one of great heat and intensity, unlike anything Collin had ever felt, filled his being and he knew that should he ever again encounter Falk, Collin would not hesitate to skewer him with his sword.

"My...my people," she continued. "How could he... Oh, by the goddess, Collin."

He gently pulled her into a comforting embrace, as her tears flowed hot against his shoulder. Although the small northern province of Calan was isolated and distant, Collin remembered well listening to his parents when he was just a child as they discussed the rumors of carnage that had taken place there. For months afterwards, the children would play "Galorians and Calanians." Although the battles staged would vary, the game always ended the same, the "Calanians" face down on the ground as the "Galorians" mocked slicing off their prisoners' heads with pretend swords. In these games of children, there were no survivors.

In reality, as Kyreen tearfully explained quietly to Collin, some Calanians had managed to evade capture, mostly those not involved in the battle—the very elderly, the very young and those pregnant with child. Aren, barely thirteen summers old, had assisted with the evacuations into the same tunnels through which Tyra had fled with her children. Even then many of those had been unable to escape the castle before the Galorian soldiers overtook it and the tunnel passage was closed. The battle had waged all of that first day and into a second. All who did not die in battle or escape were executed as dawn broke on the third day.

Collin surprised himself by taking Kyreen's face between his hands so as to tenderly kiss her tear-soaked cheeks. In the dim starlight, he was once again overwhelmed by her essence and fought the urge to kiss her lips, instead he wrapped his arms around her and drew her close to him.

"Will you share the tent with me tonight?" he asked, his question laden with hope and tenderness.

Kyreen pulled back to gaze into his hazel eyes, wanting nothing more than to disappear in their depths and forget all she had learned this evening. Eventually she sighed and Collin knew her answer before she spoke. "I cannot, Collin. We... they... I must not show weakness by taking to shelter for my rest."

"I understand," he replied, pressing a final kiss on her forehead. "Should ye change your mind, ye know where to find me." With that parting he stepped back and lowered himself through the tent opening.

Chapter 25

Kyreen waited until the tent flap had settled into place before turning towards the fire. Viggo and Aren stood in the circle, conversing quietly. Aren still held Tyra's sword in her hands, absently caressing the worn leather. In his own hands, Viggo held the evening meal he had brought Aren, simple fare of bread, dried meat and cheese. Wiping her eyes dry with the back of her hand, Kyreen moved towards the couple, who fell silent with her approach.

Aren held the sword out to Kyreen and shook her head before the girl could protest. "Arvis was right. This is your birthright, Kyreen. You keep it safe until we reach camp."

Unable to find words, Kyreen took the scabbard and avoided their gaze. Aren took the food from Viggo, who pulled Kyreen into a brief embrace. When they parted, he gazed into her face, his hands resting lightly upon her shoulders.

"I am truly sorry for your loss," he said quietly.

Uncomfortable under his deep blue gaze, sorrowful yet lacking pity, Kyreen looked away. "It is all long in the past."

"Not for you," he replied.

Casting a brief glance towards his partner, he added, "I take my leave now, ladies. Good night, Kyreen. I am happy you have found your way back to us."

Giving Kyreen's shoulders a soft squeeze, Viggo kissed Aren's cheek and the two women found themselves alone once more. Both pairs of eyes followed Viggo's departure as he disappeared into the woods. Kyreen, unaccustomed to such sincere kindheartedness, was at a loss for words.

Lowering herself onto a vacant log beside the dying fire, Aren said, "Come sit with me and share my meal. Viggo always gives me more than I need or want."

Kyreen joined her cousin, chewing the offered food and listening as Aren described the Calanian camps, kept mobile in order to evade the Galorian soldiers patrolling Calan's woods.

"Even after all these years, Dolan is relentless. He will not rest until every Calanian is exterminated. I do not believe even you will escape his wrath. Mayhap you would garner even more hostility," Aren commented before placing the final bit of dinner into her mouth.

This statement startled Kyreen.

"What do you mean?" she asked, "Why would I garner more, or less, wrath from this coward? Is it because of my mother?"

Now it was Aren's turn to be surprised. "You do not know?"

She washed down the bread with a drink from her canteen before answering. "Not because of your mother, Kyreen, but because of your father."

When Kyreen's face shows no comprehension, Aren added, "That coward as you so aptly called him is your uncle, Kyreen. Your father was Dolan's older brother."

Kyreen flinched as though physically assaulted and Aren slipped an arm around the younger woman in comfort. "Your mother never told you?"

Kyreen shook her head. "She only told me that my father died before we were born. He died in battle," here Kyreen looked at Aren, "against the Galorian emperor, Cathal."

Aren nodded. "Cathal was the oldest of the three brothers."

She stood and began poking at the fire with a stick. "We all thought Cathal was the worst, especially when Dolan left us alone for so long. We actually thought that the fighting could be over, that mayhap after losing both his brothers or because of you and your twin being part Galorian, Dolan would maintain peace but then..." her voice trailed off and the women shared a companionable, if sorrowful, silence for several moments.

When Aren next spoke, her voice was steely with resolve; her gaze never leaving the glowing coals. "I have two vows to fulfill in this life before I may enter the Great Hall in the Fifth World, Kyreen. One is to destroy the man who exterminated my people without honor, the man you now know is your uncle. The other vow is to also end a man, one with whom you are already familiar, someone you spoke about earlier, the man who lost an eye at your hand, the man who killed our Queen, your mother, my cousin."

For several moments both women stared into the dwindling fire, each lost in her own thoughts. Aren finally broke the silence, her voice conversational now. "I do not know if you are familiar of how our empathy works, Kyreen."

The girl shook her head, "Not at all."

Aren put down the stick and returned to sit upon the log. "What you have experienced all of these years has been a vague sense of something you cannot quite name, just feel, correct?"

At Kyreen's nod, Aren continued, "It is hazy against strangers, outsiders who do not share our talent. We get impressions of their intent or their feelings, but nothing as strong as when we are with our own people. Protocol, as you remember, discourages empathic exchange without permission.

"Additionally, there are two factors that lend themselves to extraordinarily strong connections. The first is familial, a connection by blood. You and I are removed but we still may have a light family connection; it will grow as we spend time together. Connections with a parent or sibling tend to be strong. You may have been too young to remember the connection you shared with your twin. It was so strong your mother sometimes joked about you two actually conversing with your minds."

"No, I was not too young," replied Kyreen softly, a familiar ache rising in her chest, "I do remember."

"Although Tyra and I were not siblings," Aren continued, "We shared a closer connection than most cousins. You heard we were related through our fathers, but also our mothers were sisters, so our connection was doubly strong. When Tyra left Calan, I felt her absence so sharply; it was almost as if she had died then. I resented her so much when I heard she had left," Aren paused so long Kyreen thought she had finished, but eventually she began speaking once more.

"Tyra could not have known what would happen. How could she? None of us that lived through it could believe it ourselves. So, so, so many of our dead I helped burn in secret, by the moonlight. So many others we had to… had to be abandoned.

"I am ashamed to admit that my resentment grew slowly over those first years, eventually evolving into a deep hatred that poisoned my heart. Viggo, with his patience, his steadfastness, and his unyielding kindness, helped to start my healing, but it was not until I bore my first child that I realized how deep a mother's love runs.

"So, you see, Kyreen, I now understand why Tyra risked fleeing with you and your brother. I can only imagine the pain she felt watching Quillan ride away with Arvis. She was a realist, your mother. She knew the odds of her survival were not good," Aren's voice tightened with emotion as she spoke. "There is little I would not do to ensure my children's safety."

Once more Kyreen interceded. "I saw you," she said, "…in the square… back in Myrddin."

Aren nodded thoughtfully, eyeing Kyreen's short curls. "Aye, one of my men reported sighting a young man of obvious Calanian descent there, in the square. I had wondered of the connection when we first met on the road."

The women fell silent again, both staring into the dying embers, lost in their thoughts. Without consciously probing, Kyreen could still feel all of the people all around her. Her people, she thought. A soft breeze rustled through the trees, obliterating the sound of any conversations, but Kyreen still felt their presence, a comforting extension of herself weaving through each person.

After several long moments, Kyreen broke the silence. "What is the other connection, Aren? You said there were two factors that lend themselves to strong empathic connections. Family is one. What is the other?" she asked, fairly certain of the answer.

A smile touched Aren's voice when she replied, "Soul mates. It happens when you are with that one person, the one who makes your world better, the one who causes your heart to sing even in times of sorrow."

"You have that with Viggo."

"Aye. Not that I wanted it mind you. No. I was never going to have a mate. I was never going to covenant nor have children. My life was going to be about revenge. Yet the moment he laid eyes on me, Viggo knew that I was his destiny. Instead of pursuing me though he stepped back. Deep down I knew it as well, but I thought I could avoid it if I refused long enough. It was a full year before I allowed myself to be close enough to him for us to even converse," she chuckled softly. "I like to say my resistance melted the first time he kissed me, but in reality, it was the first time we talked and I looked into his eyes."

"My father," Kyreen began shakily, not sure she wanted to know more. "He was not Calanian, yet… my mother… did she… did he… did they love each other?"

"Yes, Kyreen, very much. Although their time together was short and tragic, the love they shared was strong."

Without consciously meaning to, Kyreen glanced towards Collin's tent, the pale canvas shining in the weak moonlight. She remembered the feel of his hand holding hers, his lips on her cheeks and forehead so recently, and her mind drifted back to the previous day's kiss.

"How long have you known Collin?" Aren's voice brought Kyreen back to the present.

"Not long. A week," Kyreen cleared her throat, "But somehow it feels like forever."

"I sense within him a conflict." Aren chuckled when Kyreen threw her a horrified look. "He is not Calanian. He is fair game."

Kyreen could not help but laugh herself. "Go on," she urged. "You sense a conflict, but…"

"His feelings are strong for you. You say you only met recently. Are you bedding him?"

The frankness of the question startled Kyreen. In Hanoria, such questions and talk were frowned upon, not to mention all the restrictions about pre-marital relations. Realizing Aren was still waiting for an answer, Kyreen stammered, "No…not really."

Again, Aren chuckled softly, not needing empathy to interpret Kyreen's discomfort. "I do not know why not. You both are healthy young people with an obvious attraction to each other. If you harbor concerns, we have herbs to prevent an unwanted pregnancy."

Kyreen mumbled incoherently, grateful for the darkness to hide her flaming cheeks.

Aren rose, turning to help pull Kyreen to her feet. "Please forgive my frankness. All this talk of the past, your resemblance to Tyra, it all loosed my tongue and I forgot my place."

Aren extinguished the fire and bid Kyreen a good night. The younger woman listened to the other woman's footsteps recede as Aren headed toward the tree line in search of her family.

Teeth nibbling her bottom lip, Kyreen slowly moved towards the quiet tent. Her heart was beating so loudly in her chest that Kyreen was sure Collin could hear it. She wondered if the Calanians in the woods could sense her nervousness.

She halted several feet from the tent entrance, sensing nothing from its interior. Was he asleep already? Indecision clouded Kyreen's thoughts. After another long moment, she reluctantly turned away and headed for the woods.

Chapter 26

The next morning the small band broke camp in the gray pre-dawn. Once more Kyreen and Collin were in the middle with Aren and Viggo taking front and back. The band's mood tensed once they reached the main road and Aren pushed their mounts into a quicker pace, one that deterred conversation.

With only a short break to tend to the horses, the group did not pause all day. Pink streaks had just appeared across the evening sky when Aren pulled her mare to a halt. To Collin the road and surrounding area looked deserted. The spring air was cooler here and the tree line thinner, mostly tall evergreens branching in the sky, the scent of pine hanging thick in the air. Even as Collin gazed into the dusk, one of the shadows moved and a man walked out—tall, pale with dark hair and bright green eyes. He approached Aren. They spoke briefly and then the group was moving once more.

"What was that about?" Collin wondered quietly.

"She had to find out where the camp is tonight," Kyreen answered. Shortly, Aren sent word back to Kyreen, requesting her presence.

Kyreen urged the gelding forward to fall into step beside Aren's mount. For a long moment, the other woman did not speak, but, feeling the turmoil within Aren, Kyreen remains silent.

"Kyreen," Aren finally began, "We have been a nomad tribe with no home for many years. Most of our youngest do not remember Calan before... before that night. Those that do remember may not be welcoming. I do not know how some will react to you."

"Aren, I did not return to cause unrest. I merely wanted to return home. How do you wish to handle this? I will do as you advise."

"Allow me to speak first with the elders. I would ask you to remain silent, do not reveal who you are until I can gauge the situation. If the mood is not right, we should not be completely forthright, at least right now. I have been gone a fortnight. One never knows the camp status from one day to the next."

Kyreen nodded. "Whatever you feel is best, Aren."

Outsiders were a novelty in the camp. While no one stared directly, Kyreen felt the attention of the entire camp upon her and Collin as they rode into camp. The evening meal had been served and groups of diners paused to watch the newly arrived group.

A tall young man of about fourteen or fifteen summers approached as Aren pulled to a stop near the center of the camp. It was Yngve, Aren and Viggo's oldest son, followed closely by their middle child, another son, named Reidar. Other family members came forward to greet their returned relatives while Kyreen and Collin stood to the side. After greeting her brothers, Gunda once more offered to care for Collin and Kyreen's mounts. Aren motioned for the pair to follow her while Viggo remained with their sons.

Just beyond the light of the camp's single fire stood a lone tent. Kyreen noticed sentries posted around the exterior walls to discourage any who may wander too close. Upon Aren's approach one of the guards pulled back the door flap, through which Aren ushered the newcomers. Smokeless lamps lit the interior of this large space. A fine tapestry rug of gold and red created the tent floor upon which sat an oval table surrounded by several wooden high-back chairs, nine of which were occupied. The assembly stood upon their entrance and Aren introduced Kyreen and Collin to the camp's council, merely calling them travelers encountered upon the road and promised more formal introductions later.

Nine pairs of eyes assessed the newcomers without visible emotion as Aren moved to a vacant seat at the head of the table. She waved Collin and Kyreen into an empty pair of chairs opposite her. Once everyone was seated, Aren explained what had occurred in Myrddin, how Gunda had been arrested when a vendor had mistakenly accused the girl of stealing from his stand, when in reality she had merely picked up a fallen apple to place it back upon the pile, and how in the ensuing tussle the young girl had incapacitated almost a dozen of the city guard, resulting in the swift and harsh sentence of death by hanging. Aren described the gallows rescue, then told how upon leaving the city they had happened upon Kyreen and Collin on the road to Calan. Respect and politeness dictated all eyes focus upon Aren, their comrade; however, Kyreen felt attentions also rested upon the outsiders as well. All appeared calm and rote on the surface, but even Collin felt the underlying tension in the confines of this tent as all heads swiveled to physically focus upon Kyreen. After a long moment of silence, Aren finally used Kyreen's true name for the first time and a ripple of emotion coursed through the gathered Calanians.

"You have done the ritual of Knowing?" asked a steely eyed woman, her hair streaked with gray. Shadows obscured half of her face as she spoke, but when she turned to gaze upon Kyreen, lamplight glittered off the spider-web of scars crisscrossing her otherwise flawless face.

"Yes, Olina," Aren answered. "It has been done last night. Kyreen, the sword."

Kyreen stood, unsheathing the sword and placing it upon the table.

As always Collin was awed by its appearance. He heard a few quick intakes of breath from around the table, although no one made verbal comment.

"Anyone can recite words and carry a sword," the man sitting to Aren's right spoke the words everyone had been thinking. Although he remained seated Kyreen could tell he was a tall man, even by Calanian standards. His dark hair and beard were trimmed close to the skin and his green eyes were dark with suspicion. His name was Lang and even from across the room Kyreen found him extremely unsettling. Sometime later Kyreen would learn his story in what the Calanians simply referred to as "The Battle." He had been six summers old at the time. His father, a castle guard, had escorted Lang, his eldest child, to the tunnels before returning to the castle for his wife, Lang's mother, large in the final days of pregnancy, who had fallen behind with the two younger children, a boy and a girl. Lang would never see any of his family alive again. Tonight, however, she only saw an irritated man who made her feel ill at ease.

"Have you looked upon her, Lang?" another man interceded. He was one of the oldest council members, his shorn hair completely white. As he gestured, Kyreen saw his left hand had been removed at the wrist, and his shirt sleeve had been sewn closed at the end of his arm. "She is obviously Calanian and also our queen's exact image."

Collin listened as the group debated and stole a glance at Kyreen. She sat still as stone, no expression upon her face, even her beautiful eyes void of emotion. He wished he could reach over and take her hand in his, but he stilled these urges. In this tent, he was merely a bystander. Anything he did could work against her. Although the conversation appeared controlled and civilized, Collin knew from his own experiences at guild meetings things could escalate in a hurry.

"Even if we do prove she is the daughter of Tyra," asked the steely-eyed woman. Olina, Kyreen remembered. "Where do we go from there? It has been almost two decades without true primacy. Aren is an heir, yes, but without formal coronation. She is our general, not our queen. What does this stranger want from us? We do not know her. Though the blood of Calan flows within her veins, she is an outsider."

Kyreen bit her tongue, fighting the tidal wave of emotions stirring in her breast. She was yet a visitor here and had no power, no voice, no rights, until granted so by the council. They must not feel the conflict within her. She fixed her gaze upon Aren, hands resting in her lap. The sword, back in its sheath, rested upon the table in front of her.

When Aren's eyes move to her face, Kyreen knew she must also find the words to explain herself. What did she want? Why was she here? When she had left Hanoria, Kyreen had only thought of returning home, to a place she could fit in. It had never dawned on her that her homeland and her people would be more lost than she, would need her more than she needed them. The hurts of her childhood and life in Hanoria were nothing compared to what these people had suffered over the ensuing seasons. She had no right to demand anything from them. She also had no right to lead them. What was to be her role here?

Realizing everyone was waiting for her to speak, Kyreen stood. Her mind raced as she waited for Aren to settle back in her chair. Sincerity, she told herself, be sincere. With a deep breath, she stood, found center and began the Telling. As always, this story calmed her. Kyreen heard her mother's voice in her head and in the words she spoke. This time the transition between her life with Tyra and the one in Hanoria was smoother. She did not stumble as she talked of her life with Jorn and Ildri; and though Kyreen managed to continue without pause, her heart ached as she now knew the truth and brutality of her mother's death. The council watched and listened without reaction until her final words faded away and the tent fell silent.

"There is a way to know for sure," a man's voice announced from the tent entrance. "Check for the rose."

Chapter 27

As one, every head in the tent turned toward the voice. Collin felt more than a little uncomfortable that someone had entered the tent from behind him. The speaker was a man of very advanced years, quite obviously the oldest in the tent. His skull glistened pink beneath thin bristly white hair and his hand upon the cane supporting his weight was gnarled with arthritis.

Aren moved over to the elderly man, greeting him warmly in a long embrace. With a hand on his elbow, she guided him to the table. One of the younger members of the council vacated her seat and stood aside.

As Aren placed his hand upon the chair back, the man turned his sightless gaze in the direction of the newcomers and announced, "I would like to meet our visitors."

Kyreen immediately stood to approach the elder, and, at her glance, Collin did as well. Aren placed the man's hand in Collin's hand.

"Vidar," she said, "May I present Collin of Myrddin?"

The man's hand is gnarled, but his grip strong. Collin noticed Kyreen flinch at the mention of the man's name. Obviously, it was a name with which she was familiar.

"Well met," Collin responded, his curiosity piqued as the man released his hand and turned towards Kyreen.

After the introduction, the man raised his hands toward Kyreen's face, pausing a fraction before touching. "May I see you?" he asked.

"Yes," Kyreen whispered.

Up close his sightless eyes were milky-white. Dimly she remembered deep blue eyes and wondered if the memory was true or imagined. Kyreen closed her own eyes as calloused fingers began to explore her face. Slowly he traced the plane of her brow, the lines of her jaw, the curve of her lips, the swell of her cheeks, then softly across her closed eyelids. His exploration completed, he held her face between his palms.

"Ursula," he breathed so quiet that only Kyreen heard the name.

His voice, so full of tenderness and love, tugged at her heart. A single tear slipped out from her closed eyes and traveled down her cheek. Gently, with his thumb, Vidar wiped the moisture away. Kyreen struggled to control her emotions, not wishing to be guilty of the same gaffe as the previous day. Although only a mere moment passed, Kyreen felt it to be an eternity before Vidar dropped his hands.

"Thank you," he whispered before settling into his chair as Kyreen and Collin moved back to their seats.

"So, we have the word of a stranger and a sword?" said the husky man sitting beside Kyreen, repeating Lang's earlier sentiment.

Glancing over, Collin felt an immediate dislike for the man, who licked his lips nervously and glanced about the table. When the man's gaze rested upon Lang sitting next to Aren, Collin recognized the politics at play, similar to those he has witnessed in his own guild. So, the Calanians are human, Collin thought as heated words begin to fly about the room.

"Check for the rose." Although his voice is not raised, Vidar's words echoed through the room and once again attentions are turned towards the blind man.

"Vidar, what do you mean?" One of the younger councilmen asked, his words reflected in the confusion of all around the table, all except Aren.

Vidar turned his sightless eyes towards Aren, asking, "Does she bear the mark?"

Aren shook her head slowly, but not in denial, as she wondered aloud, "How did I forget?"

Collin glanced over at Kyreen, who for once also looked confused. She shrugged her shoulders and shook her head. He glanced back around the table, but everyone was staring at Aren who has risen to her feet. The leader moved around to stand behind Kyreen's chair, leaning down and whispering into the girl's ear. Kyreen's brow furrowed, shaking her head again. Aren placed a hand on Kyreen's right shoulder, then whispered some more. Again, Kyreen shook her head negatively. Aren asked a question and this time Kyreen nodded, getting to her feet to follow Aren back to the head of the table.

Aren turned to the group. "Comrades, I first apologize for my slip. We should be able to rectify my oversight shortly as Kyreen has agreed to allow inspection of her person for the royal mark."

Though nobody spoke, Collin watched as the people around him exchanged glances. He was rather pleased to see they were as confused as he.

"Royal mark, Aren? Really? What are you talking about?" Lang's tone did nothing to disguise his misgivings.

Kyreen glanced down at the bearded man, her stomach churning. In such close proximity, the unease she felt multiplied to uncomfortable proportions. Without consciously thinking Kyreen stepped away from his chair, closer to Vidar.

As if he sensed her discomfort the old man to pat her arm. "Twill be fine, young one," he said softly.

Kyreen looked down at the man's lined face, then the gnarled fingers resting upon her arm. The words, his voice, this hand, all together unchained a long forgotten memory. Once this man had similarly soothed and steadied a toddler on her first ride around the paddock.

"Sapphire," she whispered. "Your eyes were the deepest blue, even darker than Quillan's."

Vidar smiled and squeezed Kyreen's arm before turning back towards the collected people waiting.

"Every heir to the throne is marked with the Calanian seal," he said. "Before he ascended the throne, King Rolf and I were boyhood friends. I saw his mark many times. I was blessed to be present when Tyra received her mark. Then, years later I was once again privileged to bear witness as the royal twins were marked just days before their third birthday…before… the Battle."

Aren glanced at Kyreen and nodded. The girl turned to face the tent wall, her back to the gathering. She crossed her arms across her chest and waited for Aren to raise her tunic. As the cool air touched bare skin, Kyreen felt rather than heard the reactions.

"A red rose twined about a sword," Vidar announced.

Kyreen glanced over her shoulder, her eye catching Collin's gaze.

He nodded and looked over at the banner hanging to the side. Kyreen followed his gaze, suddenly remembering the painted man.

Aren pulled Kyreen's shirt down and patted her shoulder. "Thank you, cousin," she whispered.

As Kyreen retook her seat, Vidar said, "Although my presence here is honorary, I hope my opinion still weighs merit and this council will grant this child reprieve and welcome."

Aren waited for Kyreen to settle in her chair and Vidar's words to fade before she addressed the collective.

"You have all heard the Telling," she said, looking around the table. "You have all seen the sword. You have all witnessed the mark. Now is time to deliberate. Grant sanctuary and recognition or banishment and denunciation."

Chapter 28

In the ensuing silence, Kyreen sensed the camp's inhabitants beyond these canvas walls as they went about their evening routines— supper, stories, settling in for the night. Inside the tent she waited, resisting the urge to probe. Even Aren's face showed no emotion or reaction. Within the long silence inside the tent, Kyreen discovered that she can feel, without probing, the emotions swirling, ebbing and flowing from each person. No one moved. No throats were cleared. Not even a chair squeaked or a paper shuffled.

For Collin, the tension in the air swelled until he feels suffocated. He dared not move for fear of drawing the inappropriate attention. Most of the people around the table sat with their eyes shut in an almost meditative state; the rest had their gaze averted, either on the table or the tent ceiling. Even after having experienced Kyreen's ways for the few days, Collin was unnerved by the collective stillness of these people.

In the Myrddin guild, the atmosphere would have been pure energy, electric like after a lightning strike. People would be out of their chairs, hands gesturing, voices raised. Some would be arguing with their neighbor, still others simply spewing their opinion out loud without a specific beneficiary. Thoughts of his guild and Myrddin circled around to Collin's own task at hand.

Was he still gathering information? Was he still on a mission? Or had he abandoned that mission when he had kissed Kyreen in the kitchen?

Never before had Collin felt so conflicted in his loyalties. The guild had been his village within the large city since he had been a small boy and the division run by Rhun had been Collin's extended family, especially after both his father's and brother's premature deaths. There was not a single man within his sector who would deny or give a second-thought to anything asked by Collin. Until today he would have done the same for any of them. What would happen now if he returned without completing this mission? Failing not because he had not acquired the necessary information but because he could not betray Kyreen?

Dimly Collin became aware that every Calan has opened their eyes and directed their gaze upon Aren. Belatedly he wondered if his internal conflict has been felt and hoped these people are too involved within their own controversies to pay attention to his flurry of emotions.

Aren's voice, brittle and emotionless, broke the silence. She had risen to her feet without sound. Her visage, steadfast and resolute, shielded her own thoughts. No longer was she a cousin, once removed. Now she was the leader of these people.

"You have all heard the Telling. You have all seen the Sword. You have all witnessed the Mark," she repeated, pausing before adding, "Now opine."

To Collin's surprise Aren did not look to the man on her left, Lang, most obviously the second-in-command. Instead Kyreen's cousin's gaze found a much younger man, one sitting in a position of less importance.

"Eilert," she stated.

The young man, a boy actually, not much older than Aren's own children, displayed the first visible signs of unease Collin has witnessed. Eilert cleared his throat, tongue nervously wetting his lips, his eyes moving uneasily between Aren, Kyreen and Lang.

"Defer," he finally mumbled, his voice cracking with the word.

Aren's expression did not register any reaction as her gaze shifts across the table. "Signe."

The brunette woman, Signe, though just as young as Eilert, displayed much more composure than her comrade, her back ramrod straight, hands clasped together upon the table. At the sound of her name, she squared her shoulders, and turned towards Kyreen, her sapphire gaze firmly meeting the other's emerald one.

"I deem her story true and cast my vote to grant temporary residence until the harvest moon, three cycles hence," the younger woman responded with conviction.

Aren continued around the table, not in a circle or any pattern Collin can readily identify. Gradually he realized she was going from the lowest rank upwards, working her way towards the grim-faced man on her left. As another granted amnesty followed by the husky man Geir calling the story a fabrication, Collin pondered the wisdom of this system. In theory, by calling upon the younger, less experienced persons around this table first, as opposed to the leaders, the opinions voiced should be more valid. Should the leaders speak first, it would be possible Aren or Lang or others could influence some opinions. Collin wondered also about Eilert deferring. Would this make his opinion less valuable in the eyes of the others or maybe invalidate it completely?

Collin accepted he was not a factor in this discussion. These were obviously not his people or his politics. Here he was but a bystander. Still he cared deeply for Kyreen and the fact that some here doubted her story, or even suspected, her story to be false bothered him immensely.

Noticing Aren turn towards Lang, Collin pushed away his curiosities to pay full attention to the man obviously antagonistic towards Kyreen. The bearded Calanian slowly moved his gaze around the table and for a brief moment locked eyes with Kyreen's companion. In that passing contact, Collin's animosity for Lang swelled into loathing, though if asked Collin could not have articulated the exact reason or cause to his feelings.

Sitting beside Collin, Kyreen felt this change and resisted the urge to glance over at him. Instead she kept her gaze locked on Lang, suppressing the churning of her stomach. Lang, she noticed, did not even grant her the consideration of eye contact, skipping completely over Kyreen as though she were not even present.

'So that is how this shall be,' she thought, concentrating her full attention on this man, making her presence known. When Lang swallowed uncomfortably, Kyreen allowed herself a smile, until she noticed Aren staring at her. Immediately, Kyreen shut down her emotions, that small thrill of joy quickly deflating into embarrassment.

Lang cleared his throat, his gaze focusing everywhere around the table except Kyreen's vicinity. "I do not doubt the sincerity or validity of this person's claim," Lang began, his first words surprising both Kyreen and Collin.

"I do, however," he continued, "have misgivings with regard to the wisdom of welcoming her and her companion. It is with concerns about the disruption such an outsider will cause to our people, our safety, and the upcoming campaign, that I support immediate separation from these strangers."

Though Lang was not the first to vote against her, his words provoked another wave of emotions within Kyreen. Except for the clenching of her jaw muscles, Kyreen managed to physically suppress the anger coursing through her. A fleeting glance from Aren cautioned her to work harder on stemming the internal emotion.

Aren looked around the table, her fingertips resting lightly upon the wooden surface. "By my count we have two more votes towards amnesty than for expulsion. As my vote is reserved to break a deadlock, Eilert's vote is deemed redundant," she paused to glance at the most junior member. "Do not fret about this outcome. Most plebes serve their mandatory rotation here without a vote ever coming before the council. You have gained more experience here tonight than most of your peers."

Eilert, his face flushed, inclined his head toward Aren. Collin did not need to be Calanian to sense the younger man's immense relief as Aren turned her attentions back to the gathering.

"The hour grows late, comrades. Let us reconvene in the morn to finalize details with Kyreen. I bid thee all a good eve. We are recessed."

Chapter 29

Outside, the council members dispersed quickly and quietly in groups of two or three, moving into the shadows of the forest. Collin stood on the edge of the puddle of light cast from the tent's doorway, waiting while Kyreen bid good night to Vidar and Aren. He noticed Lang with Geir exiting and his antagonism ignited anew. Geir was speaking in hushed tones, his hands waving vigorously. Lang, however, had his eyes fixed on Kyreen, his expression so malevolent Collin wondered at her safety. Surely Lang would not try to hurt or even worse kill Kyreen? Between Lang's high position on the council and his unveiled animosity towards the newcomer, Collin resolved this man would need to be looked after. As though sensing Collin's scrutiny, Lang turned to stare at Collin. If possible, the Calanian's gaze darkened. Collin chuckled to himself. Let the man wonder and worry he thought with satisfaction.

"Shall we depart?" Kyreen's voice in his ear startled Collin.

"Aye," he replied, smiling brightly. When he glanced over, both Lang and Geir have disappeared into the night.

A companionable silence filled the space between them as they walked back towards the center of camp. Collin resisted the urge to put an arm around Kyreen. A moment later, his patience was rewarded when Kyreen slipped her arm through his, leaning lightly against his shoulder.

"Thank you," she whispered.

"I did nothing."

"You supported me," she responded. "I felt it and I am certain others around us did as well. In your silence, you respected the council and your position as an outsider. Aren is grateful as well."

Collin shook his head. "Your people are very peculiar."

Kyreen chuckled and he smiled at the sound. Although the last couple of hours had been stressful, he felt her tensions receding here in the dark, surrounded by these strange people. He did not understand it, but he welcomed the transformation.

When they reach the dying campfire, a shadowy figure rose to meet them. It was Gunda holding their packs in her hand. "Father asked I deliver these to you and show you to where you may rest for the night."

Collin opened his mouth to protest, but stopped when Kyreen lightly squeezed his arm as she replied, "Thank you. Please lead on."

Recognizing he may be committing a blunder, Collin kept silent and fell in step with Kyreen. At the trees' edge, they began to walk single- file along a narrow path, Gunda in the lead. Kyreen took the middle spot, thankfully placing Collin's hands upon her shoulders for he could not recall ever experiencing such darkness in the outdoors. After several minutes, Gunda stopped.

"Your accommodations," she stated, her voice very low and quiet, barely carrying to Collin's ears. He did not trust himself to speak and let Kyreen bade the girl good-night.

Once Gunda retreated, Kyreen remained silent, lightly holding his hands in hers as they stood facing each other. Ultimately Collin realized Kyreen was waiting until her cousin's daughter was out of hearing. This respite granted his eyes time to gradually adjust to the darkness, until he could make out the shadows of the trees around them, an inky black canopy overhead from which an occasional star could be observed.

When Kyreen eventually began to speak, Collin had no trouble hearing her words. Her voice was so quiet, however, he wondered how he could possibly be hearing her. For a brief moment, he worried that she might be not be speaking aloud at all, but within his mind. Then he forgot this notion and concentrated on her words.

"Aren said something to me last night, something startling, something I have pondered on much during the day," she paused, her face shrouded in shadows, staring up at him. "She asked if I was... If we were...That there was an obvious...."

Kyreen leaned in and pressed her lips to Collin's. Taken by surprise, his response was sluggish, but then he slid his arms around Kyreen's waist and deepened the kiss. After a long moment, they parted lips, but he kept holding her close, trailing kisses along her jaw line.

"Collin," she asked quietly, "will you stay with me tonight?"

Not trusting his voice in the silent woods, Collin responded with another languorous kiss. This time when their lips parted, Kyreen took his hand and led him deeper into the shadows to the waiting blankets.

Chapter 30

The following morning, Collin awoke with the weight of Kyreen's head nestled against his shoulder and smiled at the memory of the previous night. When they had finally prepared for sleep he had reluctantly agreed, when Kyreen asked, to forgo the tent. Now in the gray morning light, he looked up into the canopy of trees, marveling at the feeling of being outdoors, yet beneath the protection of this bush. The feeling was at once both intimate and disconcerting. Overhead, birds flitted pass, their forms inky shadows. Lying here, he and Kyreen were a part of nature, yet removed. At this moment, Collin was acutely aware of how insignificant one life was, yet still felt connected to everything around him.

"I may never use a tent again," he murmured.

At the sound of his voice, Kyreen stirred. "What did you say?" she asked, still half-asleep.

Collin had never seen her so relaxed. On the road, she always woke long before dawn and when he caught her dozing she would waken harshly, instantly alert and on-edge. Now she shifted languidly, nuzzling against his collarbone, her body melting against his.

"Nothing important," he answered, folding his arms around her, breathing in the sweet scent of her curls.

"Good morning," he whispered, pressing a finger to her chin, tilting her face up to his. As his lips meet hers, Kyreen stiffened and she pulled away, reaching for her clothes.

Before Collin could ask, a woman's voice came from beyond the canopy of leaves. "Please forgive me for waking you. The council is convening and has requested Kyreen's presence." Collin never heard the Calanian retreat, but when they both stood a moment later, she was gone.

Kyreen smiled at him, placing a palm against his cheek. "I am sorry," she said, pressing a kiss to his lips before moving back into the camp.

Collin could not help notice she, too, made no sound as she maneuvered through the forest. Thus, he was extremely conscious of his movements as he rolled up the bedding. He was sure every Calanian in the area could hear every move he made, every footstep he took when he eventually headed towards camp.

Viggo, seated near the central fire with Gunda and his two sons, waved Collin over to sit beside him. After morning pleasantries were exchanged and everyone eating their morning gruel, Viggo said, "Yesterday I noticed a bow among your belongings. Protection or food?"

"A bit of both," Collin answered, distracted by a feeling of unease.

Something was unusual here and for a moment he was unable to name it. Then he realized, everyone in camp was awake and moving about their business, yet the camp was silent. Beyond the people still eating, the older children played, running about in game, yet they did not cry out to one another. Mothers and fathers interacted with their younger children in hushed tones.

Viggo noticed Collin's glances around the clearing. "Sound carries farther in the calm of the morning and soldiers are most alert," he offered as explanation then changed the subject. "Aren spoke about taking Kyreen out for a ride this morning after council. I am thinking about hunting. Would you like to join me?"

"That would be nice," Collin nodded, then his politeness yielded to curiosity. "Why are you not in the tent, Viggo? Are you not permitted on the Council?"

The Calanian chuckled, a calloused hand stroking his beard. "Aren is the strategist whilst I prefer more tangible endeavors. I am a tracker like my father before me."

One of the boys, the oldest, Yngve, rose to his feet and took Viggo's dishes. The other two children finished up and followed their older sibling. As Viggo watched them walk away, his expression pensive, Collin finished up his meal.

"My father was not just any tracker; he was the best tracker," Viggo said, his tone contemplative. "It was he who tracked the queen and discovered she had parted ways with Arvis. I was a teen at the time, just beginning my apprenticeship with him so he took me with him. The queen left in such a hurry amidst so much chaos. Shortly after her departure, the council discovered the plot against Queen Tyra and her children, so he led a contingency of soldiers left to keep her safe. When we saw the tracks separate, we knew not which to follow so returned. It is the reason I did not participate during the Battle. If not for that...." his voice trailed off and both men sit in silence, each preoccupied with his own thoughts.

Aren and Kyreen joined the men as they were saddling their horses. Gunda had already tacked two horses for the women and now asked, obviously not for the first time, if she may accompany them. Both her parents immediately shook their heads against the idea. Without a word, the girl turned to leave, but her mother stopped her with a hand to the girl's arm.

"Do not follow us, Gunda," she ordered, her voice soft, taking the sting from her words. "You have duties here in camp. Vidar is trimming hooves. He requires your assistance. Promise me?"

The girl shrugged, avoiding her mother's gaze. She attempted to pull away, but Aren tightened her grip.

Finally, Gunda looked squarely at her mother. "I promise," she whispered, emerald eyes shimmering with angry, unshed tears.

Satisfied, Aren released her daughter's arm and watched the girl stride towards the band of horses assembled across the field. Viggo kissed his wife's cheek before swinging himself up into the saddle.

"Every day," Aren said, reining away from camp, "Gunda reminds me more and more of Tyra."

"I was thinking she became more like you every day," Viggo replied, his tone light and teasing.

Aren chuckled. "You met me when I was more like Tyra and less like myself."

"My mother was angry and defiant?" Kyreen felt uncomfortable intruding on an intimate moment between partners, but relished any opportunity to learn more about her mother.

"Do not get the wrong impression from that interaction, Kyreen," Aren explained. "Tyra was confident and so self-assured in everything she did. She knew her own mind and never hesitated to speak it. Some may call her hard headed, outspoken, rebellious, stubborn. All deserved but she was not arrogant. She was just...." Aren paused, lost in her memories or grasping for the correct word.

"Tyra was perfect in everything she did. The sword in her hand became an extension of her body. Her hand-to-hand combat was a dance of beauty. You reminded me of her in the clearing yesterday. You not only look like your mother. You also have her grace. It was not just in combat that she excelled. Horsemanship. Games. She was the best at everything she attempted, but she possessed dignity, yes even humility. Though she knew how good she was, Tyra never lorded that over anyone, never made one feel less in her presence."

The horses reached the edge of the forest and Viggo took the lead on the narrow trail. Aren motioned for Kyreen and Collin to follow Viggo, while she trailed in the rear position.

Riding in the forest made conversation difficult, so each person was left to their own thoughts—Kyreen her mother; Aren her daughter; Collin his mission; and Viggo the trail. Once Viggo halted his horse, holding up a fist. Beyond the Calanian, through an opening in the trees, Collin saw a road, obviously once well used, now overgrown and deserted. Mere seconds later a group of Galorian soldiers, relaxed and conversing with each other, casually rode by. Once the soldiers had passed, Viggo led his group of riders across the road and back into the thick forest.

As the sun hits midpoint in its morning jaunt, the trees became thick and low hanging, forcing the riders to dismount and lead their horses. Collin could not imagine hunting in this type of surrounding, but had a feeling there may be a stop before he and Viggo got to the business of hunting.

Very shortly, his suspicions were confirmed when Viggo paused before a wall of brambles. Thick low-hanging branches heavy with dark green leaves and thorns as long and thick as Collin's thumb rendered the path impassable. Glancing right, then left, Collin verified that the copse continued in both directions as far as he could see. Viggo picked up a stick from the ground and thrust it into a grouping of thorny bushes, wrestling it open, creating a gate.

Though Collin had thought he was beyond surprise at the resourcefulness of the Calanian people, he issued a soft whistle of appreciation. Viggo grinned and waved them through, replacing the brambles once all had passed. After a short walk, the dense overgrowth began to thin away, the sunlight overhead again penetrating the thinning vegetation. Not long afterwards, Collin stepped out onto a grassy hilltop. He stood still, gazing down, while his grey gelding eagerly began to graze.

The vast, verdant green valley spread out before him, acres upon acres spotted with horses. A river, glinting dark blue in the distance, meandered across the plain, cutting the valley into two almost equal halves. The ride to the other side would be a half a day's hard ride.

Awed and confused, Collin asked, "Why do ye not settle this land?"

Aren exchanged glances with Viggo, then looked to Kyreen, clearly waiting for the younger woman to answer.

For a long moment, Kyreen's brain raced, then she nodded.

"The horses need this land, the open spaces, the grazing," she said, her voice soft. Her gaze drifted to the far end of the valley, where fields have been cultivated, "and the people need food."

"And…?" Collin is still confused.

"If all the Calanians disappeared from the forest, the Galorians would follow," Kyreen answered, her eyes sweeping across the valley before turning to rest upon his face, "And they would find this place."

"You saw the soldiers, Collin," Aren said, "They are unconcerned, victorious. In their minds, the war is over and they have won. To them, we are no longer a threat."

"The Galorians have no idea our numbers. To them we are a band of stragglers, vagabonds living off the land," Viggo added, his eyes narrowing at Collin's expression. "You agree?"

"I have no quarrel with the people of Calan, but, yes, I lean towards the Galorians' impression. How many people are in your camp? Sixty? Seventy? Nearly half of those are children Gunda's age or younger? How can you launch an attack with such numbers? It has been almost a generation since the Battle," Collin replied, his voice trailing off as he witnesses Kyreen's reaction. "What did I miss?"

"You think that is the extent of the Calanian people?" Kyreen asked, her smile and tone both soft, tempering the sting of her words. "You think they would take us, complete strangers, to the main camp? Show us their true numbers? Their strength? Without first examining us? Our intentions? Our loyalties?"

Aren chuckled softly as Collin looked between the three with confusion. "He is not of us, cousin. The city is a different place, with different rules." She nodded farewell to Viggo, who turned his horse back towards the forest, before glancing over to Kyreen's companion. "If you do not mind, Collin, I need to speak with Kyreen. Mayhap you two men can bring home fresh meat for supper?"

After the men had ridden away, Aren led Kyreen down the hill, explaining the trail up the river is a quicker way back into Calan's borders. A few of the grazing horses, sorrel mares with spindly-legged foals, raised their heads to watch the pair as they pass. At the river, Aren dismounted to let her mare drink; Kyreen followed suit.

"I believe my mother knew something terrible had happened here," Kyreen said, tentatively, replaying memories of her life with Tyra, "I do not believe she had imagined something this… wicked," she paused to remount the gelding, her voice and eyes firm as she looked down on her cousin, "You have been testing me this morning, Aren. How have I done?"

"Have I offended you then?" Aren asked, swinging back into the saddle herself and heading the horse north, upstream. Both her voice and posture confirm her next statement, "That is neither my concern nor problem."

"Then what is on your mind, cousin?" Kyreen asked sharply, not sure she wants the answer.

"You understand the basics of our society, Kyreen, but you…" Aren paused, obviously searching for a word, "…your presence complicate matters."

Kyreen's anger deflated as quickly as it had erupted. Shamefaced, she apologized, "Aren, please forgive me. I should not have come here. I did not mean to…"

Aren put up a hand, cutting Kyreen's words off, and reining in her horse. The two women sat still, listening to the sounds of the forest for many long moments before Aren relaxed. The older woman turned in her saddle, emerald gaze boring into the younger woman.

"I said 'complicate' that does not mean your return is a bad thing. I do, however, need to know what your intentions are here. Will you leave us at the first sign of conflict? Or will you sacrifice everything for your people? You need to know that there is a division in the council. Some wish you to take my position, to lead as our general. A few others feel you should ascend the throne to boost morale of the people. The rest, well, they find you a distraction and they have strong convictions."

"Lang," Kyreen stated, not needing Aren's nod to confirm that the hard-faced man had spoken out yet again this morning.

"He was adamant that you go back to Myrddin. Lang's arguments are sound and many on the council already suspicious of your return have sided with him. If I am to rally for you, Kyreen, I must know your intentions," Aren raised a hand as Kyreen opened her mouth to speak. "Do not answer now, cousin. We have a long ride ahead. Think hard about your future. As Collin pointed out many years have passed. A few more hours will not harm our cause."

Without waiting for Kyreen's response, Aren straightened in her saddle and urged her horse forward, clucking to coax the leggy mare into a hard run. Nibbling her bottom lip, Kyreen followed her cousin's lead, letting loose the gelding's rein. Not needing any encouragement, the sorrel erupted and easily caught Aren's horse, despite the mare's head start.

For the next few minutes, all thoughts of Calan and the conflict, everything left Kyreen's consciousness except the thrill of riding her horse. She relished the breeze stinging her eyes, the blur of the ground as the gelding's long strides lengthened. When finally the edge of the woods loomed ahead, Kyreen grudgingly pulled up the gelding, her breath almost as ragged and quick as her mount's.

"Thrilling?" Aren asked when she caught up to the younger woman, her smile warm and genuine.

Kyreen nodded, her eyes sparkling, her cheeks flushed with excitement. "Tis been too long since he has felt the freedom of the run."

"You, too, by the looks," Aren commented, before reining her horse into the woods.

Once in the shadows of the trees, following Aren, Kyreen pondered their conversation. Her brow furrowed, teeth nibbling her bottom lip. Her life had seemed so complicated before she rode away from Jorn just a fortnight hence. She had come to Calan expecting to slide back into her own community with her own people. With a deep sigh, Kyreen silently acknowledged not for the first nor last time that leaving Hanoria had failed to simplify her life.

Chapter 31

The quick excursion into Calanian land was uneventful. The women encountered only one patrol, this one even more casual and relaxed than the earlier patrol. After too short a time, Aren indicated they must return to camp. On the way, she pointed out another Calanian settlement in the distance, explaining, "That is where the family units reside. The other camp, our training camp, is secluded along the coast, a couple of days' ride away."

"Yngve is scheduled to move there after Harvest," Aren commented. Thought Aren's tone was casual. Kyreen picked up on an underlying tension and quirked a brow at the other woman, who shook her head, continuing, "A mother in denial, Kyreen. I do not want to believe my son, my baby is old enough to go to…to battle."

Silence descended between them, but Kyreen sensed Aren has not finished with the subject.

After a few moments, Aren began to speak, her voice soft and full of emotion, pain reflected in her eyes, "I have lost too many loved ones, family and friends, in battle, Kyreen. War is not pretty. It is ugly and nasty. The rawness of emotion, of pain. It is intolerable and it tears at your soul. My greatest fear is to feel one of my children die in combat under a Galorian blade."

Aren reined her horse to a halt, twisting in the saddle to face Kyreen. "There are strategies, lines of attack, options available to us to regain us not only the castle, but our independence, our sovereignty, our quality of life and dignity. Some are riskier than others. If you are to be a contributing factor in these I need to know the extent of your commitment to us."

"The other night you said something," Kyreen paused, involuntarily remembering another conversation with Aren on that first night, her cheeks flushing at the memory of last night with Collin.

"Yes, I said many things that night," Aren commented, her mouth twisting into a wry smile, "but I doubt our conversation regarding Collin is the one you mean to discuss right now."

The blush in Kyreen's cheeks deepened. "You are correct," she admitted, coughing self-consciously. It took her a moment under Aren's amused gaze to regain enough composure to continue.

"Aren, you said you have two vows to fulfill in this life. With your acquiescence I would join you in both of those vows. I will not rest until justice is dispensed against both Dolan and that other man. Though I know not his name, I will recognize his face as the man who murdered my mother.

"And, by your leave, Aren, I would add one additional vow," Kyreen continued. "Earlier you inquired as to my intentions here. Would I leave at the first sign of conflict or would I sacrifice everything for these people? I make this vow to you, cousin, that I will not stop until our people are safe, all of our people, every man, woman, and child, until Calanians once again reside within the castle, and peace is returned to our lands."

"Peace is an ambitious vow, Kyreen," Aren responded. "Are you sure? Peace has been tentative at most for more generations than can be recalled."

"This needs to stop," Kyreen said, the words coming from somewhere in the back of her memories. "Peace was on the horizon. My grandfather thought it could be done and he died in its pursuit. If I cannot bring peace to my people, then what be my purpose here?

"I know of places which have not experienced war. I lived in such a place, Aren. Although Hanoria was not perfect and there were conflicts of sorts, the people there do not live under constant threat, perpetually priming for attack. It was safe there. That is what I vow. That is my commitment."

Aren's gaze quietly searched Kyreen's face for many long moments. At last she nodded and extended her hand. "I accept your vow, Kyreen. By the goddess, I pray you success."

Kyreen clasped her cousin's forearm, thus sealing their covenant, though she had no idea how to accomplish such a feat. As they began their ride, Kyreen felt within Aren a shift of emotions, an acceptance that had not been present just moments earlier.

Upon their return to camp, Aren excused herself to convene the council while Kyreen helped Gunda care for the horses. The young girl, her outburst of the morning long forgotten and as though feeling her mother's new level acceptance, opened up to Kyreen, speaking animatedly about the camp, her family, friends, the horses. Listening to the cheerful banter, Kyreen brushed the gelding's coat until is shone golden in the late afternoon sun. As always, there was something comforting about the chore.

As they were turning the pair of horses out with the herd, Gunda exclaimed joyfully, "Poppa is back."

The girl ran towards the camp with Kyreen following at a more sedate pace, her smile widening when she spied Collin. The men had killed a stag, which several people helped unload and carry away to be processed.

Viggo, enveloped in a hug from his youngest, nodded a greeting to Kyreen over Gunda's head. Impulsively, and to the surprise of them both, Kyreen wrapped her arms around Collin, brushing her lips softly to his before hugging him close.

"Good hunting?" she asked, pulling away to gaze into his face.

"Aye. And ye? Did ye have a good ride with Aren?"

Kyreen nodded. Before she could reply, a motion from the council tent caught her eye. Aren had emerged and was moving towards them. Just behind her cousin, Kyreen spied Lang leaving the tent, his expression as dark as ever. For a brief second their gaze locked, sending electric shock waves through the young woman.

"Alright there, Kyreen?" Aren asked, stepping in front of Kyreen, forcing a break in the eye contact.

Kyreen nodded again, unable to trust her voice. A furtive glance over Aren's shoulder showed empty space where Lang had just been standing. Mentally shaking away her unease, Kyreen smiled up at Collin, who began to talk about his and Viggo's hunt.

Evening meal that night included the venison, a treat for the people of the camp, who sought out Viggo, the usual purveyor of fresh meat, to give their thanks. As each person approached Viggo, the tracker introduced Collin, who could not help but feel a rush of pride that it had been his arrow which felled the young buck and brought nourishment to these nomadic people.

After dinner Aren once again retreated to meet with the Council, again without Kyreen. The third or fourth time the young woman glanced towards the tent resting along the edge of camp, Viggo moved to sit beside her.

"I hope you do not take offense for it was not my intent," he said, pulling a jumble of leather out from his knapsack. "I made you a harness for your scabbard, to let you carry the sword upon your back."

Kyreen's cheeks flushed bright red, her hand slipping to the sheathed sword resting on the ground beside her. "Viggo, this is... you did not need... I do not know what to say."

Collin leaned over, whispering loudly. "Say 'thank you' and accept the man's gift."

"Thank you, Viggo," Kyreen said, elbowing Collin playfully. She stood so Viggo could begin to strap the leather strap across her torso.

"You are welcome, though it was not a difficult task. Aren carries a comparable strap for her sword and you two are similar of size," Viggo commented. Making final adjustments to the scabbard angle, he stepped back. "How is that?"

Kyreen flexed her shoulders, testing. Reaching back, she easily found the grip and slipped the blade from the sheath. Replacing the sword, she grinned at Viggo. "Remarkable. I can barely feel the weight, yet easily accessible. Thank you, Viggo," she repeated.

"My pleasure. Have you ever practiced with the blade?"

"Morning ritual," Kyreen replied warily. The morning after the snowstorm, Kyreen had felt pulled to hold the sword. Moving through the various stages, she had been very surprised at how balanced, how natural the weapon had felt in her hand.

"Have you ever sparred?"

She shook her head negative.

"So now I must confess my ulterior motive. Will you join the youth tonight as they practice evening exercise?"

At Kyreen and Collin's confused expression, Viggo explained, "A handful of them, Yngve included, will be transferring to training camp this Harvest, so have decided to begin now, hoping to gain an edge upon their colleagues."

Viggo lowered his voice, glancing around to ensure none of the youth were within earshot. "It has not occurred to any of our youth that mayhap other youth in the other camps will be doing precisely the same thing," he added with a chuckle.

As the sun set to the west, Collin took his place next to Viggo. The two men were the oldest by far in this human ring. Across the way, Yngve flashed a grin at his father and Collin before turning his gaze onto the two individuals facing each other in the middle of the circle.

Kyreen had drawn the first spar against a husky young man named Ebbe. In terms of size, Ebbe stood almost a head taller than Kyreen and outweighed her by almost twice. This aside, Collin felt rather certain Kyreen held all other advantages. She stood completely still, her gaze steady upon her opponent, an image of complete casualness. Ebbe on the other hand, shifted nervously on the balls of his feet, flexing and loosening his hands, his gaze flicking between Kyreen and the young woman stepping forward to officiate.

"Round One," the lanky brunette said, her soft-spoken voice barely carrying to Collin's ears. "Hand-to-hand combat…Begin."

Even as the last word faded, Kyreen slid to her right and stepped in towards her opponent. Ebbe's reflexes were quicker than Collin had expected, but Kyreen still managed a tap to his rib cage. Instead of stepping backwards, she slid again to her right, forcing Ebbe to scramble back and left to avoid another strike.

"Kyreen, one point," the umpire announced.

The dance continued for several moments without either combatant landing a blow. Eventually Kyreen did gain one more point with a strike to Ebbe's shoulder. Two points ahead she settled into a defensive strategy while managing to thwart all of Ebbe's attacks.

Collin glanced around the circle. Though all present were actively engaged, no one spoke out loud. The only sound in the clearing was the sound of two combatants. In his guild, training sessions were noisy boisterous events. Now it took discipline and self-control for Collin not to react verbally, especially when Kyreen grappled Ebbe to the ground just as the round finished.

After a short break, mainly time spent donning protective leathers, Kyreen and Ebbe once again face each other. This time Ebbe appeared much more at ease with a leaf-blade short sword resting easy in one hand and a round shield strapped to the other forearm.

At Viggo's suggestion, Kyreen held her mother's sword in her hand. When she had protested, he had pointed out the sword was meant to be a weapon and if Kyreen planned on carrying it she must have practice. Admittedly the blade felt comfortable and natural in her hand. The round shield, however, identical to that Ebbe wore, felt awkward and heavy strapped to her arm.

"Just relax and let your body move," Viggo had suggested, tightening the straps on Kyreen's forearm. "The movements of ritual are just as valid with the shield as without."

Ebbe stood ready, sword and shield in middle position. Kyreen mirrored the youngster's stance, maintaining an external appearance of calm.

This time Ebbe took immediate action at the spar's recommencement. Leading with shield side, he stepped in quickly, dropping his sword in order to deliver a swift upward slash. Kyreen managed to drop her shield at the very last second. Still, Collin visibly winced at the wicked sound of Ebbe's steel on wood. Even as Kyreen stepped back, Ebbe thrust the shield forward, pressing close as he raised his sword for a downward slash. Again, at the last second, Kyreen maneuvered away from the strike, pirouetting away so the blade swished harmlessly past her shoulder.

Collin did not realize he had been holding his breath until a strong urge reminded him to exhale. He sucked in his breath as Kyreen side-stepped a quick jab. Ebbe moved in almost immediately striking diagonally upward, his blade just nicking the edge of Kyreen's shield. Every time Ebbe's slash or thrust missed, he seamlessly recovered, never relenting long enough for Kyreen to take the offensive. Although Collin's stomach clenched with stress, Kyreen's calm expression never changed. Only the light in her green eyes reflected any emotion, one of composed deliberations.

After a dozen or so interactions, Kyreen, gaining more confidence in the unfamiliar guard, began greeting Ebbe's strikes. She no longer twisted and moved away. Instead she used the weapon strapped to her arm, deflecting low, blocking left, parrying a horizontal attack.

Gradually Collin perceived a shift in the rhythm of the exchange. No longer were Ebbe's strikes near misses. Kyreen was anticipating her opponent's next move and placing the shield with plenty of time. Ebbe, apparently unaware of the change, continued alternately stepping in with shield and following up with a forward pass. As the tempo settled into a steady and measured rhythm, Collin realized Kyreen was orchestrating the cadence, lulling Ebbe.

Even as this awareness dawned in Collin's mind, Kyreen dropped her shield and stepped forward. With a blur of steel, she feinted high, switching direction at the last moment to strike low, catching her opponent on the outer thigh with the flat of her blade. Had she led with the blade edge, Collin reckoned the strike would have been extremely unpleasant, maybe even fatal.

"Kyreen, one point."

Collin noticed several surprised glances exchanged between the young spectators. Clearly Ebbe had been the favorite in this contest. He smiled to himself, feeling a rush of pride at Kyreen's performance.

A moment later the spar was called finished and Kyreen declared the winner. If his loss bothered him, Ebbe did well concealing it. He immediately shook off his shield so as to extend a beefy hand to the victor as others pressed in around the combatants to offer their congratulations.

"Good show, Kyreen," the youngster said. "You snuck that one in on me at the end. Could have been a nasty, eh?"

After watching a few more pairs face off, Viggo motioned for Collin and Kyreen to follow him. They headed back to the campfire where Aren and others from the council were relaxing, their meetings completed for the night. Kyreen glanced around for Lang, her stomach in knots, but he and Geir were both absent.

"Kyreen defeated Ebbe," Viggo commented, dropping to sit beside his mate.

"In sword play?" Aren glanced at Kyreen, visibly impressed. "He is one of our most skilled swordsmen."

When Kyreen did not respond, Viggo added, "In all the camps, not simply amongst our youth."

"Kyreen, you met his mother, Olina, at council," Aren continued, "And his father is the weapons master at training camp."

"He is young," Kyreen replied, shrugging her shoulders. "All I had to do was fend him off until his attentions wandered, though he did almost nick me a time or two."

Collin noticed Aren and Viggo exchange a dubious glance. As the conversation turned toward more mundane topics, he realized he was learning to read the Calanian people. Though they did not always make their internal feelings known, they did on occasion slip, or as in this case, communicate their emotions physically. He wondered silently if Aren and Viggo had perceived Kyreen's fatal flaw, the one thing about her that so annoyed Collin—her self-deprecating nature. As callous as Collin felt the Calanian people had been towards Kyreen with regards to her return, he knew she treated herself much harsher. If only she could see herself through his eyes, he thought.

As though sensing his thoughts, Kyreen reached over for his hand and smiled. A few minutes later, as velvet darkness settled upon the camp outside the firelight, they excused themselves for the evening.

Chapter 32

Kyreen and Collin's sixth morning in the camp dawned gray and foggy. Silence hung over the camp like an ominous blanket in the gray mist swirling about the people. Their presence in camp had been settling into a comfortable routine, although there was always a feeling of waiting tickling the edges of both their minds.

Kyreen had been spending her days with Aren and those members of the council who were friendly towards her, catching up on her lost decades, learning more about her culture and history since the Battle. Collin occupied his time hunting with Viggo, learning how to track through brush and practicing patience when there were no tracks to follow. In the evenings Kyreen participated in training sessions with the youth, adapting to a variety of weapons—her sword, battle axe, spear—while bonding with Yngve and his friends. At night, in each other's arms, the outside world faded away.

On this particular morning, Collin knew Kyreen well enough by now to sense her stress, although outwardly she gave no sign. Most mornings her gaze would wander, mainly following the toddlers around the communal square or the older children at their quiet play. Today, her eyes focused on the ground at her feet as she absentmindedly spooned the gruel into her mouth. Collin finished his own breakfast in silence, watching Kyreen.

Finally, when no one was near, he leaned in so that their shoulders touched and asked, "What bothers you?"

Kyreen did not immediately react and remained silent so long, Collin thought maybe she had not heard him. His mouth was opened, about to ask once more, when she finally looked over at him and answered, "Today Aren is taking me to the castle," her voice was so low he strained to hear her words. "It shall take four, maybe five days."

Collin was surprised. From his conversations with Viggo, Collin knew the castle lay deep within Calan, situated upon a major river just a few miles upriver of the large deep-water bay which served as a gateway to the ocean. Thus, it was considered too far, too dangerous and was off-limits.

"Why would you go?" he questioned aloud, his brow furrowed with concern.

"I need to see it, Collin," she replied quietly.

"The council, even Aren, is against this trip, but…" Kyreen's pain-filled voice trailed off as she idly fidgeted with her spoon, making designs in the remaining gruel.

"You won't feel like you are home until you set eyes upon it?" Collin finished for her after a few moments' silence.

She nodded, shrugging her shoulders.

"I know it is silly, but still I cannot settle my mind," she explained, setting her head upon his shoulder as he slipped an arm around her. "These last days have been the best since my mother... since we left Calan, but I need to decide where to go from here. Some on the council believe I should leave. They feel I am a distraction and offer nothing to the people or the cause. Others see my mother's face and remember her leadership. Aren and a few others are encouraging me to join the training camp with the youth this Harvest."

Her voice trailed off, leaving the pair to sit in silence, both considering their future and their options. Collin knew he could no longer complete his mission. In his heart, he had known that even before he and Kyreen had spent their first night together. Truly his mission had been abandoned that afternoon in Glain's kitchen when he had first kissed Kyreen.

Collin knew there was no possible return to Myrddin for him now. Dwyn would relish in the opportunity to disgrace Collin, expelling him from the guild. On the other hand, where else could he go? Kyreen was heir to the throne here, a true Calanian yet her people had not welcomed her with open arms. If they rejected this woman beside him, one so obviously their own, how accepting would they be towards him, an agent of the mercenaries who helped destroy their nation?

Collin wondered, not for the first time, if this was the time to confess all to Kyreen. Should he tell her or wait? Even as he decided, the decision was taken from his control.

"Kyreen, we should leave. The rains approach and will slow us down," Aren's hushed voice interrupted his thoughts and Collin's opportunity faded.

This moment would loom in his memories and he would often wonder how different matters might have been had he spoken then instead of later. Nonetheless, they rose to their feet together and Kyreen pressed a soft kiss to his lips. For a long moment he held her close, reluctant to release her. Eventually she extricated herself gently, pressed a palm to his cheek and her emerald eyes smiling into his hazel eyes, turned and disappeared into the mist, where Gunda stood ready with the horses.

Two sunrises later, Kyreen lay on her stomach in the wet grass. Aren was similarly situated to her left. Oblivious to the damp, their attention was focused on the large structure looming far in the distance. The rising sun glistened brightly on the dew laden blades, as the morning mist quickly dissipated.

The rains had begun shortly after Aren and Kyreen had left camp. Their moods had been somber, but Gunda, excited to be accompanying them, was animated. Finally, just as Aren was about to tell her daughter to be silent, the dark clouds overhead had opened up; thunder clapped after unseen lightening and the rain fell in nonstop torrents. After slogging for hours through the rain, the trio had reached the edge of the outer valley. Aren had decided to set camp and the following morning, had sent Gunda and the horses back to camp with instructions to return in three days.

The two women had then set out on foot. The going had been soggy, but they had made good progress across treeless valleys as the rain had kept visibility low and the Galorian patrols to a minimum. The entire day had been gray and sunless; dark fell early but Aren pushed on well into the night. Finally, when Kyreen was as wet and miserable as she could ever remember, they had happened upon the final hill with brush for cover. After forming a lean-to from brush for shelter and a fireless meal, Kyreen had rolled up in her blanket and fell into a deep sleep. Sometime, shortly before dawn, the rain had dried up and with dawn the clouds had disappeared.

Now she was looking down upon her first home, the last place she had been truly happy and carefree. The castle shimmered and she blinked away the tears.

"The castle is used as a garrison for the soldiers who patrol," Aren explained quietly, neither woman's gaze leaving the scene below them. "The Galorians learned early not to make camp outside its walls."

Kyreen nodded. She had known there would be a reason the soldiers did not venture far into the countryside. The castle perched up high, backed to a steep cliff, the turrets positioned along the stone walls creating a complete view of the surrounding valley. A single road, well-worn with wagon wheel ruts, ambled down from the castle gates, forking into two roads—one meeting up to follow the river towards the ocean to the west and another rambling northeasterly into the hills, towards Galor. The southern road leading in the direction of their position, the interior of Calan, towards Myrddin and civilization, was grown over, absent the wheel ruts. Aren explained that Galor did their trade with vessels that arrived in the bay. Men and merchandise moved overland very rarely made it in or out of the province.

"We have been unable to do much against their presence in our land, but we have made a nuisance of ourselves over the years," she added with a grim smile.

Kyreen nodded again, examining the scene before her. Very little activity appeared to be transpiring outside the gray stone walls. The hour was early enough that the heavy wooden gate had not been raised for the day. Was the portrait of her grandparents still hanging in the war room? Had the big chair and table survived? She doubted it. Her mind conjuring up images of slashed paintings and broken furniture. While she ached to see the inside of the castle, another part of Kyreen wished to turn around and ride away forever.

Reliving those last moments spent in the castle, Kyreen remembered the tunnels and asked Aren, "I suppose they have cut off access to the tunnels?"

"Actually," Aren answered, "We did or more specifically Vidar and Viggo's father did following The Battle. The Galorians had known about the tunnels. Someone betrayed us, Kyreen. A Calanian."

Aren paused and for just an instant Kyreen could feel the struggle of emotions within her cousin. After a few moments Aren continued speaking, her voice low and tightly controlled, "Vidar was more than a blacksmith. He also experimented with alchemy and had discovered a combination of elements that could create an explosion. He was one of the first to be injured in battle and was evacuated out early, before we… knew. Once Vidar had recovered, he realized his creation would give the Galorians power, too much power. After what Dolan did to our people, Vidar could not risk it. So, one night he and Viggo's father returned to the tunnels to recover this concentrate and use it to seal off the passage entries in the castle.

"At the last entranceway, the one into the war room, the pair was surprised by the door opening, a group of Galorian soldiers being dispatched into the tunnels. In Vidar's haste, the powder was not set correctly. Vidar was caught in the explosion and was knocked unconscious. Viggo's father defeated the Galorian soldiers, barely, and was injured in the fight. He escorted Viggo out to where we were waiting for them. The last bit of Vidar's creation was used to seal off the tunnel, but in a controlled manner, one we could reverse when and if necessary."

"Viggo's father?" Kyreen asked, instinctively knowing the answer.

"He died shortly afterwards and, as you most likely surmised, Vidar lost his sight."

The two women fell silent, both lost in their own thoughts. After a few moments, the gate of the castle was raised. A contingency of five soldiers rode out, heading down the southern road. Just as Kyreen was about to ask Aren if they should leave their position, the soldiers turned off the road and rode over a lightly wooded hill.

"They check the tunnel entrances every morning. It is their first stop," Aren explained. "The next group to leave patrols the road to Galor, escorting caravans if one is headed back, and the third patrol maintains the road to the docks. A fourth patrol may or may not be dispatched to patrol the southern road."

"What about the one we saw the other morning, on our way to the Valley?"

"Every so often they send out a survey crew with a couple of soldiers. We learned early on that such units are sent out as disciplinary measures for disobedient or indolent soldiers. So, for the most part we now leave those parties be. Why should we be disciplinarians for the Galorians? As I said, Kyreen, these men are not worried about us anymore. As long as they contain themselves to this valley and do not push south, we are safe."

"Safe, maybe, but this is our home," Kyreen said. "It is not right."

"I am glad you feel that way, cousin," Aren flashed Kyreen a smile and motioned that they should move back down the hill. Once they returned to the cover of trees, Aren continued her tale of The Battle.

"With Vidar injured and Viggo's father killed, we retreated and set about organizing the survivors. It has taken us an entire generation to grow in strength to where we are now. We have been planning our strategy for an attack later this summer. I wanted you to see this for yourself, cousin, before I asked if you would join us."

"Why would I not?" Kyreen asked her heart leaping. "I gave you my vow, Aren."

"I know you are Calanian by birth, Kyreen, but you did not grow up here. You could walk away and live outside with ease. You have spent time here, learning the situation, so I offer you this chance to renege."

Kyreen flinched, a myriad of emotions assaulting her senses. Aren's words stung like salt ground into an open wound. All of her life Kyreen had dreamed of returning to Calan. For the first time in memory she felt comfortable and relaxed, like she belonged somewhere, here. How could she walk away with ease? Kyreen did not say anything but instead relaxed the hold she had been keeping on her emotions.

Aren held up a hand. "This is not the place to have such a discussion. Follow me."

As Aren turned away, Kyreen finally felt what her cousin had obviously felt. A group of mounted riders had left the castle and were traveling down the southerly road, their route taking them very close to the grove in which the women had been standing. Silently cursing herself Kyreen followed after Aren. Every day she was reminded how atrophied her skills had become over the years. She lacked the ability to completely rein in her own emotions. She found it near impossible to pick and choose who she scanned while at the same time not scanning those around her who could perceive her intrusion. These were abilities young Calanians grasped with ease by their third or fourth season.

Distracted by her thoughts, Kyreen misstepped, the loud crack of a twig snapping bringing her fully back to the present moment. Both women paused, frozen in place, their senses highly alert. Horrified by this gaffe Kyreen's face burned with shame as she waited, but everything around them remained quiet. The patrol was obviously, mercifully, out of range.

Kyreen opened her mouth, intent on apologizing, but a look from Aren silenced the words unspoken upon her tongue. How Kyreen wished she could sense what Aren was feeling at this moment. As the women resumed their trek, Kyreen concentrated on the trail before her, fighting back the swirl of emotions barraging her senses.

Chapter 33

"Aren, I am so sorry. How can you forgive me?" Kyreen blurted as soon as they stopped for the midday meal. They were standing beside a small spring fed by an underground river. Sunlight filtered through the canopy, glittering off the rippling surface. Far overhead fir trees swayed in a light breeze, dark green moving against a bright blue sky. The women had worked away from the castle, paralleling the main road for a long time before angling away to penetrate the forest. Kyreen was certain they had passed this pond previously, on their journey towards the castle. Traveling in the dark and the rain, however, Kyreen could not be certain of their exact path, yet another ability in which she was deficient.

Kyreen realized Aren had not spoken. The woman gazed upon Kyreen, her expression neutral. Kyreen could not meet Aren's eyes, so her own gaze dropped to the ground. Uncomfortable under the scrutiny, Kyreen willed herself to not fidget, but could not stop nibbling on her bottom lip.

After a perceived eternity on Kyreen's end, Aren sighed quietly and turned towards the water. As she knelt to begin refilling water skins, Aren said, "It is I who should be asking forgiveness, Kyreen. I see your face and I forget."

"Forget what?"

Aren proceeded to fill the canteens without answering. Kyreen, though anxious to hear the answer, remained silent, having learned her cousin's customs. Aren would speak once her thoughts had been gathered and she could concentrate on the message. It was yet another reminder to Kyreen of how she differed. Although Kyreen's words and actions were much more measured and careful to those people around whom she had grown up, here Kyreen was perceived careless and injudicious.

Finally, Aren stood and faced Kyreen. Her gaze reflected an emotion Kyreen could not exactly name. Pity? Disappointment? Unease? Whatever it may be, Kyreen knew she would not welcome the words she heard from her cousin. In this she was correct.

"I forget, Kyreen," Aren answered, her quiet voice laced with emotion, "That you are not Tyra."

Kyreen's eyes filled with tears. Eventually, she lost her fight to contain them and turned to move away, knowing Aren could feel her emotions, but needing the space nonetheless.

For the majority of her life, Kyreen had fought to belong among people who judged her poorly because her physical looks differed so much from them. Now she had returned to her people, her home, only to discover that she now looked too much like her mother. Maybe Lang and his contingency were correct. Maybe Kyreen did not belong here.

But where? Kyreen wanted to scream to the heavens. Where could she belong if not in Calan. Even before the incident with Markku and the stolen stud colt, Hanoria was never her home. Myrddin was not an option either. Kyreen squatted in the shadows of the forest, hands covering her face and struggled to regain control.

After several long moments, she stood once more. Taking a deep breath and swiping the back of a hand across her eyes, she returned to the clearing. Aren sat upon the ground in a puddle of sunlight near the pond eating her rations. Kyreen felt the other woman's gaze upon her as she wordlessly filled her own water bags. That task completed, Kyreen took a seat close to Aren, but in the shade, and began to eat her meal.

Aren continued to examine Kyreen, silently chewing. The pity was gone, replaced with curiosity. When she finally spoke, Aren's voice was neutral. "Why do you do that, Kyreen?"

Her feelings still wounded, Kyreen mumbled, "I have no idea what you are asking, Aren."

"Turn away. Shut down. Shut up. Retreat," Aren said. "You never truly confront me, the council, anyone. I dismiss you, insult you, bait you, yet you never, ever respond openly."

"What would you have me do?" Kyreen snapped, losing some of her hard won control. "Rant and rave? Shout at you in a fit of temper?"

"If necessary, yes. There are times for emotions, Kyreen. We are not a people of indifference. We are very passionate and rage is a part of those emotions," Aren paused, then chuckled. "Your mother was one of the most fiery, quick tempered people I have ever known. She would have taken my head off back there to suggest she did not belong with her people."

While she normally enjoyed reminiscing about her mother, Kyreen remained somber. "What if you are right, Aren?" she asked quietly, "What if I do not belong here?"

Aren responded almost before the words were out of Kyreen's mouth, rolling over to kneel before Kyreen, their faces just inches apart, fingers gripping at Kyreen's shoulders.

"Do not ever say that, Kyreen! Do not even think that!" she hissed fervently. "Dolan has taken so much away from all of us, but most especially you. Do not give him one more thing! If you are to do the work you have ahead of you, if you are to fulfill your vows, you must believe, you must know that Calan is your home."

For a long moment, the two women stared at each other in silence. Finally, with a soft exhalation, Aren moved away, lying back on the ground, her hands propped behind her head, eyes looking up at the splash of bright blue sky visible overhead. Kyreen, her heart racing, finished the last of her meal, washing it down with a sip from her canteen. The silence between the two women continued, each lost in her own thoughts, with just the sounds of the forest surrounding them.

After a few minutes, Aren sat up, glanced at Kyreen then stood, brushing her hands against her britches.

"We should move on," she said, offering a hand to Kyreen, who takes the unnecessary assistance after a second's pause.

As they begin walking, Aren said, with a glance around the clearing, "We are fairly safe now, far enough from the road that we can speak and move a bit faster."

Kyreen nodded, speeding up to maintain pace with Aren.

"I am filled with doubt most of the time and about most things, Aren," she said. "But I do feel more at home here and this place feels the most right, like I could belong. You said you needed my help in something. If it helps get your people back into Calan, then I will do anything."

"Us, Kyreen. Our people. If this plan works, it should get us, our people, back where we belong," Aren replied, pausing to spare a glance towards the younger woman before adding, "You really should hear the plan before you agree to it."

"Tell me, but be assured I will do whatever it takes."

"As I have mentioned before, we have been waiting until our numbers were large enough, strong enough to take back the castle. Our ancestors set up the castle as a stronghold. It is quite easy to defend for long periods of time and virtually impossible to breach."

Kyreen nodded. "The land remains clear around the castle, with eight turrets being manned visibility is maximized. Even in the cover of a moonless night, it would be difficult to approach without being detected."

"Exactly. Those mercenaries hired by Dolan entering the castle disguised as Calanians were the only reason the Galorians were able to breach the castle security," Aren glanced over at Kyreen. "The rumor is you were the one who raised the alarm. Dolan's plan may have succeeded save for you."

Kyreen shuddered, the long suppressed memory of inky shadows and a blade glinting in moonlight bringing a taste of bile to her mouth.

"Maybe," she muttered.

Sensing Kyreen's discomfort, Aren continued. "The castle is being used primarily as a weigh station for goods being transported from the bay into Galor. The garrison of soldiers is secondary; the total number of men there is small. For years we have tried various ways to infiltrate the castle walls, but since all attempts have failed, the war council has decided a full-on attack of the castle is our only option."

Surprised, Kyreen stopped walking. "But that would mean…" her voice trailed off.

Aren nodded grimly, "Yes. Massive casualties."

Kyreen fell back in step with Aren, her mind racing. "Surely there must be another way, a safer way. What about the tunnels?"

Aren grinned, casting a sly glance towards her cousin, "I was hoping you would say that. The tunnels have not been a viable option… until now."

"Why not?" Kyreen asked, her brow furrowed with confusion.

"The Battle was a long time ago, Kyreen. What do you remember of your flight through the tunnels?"

The two walked in silence while Kyreen conjured up the long suppressed memories. "I remember Mama rushing Quillan and me down to the war room. Lots of people talking. Uncle… Uncle Arvis smiling at me and ruffling my hair. Then Mama swept me up and into the tunnels. Arvis carried Quillan. We went down the stairs and ran for what felt like hours. People met us at the mouth of the tunnel with horses. I could hear the battle noises when we broke out of the tunnel. It was early morning, but still pre-dawn. I…I was terribly frightened."

"Was there anything else?" Aren prodded gently. "In the tunnels, specifically. Do you remember anyone, anything that accompanied your group through the tunnels?"

"The gargoyle!" Kyreen exclaimed quietly, her eyes lighting up. "Always, no matter where we entered the tunnel, he was there, waiting."

"He is still there," Aren replied, "We cannot access the tunnels because of him."

Confusion clouded her eyes again and Kyreen asks, "Why not? He is the tunnel guardian, for Calan, not Galor."

"No, Kyreen, he is a guardian for the royal family. He is the last of his kind, but still relatively young for a gargoyle. They are magical creatures with long lifespans and absolute loyalty to those whom they were bred to protect. Outsiders were tolerated, but barely. It would take months, sometimes years, for castle guards to gain the tolerance of these animals.

Viggo's father was the last surviving guard with access to the tunnels. That is why he had to escort Vidar out. Had Vidar continued on his own, the gargoyle would have torn him to pieces. In that manner, our timing in sealing the tunnels was unfortunate. Had the Galorians entered the tunnel before or after Vidar's mission, they surely would have been killed."

"But what has changed?" Kyreen inquired. "You do not plan to kill this creature, do you?"

"No, Kyreen. That has been discussed, but again these creatures are not only tough and resilient, they possess powers we do not understand. There is no telling how many lives would be lost just to subdue the gargoyle," Aren paused to look at Kyreen. "You truly do not know? It is your arrival which has changed the situation."

"Me? I have not been here for nearly two decades, as many are quick to highlight." Visions of Lang arguing against her rose unbidden in Kyreen's thoughts.

Aren, in her excitement for once seemed oblivious to Kyreen's discomfort, rushed to explain. "Viggo and I have discussed this in depth. We do not believe your time away matters. The gargoyle imprinted upon you and your brother at birth, just as it had done with Tyra and her father and all the royal babies before them."

Seeing the question in Kyreen's eyes, Aren added, "The gargoyle imprinted upon my father, as the king's son. It did not imprint upon me because my father never assumed the throne. The crown went directly from Uncle Rolf to Tyra. Only descendants of the reigning monarch are imprinted."

"So, you think the gargoyle would recognize me?"

"Yes! These creatures share a bond with their charges. That is how it would always know where you were in the castle and could meet you at the entrance."

As they continued walking, Aren explained the plan. Calan troops would skirt through the woods to the north side where the tunnel entrance was obscured from view of the castle by a knoll. As the Galorian soldiers did not patrol at night, the Calanians would use the cover of dark to move into the tunnels, away from the entrances. Then it would not be difficult to locate and reopen one of the castle entrances and sneak in then following evening, when the soldiers slept.

"The beauty of this plan, Kyreen, is that it minimizes our casualties," Aren finished.

Kyreen had to agree with her cousin. The plan seemed much more feasible and less dangerous than a full attack upon the castle.

"Anything I can do," she repeated her earlier words, "I will help in any way possible."

"Thank you," Aren breathed out, a smile dawning across her face. "I thought you would agree, but others on the council were unconvinced. There are several who are against the tunnel plan. Some, especially Lang, do not believe the gargoyle will let you pass. He has memories of his father working in the tunnels, unfavorable memories of the gargoyle. Lang has campaigned for many years that we destroy the creature to gain control of the tunnels. Fortunately, his is the most radical voice on the council and not many members side with him."

"I trust you, Aren. If you believe this plan is viable, then I will do my part."

"Good," Aren clasped Kyreen's shoulder. "Now, let us pick up the pace. I miss my family!"

As Aren took off at a slow jog, Kyreen suppressed a smile.

Although she would never readily admit to it, she, too, was anxious to be back in camp. Collin had been in her thoughts these couple of days and she looked forward to seeing him again.

Chapter 34

The women met up with Gunda the following day, but the rains returned and the journey was slow. When they found the main trail washed out, Aren had to find another way through the woods with the horses. Eventually, however, they made their way into the camp, which had relocated during their absence, also slowing down their return.

Muddy and road weary, Kyreen's heart rate jumped when they rode into the camp. Viggo, already waiting, practically pulled Aren and Gunda from their mounts. He engulfed them in a tight embrace, nodding a hello in Kyreen's direction. Despite his friendly gaze, Kyreen sensed something amiss and began scanning the clearing for Collin. It was close to evening and many people were gathered around the community square for evening meal. He was not one of them.

Just as she was about to ask Viggo, Kyreen spied Collin emerging from the woods, bow strapped across his back, carrying a turkey carcass. She waved and rushed towards him. When she was close enough, she threw her arms around him in a tight embrace, surprising them both.

At first, she was so glad to be near him that it took a moment to realize Collin was not hugging her back. Kyreen pulled back to gaze into his face. Collin was obviously uncomfortable and refused to look at her directly.

"What is wrong?" she asked quietly, forcing herself to step back from him, arms dropping to her side.

"Kyreen!" A voice squealed from behind Collin.

Recognizing the voice, but not truly believing it until she saw for sure, Kyreen looked past Collin's shoulder. Astonished, Kyreen watched Engla running towards her, followed by Stian walking at a more leisurely pace. Kyreen cast a questioning glance at Collin before stepping around him to greet her friends. Though a full head and a half shorter, Engla nearly tackled Kyreen with her enthusiasm. The words were tumbling from the Hanorian girl's mouth so quickly Kyreen had trouble following the discourse. She registered the words "Jorn" and "farm" and "inherit," and looked to Stian. He shrugged, giving her a hug around his sister, who was not letting go of Kyreen.

"Jorn?" Kyreen whispered over Engla's chatter, her gaze still on Stian. "Is dea....has crossed over?"

Stian nodded. "We...Engla thought you should know."

"And," Engla interceded, looping one arm through Kyreen's and the other through Stian's to lead them towards dinner, "you ran off in such haste I did not get a chance to say goodbye. Father forbade me to follow you, but for once I had to disobey. After Jorn crossed, I made my decision and took off in the night."

Kyreen stopped walking. "You? Alone?"

"Aye, alone," Engla answered, lifting her chin defiantly. "Twas not a problem."

"Because I caught up with her the next day," Stian added. "Just in time, mind you. My sister was just about to give money to a flesh-peddler to spend the night in a bawdy house."

"Stian, your tone makes it sound so bad!" Engla swatted playfully at her brother, her high voice carrying through the dusk air as she continued with the story of their journey here.

Half-listening to her friend, Kyreen's gaze wandered around the clearing, acutely aware of the rest of the camp's attention on this group. Finally, she rested her sights upon Collin standing near the horses, speaking with Aren and her family. He glanced over at her, flashing an uncomfortable smile before looking away, his discomfort completely evident even from this distance. Kyreen pushed her thoughts of him to the back of her mind, returning her attention to Engla.

"When we arrived in Myrddin, Stian found a stable," Engla was saying. "By the Lord of Fortune's grace, it was the same one you and Collin had put your horses in. The man there was not very friendly, but he did send us to Glain. Is she not the most wonderful person? Did you see her garden? How anyone can grow anything in such a crowded city is beyond me, but she does. The herbs she has for cooking are impressive. She took me to the apothecary and I could not believe the price for medicines there. It is outrageous. There is only one serving that entire city and he is a thief. No, Stian, he is! How one can charge that much for such a small dingy clump of...."

"Engla," Stian prodded gently. "Get on with the story."

The girl gave her brother an admonishing look as she continued, "Anyway, Glain told us you were heading up here, so we headed north. That is a lonely road, Kyreen. So desolate and..."

"When we came through the pass, the guards stopped us," Stian managed to interrupt again when Engla paused for breath. "I did not expect them to help us, but when I mentioned your name, one of them led us here. That was five days past."

Five days? The siblings had been in the camp five days?

Before Kyreen could respond, Aren approached and Kyreen made the introductions. Aren greeted the siblings cordially then suggested everyone partake of the evening meal. When Stian and Engla turned away, Aren gestured Kyreen to fall back with her so they may talk quietly.

"The sentries recognized the horses in addition to your name," she said. "That is why your friends were allowed to talk and were brought here."

"Aren, I am sorry," Kyreen whispered, sensing disapproval from Aren. "I had no idea these two would come after me."

"I realize that, Kyreen, but they cannot stay. It may appear calm and peaceful here, but it is not," Aren hissed, now her anger barely in check. "Strangers put us in danger, all of us! That girl's voice can be heard across half the forest!"

Kyreen glanced over her shoulder, watching her friends gather food. Their arrival warmed her heart. Kyreen's departure from Hanoria, which felt a lifetime ago, had been so sudden and abrupt. She now realized that she had been engrossed in the sting from Jorn's betrayals that she had maltreated the only two friends she had had growing up. While Kyreen's actions had been wrong, Stian's and Engla's presence here was inappropriate.

"They did not know, Aren," she said quietly. "As I did not. Hanoria is so isolated, just as Calan is. News from the outside world rarely made it to our ears. Most of what little news did some in was seasons old before it arrived through the tavern, falling upon the ears of drunken men who may or may not choose to share it with the women."

"What a strange place for Tyra to leave you," Aren commented. "Do you think she knew?"

Kyreen shrugged. "She knew it was isolated and she knew she could trust Jorn to keep me safe. As you have said, she had no idea how terribly wrong the battle would end. She never expected me to stay there for long. I will speak with my friends, Aren, and suggest they journey back home in the morn."

"Thank you, cousin," Aren replied, giving Kyreen a smile before heading towards her family to eat.

Chapter 35

Kyreen gathered her supper before returning to the fire and taking a seat beside her friends. She glanced around, looking for Collin, but before she could voice her concern, Stian asked about her trip from Hanoria. As she spoke about Kare's family and meeting Collin, Kyreen sensed there is something more that Stian wanted to speak about. Soon enough they have finished their meal. Stian asked Engla to take his dishes, which she did cheerfully, taking Kyreen's at the same time.

As soon as Engla is out of hearing distance, Stian leaned in close to Kyreen, his voice low.

"In Myrddin, at the stable, I saw Markku's horse, the flashy blood bay gelding with the four stockings and blazing stripe? When I asked about it, the stable manager said the man was looking for a horse thief! Viggo said you arrived here with two horses. Kyreen, I have had enough time to put things together. Did ye take the stallion?" He paused, putting a hand up. "Do not answer. I do not want to know. Alright, yes, I do want to know. Did ye steal the horse?"

"Stealing would imply taking something which did not belong to you," Kyreen replied calmly. "The stud is mine. Jorn had no right to sell him and Markku had no business owning him. You did not see the abuse inflicted on the stallion, Stian. Markku did not deserve the animal."

Stian leaned back, running a hand over his face. "By the Lords of Hayrik, Kyreen," he said, barely winning the struggle to keep his voice low. "What were ye thinking? Markku will not relent until he finds ye and has ye arrested, or worse hanged."

Kyreen saw that Engla was deep in animated conversation with Gunda and placed a hand on Stian's knee. "Do not fret, Stian. Markku cannot, will not find me here. I appreciate the concern and am grateful for your journey here, but, my friend, it is not safe here. You know what happened here? You have heard the story of my people?"

Stian nodded.

"From Collin and Viggo upon our arrival," he said. "It is truly awful, Kyreen. Are ye sure ye wish to remain here? Ye know ye are always welcome to stay with me on Jorn's farm."

Inwardly Kyreen flinched. As much as she cared for Stian, he was a Hanorian man and as such would never understand why she could never be content in a society that considered her to be a lesser person.

Aloud Kyreen said, "This is my home, Stian. For the first time in a very long time, I am where I should be, need to be, and want to be. But you do realize this is not where you should be. I fear Engla does not comprehend."

"Aye. Ye are correct," Stian sighed. "Ye may not believe it, Kyreen, but I have been here long enough to understand why ye could nay be happy in Hanoria. I see the difference here and I admit it baffles me, but it does explain why ye are who ye are."

"Why Kyreen is who?" Engla asked, settling down between her brother and her best friend.

"I was simply explaining to Kyreen that I understand why she cannot return to Hanoria," Stian explained, "and bidding her farewell."

"What? But she just... we just..." Engla looked between the two, her blue eyes large with distress. "I do not understand."

"You would not, Engla. This regards matters beyond your comprehension," Stian rebuked. Although his tone is not unkindly, Kyreen physically winced this time, though neither of the other two noticed.

Engla threw her arms around Kyreen, pressing her face into Kyreen's shoulder. "I will miss ye, my friend," she said, her voice muffled.

Kyreen hugged her friend, glancing anew around the clearing. Still no sign of Collin and she assumed he was taking care of the game he had brought back from hunting. Dusk had given way to darkness and most of the Calanians had retired to the woods for the night. As she spied the white shadow of a small tent on the edge of the trees, Kyreen realized she had not seen the war council tent. The camp must be moving again in the morning.

After another moment, Kyreen released Engla. "It is late, my friends. Dawn arrives early during the Growing Season."

After walking her friends to their tent, Kyreen made her way to her own spot amongst the trees. Rolling out the blankets, her mind returned to earlier, when she first arrived in the camp. Something was amiss, but what it could be Kyreen had not a clue. It must have something to do with Stian and Engla's presence in the camp. Had they committed a gaffe? Hanoria and Calan cultures differed, but not so much that Stian would not be aware of protocol. Neither would that explain Collin avoiding her.

Kyreen lay awake for a long time, her mind puzzling the situation, but a solution never arrived. Neither did Collin. When she awoke in the morning Kyreen was still alone. She rose quietly, the bushes around her dark contrasts in the gray predawn. Once her bedding was bundled, ready for travel, she entered the clearing. A few people sat around, quietly talking amongst themselves. Kyreen did not see Collin, but Viggo motioned for her to join him.

"Good morn, Kyreen," he said as she took a seat beside him. "Collin and Reidar left yester eve to check the snare lines."

Kyreen sighed, "I had forgotten."

Since their arrival at camp, Collin had been hunting with Viggo almost every day. Many times, Aren and Viggo's youngest son Reidar would accompany them on these outings. Much as Kyreen had bonded with Gunda, Reidar had become attached to Collin. Before Aren and Kyreen had left for the castle, Reidar had been preparing to set his first trap line along the northern mountain ridge. Normally a parent or older sibling would accompany a youth on their first trap line, but Reidar had requested Collin's company. Kyreen felt foolish. Obviously, the line would need checking and as the start of the trap line was a half-day's walk from this camp, it made sense that they would leave last night to be in position to begin with morning's first light.

Kyreen felt Viggo's gaze upon her and realized he had more to say, but waited for her invitation. Recalling the distress she had sensed last night, she said, "I welcome your thoughts, Viggo, unless you feel this is something better discussed between Collin and me."

He smiled, "You learn quickly, Kyreen. Yes, you and Collin should talk. I merely wish to tell you that Reidar had not planned on checking his line until after the camp moved this morn. It was Collin who requested they leave last night. Did he not see you before their departure?"

The arrival of Aren and others saved Kyreen from having to answer. It also allowed her time to ponder the statement, but not for long. When Stian and Engla emerged from their tent, Kyreen assisted Stian in stowing their gear. Shortly both the camp and Kyreen's friends were ready to leave the clearing. Gunda stood nearby with the Hanorians' horses. The girl's face was set firmly neutral, but even without trying Kyreen could feel the hostility radiating off her cousin's daughter.

"Kyreen, please come with us. Ye grew up in Hanoria and although it was nay always ideal, it was your home, correct?" Engla implored once more, but Kyreen knew her friend was merely saying the words out of social obligation. Even Engla could tell these were Kyreen's people and here was where the tall dark-haired girl belonged.

Kyreen hugged her best friend with bittersweet sadness. "I shall always think of you with the fondest of memories," she whispered in Engla's ear. "Thank you for being my friend."

Engla now allowed the tears to flow freely. With a final pat to the young woman's shoulder, Kyreen turned to hug Stian farewell. While he was not as openly emotional as his sister, Kyreen felt the conflicting emotions within her friend.

"The farm is yours without foul. I hold no claim to the land nor do I take offense to your gain," she murmured quietly into his ear, releasing him from the guilt.

Stian nodded his thanks before turning towards Viggo and Aren. In a few moments, the farewells were complete and the Hanorians had ridden out of sight. Kyreen remained there for a long time, lost in her memories of Hanoria. Every good memory she had of that place was linked to the people she loved—Engla, Stian, Ildri, and even Jorn. Now, considering the distance between their two homes, it was doubtful she would ever see her friends again.

Finally, she sighed, turning back to the task at hand. For the rest of the day Kyreen concentrated on helping with the camp move, thankful for the distraction.

Chapter 36

Collin and Reidar return the following afternoon. Kyreen, having been summoned into the council tent did not feel their return, but Aren's disquiet alerted her. Plans for the attack on the castle had moved forward. Aren secured approval from the council to infiltrate the tunnels, under the final new moon of the Growing Season, although Lang and his contingency still pushed for a direct attack. Word of the plan had been sent to the other camps and already some people had begun the trek into Calan.

Kyreen herself was scheduled to leave in the morning. After sensing Aren's uneasiness Kyreen wondered if her delay had been deliberate. After what felt like an eternity, the meeting was concluded, but not before Lang once more expressed his displeasure at the plan.

"Everything hinges upon this one detail," he said, slamming a fist into the table. "If this creature rejects… her, then we will be more vulnerable than if we just conducted a frontal attack under cover of darkness with maximum surprise."

Lang stood tall at his spot at the table, gaze sweeping around the room, skipping over Kyreen. Whenever able, he would avoid looking at Kyreen and if at all possible shunned speaking her name. Animosity radiated from him whenever Kyreen was near. She wondered not for the first time if his objection to the tunnel plan was more because of her than the gargoyle.

Still Kyreen's position with the council was precarious so she held her tongue. A distraction such as an open confrontation with Aren's second-in-command would not only be unwise, but also unnecessary. Once the attack was over, for better or worse, she would have opportunity to confront Lang and his issues with her.

Right now, however, Kyreen had other issues to address and she anxiously awaited adjournment. Lang, however, had other plans for Kyreen. As she stood to leave, Kyreen noticed the tall man heading her way. Though she turned quickly to duck through the door, he almost immediately caught up with her once outside.

"Walk with me," he instructed quietly.

Her stomach in knots, Kyreen fell into step with him. She realized she had never been this close to Lang. The experience was not at all pleasant. His essence practically vibrated with such strong waves of emotions that Kyreen wondered momentarily if she should worry about being alone with the man. As she struggled to control her own racing heart, they moved away from camp, into the forest, eventually emerging along the shore of a large lake.

Approaching a large outcropping of boulders, Lang waved Kyreen over to sit upon one while he positioned himself a distance away, standing with his back to the forest. Relieved to be out of his proximity, Kyreen did as directed, then waited. Lang requested this meeting; Lang would speak first.

"I do not like you, Kyreen," he began, pausing almost imperceptibly when he spoke her name. "I believe Aren has misplaced her trust and the safety of our people out of sentiment for Tyra."

Lang paced as he spoke, eyes fixed on the gravel at his feet. "We have waited for this summer, this new moon, this time for many years. Years you spent somewhere else, with other people, learning other ways. Outwardly you give a good show of being Calan. Stop!"

Lang raised a hand towards Kyreen when she jumped to her feet. He took a few steps backwards, gaze averted. "Let me finish…please."

Clenching her jaw angrily, Kyreen sat back down. "Tread carefully, Lang," she warned through gritted teeth, suppressing the grin when Lang flinched hearing his name upon her lips.

"My point is you are not trained. Your abilities are undeveloped. I fear you will be a distraction in battle, a distraction none of us need."

"You wish me to stay behind?" Kyreen was incredulous. She had known Lang distrusted her but had no idea his animosity ran this deep. She looked at him, standing along the shoreline, his eyes firmly fixed not on her, but a point somewhere over her shoulder. The setting sun's light reflected off his face, his eyes flaring like a brilliant emerald fire.

At that moment Kyreen's entire being froze, her breath caught in her throat, adrenaline flooding her veins. Even as she struggled to contain the overwhelming urge to launch herself at Lang, a voice rang out.

"Kyreen! There you are!" Collin had emerged from the forest behind Lang, oblivious to the conflict between Kyreen and Lang.

Lang finally looked straight at Kyreen, his eyes boring into hers. "Watch yourself in the castle," he hissed, turning to stride back towards camp, passing Collin without acknowledging his presence.

Close enough to hear the tone but not make out the words, Collin stopped walking. After watching Lang stalk into the forest, Collin glanced at Kyreen.

"I interrupted something. I am sorry," he apologized. "I did not realize…"

Kyreen waved off his words. "Lang simply wanted to make sure I knew I was not worthy to go into battle, that I am not trained, I did not grow up here, as if I needed reminding."

Rising to her feet, she walked over to Collin. Without reaching out to touch him, she looked into his face. "You and I need to talk," she stated, a calm settling over her after the encounter with Lang.

Collin fidgeted nervously. "Aye," he mumbled, avoiding her eyes.

The muddled mix of emotions flowing from Collin washed over Kyreen. Turning away, she takes a few steps towards the water and said, "What happened in my absence?"

"Nothing!" The exclamation came so fast and so loud that Kyreen flinched.

"Nothing," Collin repeated softly. "Nothing happened."

Kyreen bent down to scoop up a flat rock. With a flick of her wrist, she sent the stone skipping over the calm waters, sunlight glinting off the ripples. Holding her silence, Kyreen bit her tongue, resolved not to speak until he did. She felt the conflict seething inside Collin. This conflict was different than the one Aren had mentioned on that evening so long and so short ago when she and Collin had first encountered the Calanians. That conflict had been a quiet struggle, obviously something of which Collin had already decided his path but had not resolved all issues.

Today's conflict was fiery and full of angst, like every fiber within him was conflicted. In that instant, Kyreen knew intuitively that she was the root cause of this concern within Collin. His way had been chosen and the anxiety he felt was all concern for her. Still, she remained quiet, her chest tightening in anticipation of the pain to come.

"I did nay…what I mean to say, is…it was not my plan," Collin stumbled for the words.

It would be so much easier to pull her to his chest and hold her close, he thought. Easier tonight, but not forever. Somehow these people knew and they were inflexible. Even Gunda had been cool towards him. She cared for the grey gelding because it was her job, but gone were the innocent flirtations and starry-eyed smiles. Now she was a miniature of her mother—grim faced, suspicion glinting in her eyes.

Collin stared at Kyreen, her back towards him, standing tall, her posture ramrod straight, waiting for him to speak. Would it be easier if she were looking at him? He doubted it. Nothing about this talk was going to be easy and she definitely was not going to help him. He wondered if she would understand, casting aside that notion as soon as it formed in his thoughts. How could she understand? Although he had not done anything, he had betrayed her. There it was! That was the word that had been eluding him— betrayed. Yes, he had betrayed everything they had shared over the last fortnight.

Now he must admit this treachery aloud. He struggled to find the words to tell her, loathed to erase the good memories. Realizing she would stand silent all night if necessary, Collin began anew.

"I am sorry, Kyreen," he said, unable to resist moving towards her to place his hands upon her shoulders.

Though she flinched at his touch, Kyreen did not otherwise visibly react. The touch of his hands burned, but she did not push him away.

Despite the dread growing within, she still yearned for his embrace, for one more kiss, one more caress, one more moment of bliss. Whatever it was he was confessing had to be terrible. Various scenarios and possibilities raced through her mind. Despite a vivid imagination, Kyreen was not prepared for his next words.

"I am in love with Engla," he says quietly, forcing the statement out quickly before losing his courage. Once started he could not hold back the words as they continue to tumble from him.

"I did not mean for this to happen, Kyreen. When she arrived, I could not get Engla out of my mind. I tried to avoid her but then she asked me to be her escort into the woods. She is a wonderful lass, Kyreen. She is afraid of Stian's reaction so she asked me to say nothing until you and Aren returned to camp. Then you... we did not think you would send them away so quickly. She is going to tell her brother and I am to meet them in Myrddin..."

Tears filled Kyreen's eyes, blurring her vision. The light sparkling off the lake shattered into millions of shards reflecting the splintering of her heart. She was sure Collin and everyone within the camp could hear and feel the pain cracking so deeply within her. It took all Kyreen's resolve to remain standing upright. Collin tightened his grip, shifting closer, but Kyreen stepped away. Without turning she shook her head once.

"Go," she whispered, her voice low and forceful. Speaking any more was impossible as her throat constricted and she desperately clung to control her emotions.

He stepped back, unsure of what to do, where to go.

"Go. Away." Kyreen demanded through clenched teeth. She hugged her arms around her body tightly as though this motion could contain the emotions raging within.

At long last, Collin turned away. Kyreen listened to him walking away, his footsteps echoing on the gravel. With every crunch of his boots, a new crack formed in her heart yet she yearned for him to come back, to embrace her, to whisper in her ear that this was just an awful dream, that nothing had changed.

Once the sound of his departure faded away and she was sure he would not be coming back, and this indeed was not a dream, Kyreen crumpled to the ground, welcoming the bite of the gravel under her body. Sobs rocked her body as the pain and fury raged within. How could she have been so foolish? How could she have let down her guard? How could she permit this to happen? The questions, the anguish, the anger swirled round and round, one chasing the other without resolution.

The final sliver of sun slid behind the mountain, its light winking out upon the water. Kyreen noticed neither the arrival of evening nor the approach of someone from the forest. Thus, the soft greeting startled her, both in its presence and identity.

"Kyreen?" Viggo stopped several paces from the prone body, knowing better than to startle the young woman in close proximity.

Kyreen rose to her feet, surreptitiously swiping a hand across her eyes. "My apologies, Viggo," she mumbled, then turns to stare at him in horror. "I did not… Collin did not… Oh, by the goddess, Viggo, could you… in camp?"

"No, no, no… no!" Viggo quickly reassured her. "When Lang returned, he and Aren began discussing the battle. Then I saw Collin return alone. I merely wanted to make sure you were alright. Aren, Gunda, we all have been worried about you," he paused, as if reluctant to continue, finally adding, "…and your relationship with Collin."

Kyreen snorted, settling down upon a boulder and wrapping her arms around her body again. "There is no longer a relationship."

Nodding, Viggo took a seat upon another boulder near Kyreen.

Overhead the hush of bat wings whispered quietly as the nocturnal animals began their nightly feeding. From across the inky waters of the lake a wolf's howl echoed over the pine tops. A moment later a lonesome answering wail wafted from across the valley. The gray dusk ebbed away, leaving the sky velvety black and the stars emerging. Still neither person felt inclined to speak. Sitting in the dark, beside her cousin's mate, the boulder rough beneath her, the rhythms of nature flowing over, around and through her, a calm settled upon Kyreen, dulling the sharp edge of pain tugging at her core.

Just as Kyreen was about to ask if they should head back to camp, Viggo asked, "Do you know why I always meet Aren upon her return?"

Surprised by the question, Kyreen admitted she has no clue.

"Being apart is physically painful," he said, quickly adding with a chuckle, "Not that I need to be in her presence night and day. No, that would not be ideal at all. I am sure your brother's absence hurt you just as deeply."

When Viggo did not continue, Kyreen answered, "Yes. Most days I struggled to keep up with my mother, but there were long stretches of riding or sitting very still when my mind would wander. Always I thought of Quillan, wondering where he was, what he was doing, was he safe?"

"Then you understand the joy and relief I feel when once again I can feel Aren. Truly it takes every bit of self-control not to leave camp and meet her on the trail," Viggo paused, choosing his next words carefully. "Unlike family ties, it is a bond that develops over time, lots of time, and…"

"I have only known Collin a short time. He is not Calan. We do not, did not, have the bond you and Aren share," Kyreen interrupted impatiently. "Viggo, please. I do not need a lecture."

Viggo's reaction to Kyreen's outburst surprised her. Instead of responding verbally, he moved to stand before her. Grabbing her hands in his, he pulled her to her feet and leaned in close, so that their noses almost touched. His movements were silent and sure, his touch as gentle as his voice. "And it is reciprocal, Kyreen," he whispered. "If Collin does not feel the same as you, there will be no bond. I know that you feel hurt and betrayed. Your insides ache as though your heart has been torn away, but this will fade I promise," he paused a heartbeat before adding, "if you allow it."

Kyreen felt the tears well up anew as she gazed at Viggo. A part of her wished he would have yelled at her, given her a reason to lash out at him.

The pity and compassion in his tone and his expression were almost as unbearable as the pain Collin had inflicted. Instead she allowed Viggo to wrap his arms around her, pulling her head to his chest, and to hold her tight until the tears were once more spent.

This was how Aren found them a few minutes later when she emerged from the forest after her lengthy dialogue with Lang. Though Kyreen felt self-conscious, if seeing her husband holding Kyreen upset Aren, she gave no outwardly sign.

Instead she placed a soft hand upon Kyreen's arm. "Alright there, Kyreen?"

"You knew?"

"Gunda filled me in," Aren admitted with a sheepish smile to Viggo. "While it is difficult for outsiders to hide a secret around us, Engla also let the news of her and Collin's relationship slip to Gunda."

"Gunda?" Viggo asked, his gaze moving towards the forest from which Aren had recently emerged.

The two women turned their gaze as well, watching the girl sprint towards them. Despite the darkness, she was lithe and quickly reached them. Apprehension radiated from her, raising the alarm of all three adults.

"Is it an attack?" Aren asked quietly, her gaze moving towards the vicinity of the camp, trying to feel the alarm.

Breathless, Gunda shook her head. "No. Not the camp. Kyreen's friend Stian," she said haltingly. "He is here. Alone."

Chapter 37

Kyreen did not wait to hear more. She sprinted down the beach and through the forest, finding Stian on the outer edges of the camp standing beside his horse. Collin was speaking to him in hurried rush tones, but fell silent when Kyreen approached. She pointedly ignored Collin and set her gaze upon Stian.

"What happened?" Stian, one eye swollen shut and dried blood caked to his face, looked more fearful than Kyreen had ever seen him. His voice shook when he answered, "They took Engla. He said ye must meet him by the new moon or else…"

"Or else what?"

"He who?" Kyreen and Collin both spoke simultaneously.

Without looking at him, Kyreen pushed Collin back. She already knew who. It had to be Markku. They must have met on the road. There was no way Stian and Engla could have made the journey to Myrddin so quickly. Why was Markku on his way here? How had he known which way to go? Who was with him? These questions Kyreen quelled as she waited for Stian to regain his composure enough to speak.

"Or else he would be forced to accept Engla as payment for the stallion," Stian mumbled.

"What stallion?" Aren demanded, having walked up behind the group with Viggo and Gunda.

"My stallion," Kyreen started to explain.

"Tis not your stallion!" Stian shouted. "Markku bought it from Jorn! You stole it and now he has stolen my sister!"

Everyone's gaze turned to Kyreen and she felt their unspoken questions as Stian's voice faded away. Although she knew she had been right in taking the stud, Kyreen also understood now was not the time to argue with Stian. At the moment Stian's distress was affecting Kyreen; she felt queasy, unable to think clearly. As though sensing Kyreen's dilemma, Aren stepped forward and took control.

"Gunda, bring me Kyreen's stallion and Collin's gelding," she paused to look at Stian's weary mount. "Bring another horse for Stian while you're at it. Viggo, they will need provisions." Her husband nodded wordlessly, disappearing into the night with their daughter.

Aren drew Kyreen aside, speaking quietly, "Horse theft is serious,

Kyreen."

"You think I do not know this?" Kyreen replied. "Foremost, Jorn had no right to sell those horses to Soren. Second, you were not present in Wentworth. Any claim I may have granted Soren and his kin, Markku forfeited that night with his abuses upon that animal."

"Be that as it may," Aren urged. "The attack is just two days hence. The people are already assembling. You are needed here. Remember your vow. Collin was leaving anyway. Let him take the stallion."

"No!" Stian interrupted. "He said Kyreen must bring him the stallion."

Aren's eyes narrowed suspiciously at Stian. "Kyreen? Why?"

Kyreen shrugged Aren's arm away. "Markku is a brute and a bully. He's never much cared for me and this is his attempt at settling scores."

"Not Markku," Stian said. "The other man with him, the one-eyed man with the scar."

Cold spread within the deep pit of her stomach as Kyreen's mind flew back through the years. Once again, she was a young child, snuggled against her mother for warmth. The sound of footsteps in the woods. The hand reaching into the briar patch. Her mother's dagger, large and heavy in her small hand. The man's scream piercing the snow-laden woods. Blood, dark and thick, running down the face knotted in pain.

"What do you know of this?" Aren's sharp question drew Kyreen back to the present, and to Kyreen's surprise the woman looked not at Kyreen, but at Collin.

Collin stared back, silent a heartbeat too long, breaking Kyreen's heart anew. "His name is Falk."

"I. Know. His. Name," Aren hissed. "I want to know your connection to him."

"He has formed an… alliance with… my guild," Collin replied cautiously, his hazel eyes moving between the two women. "He desired assistance to…"

"To…" Aren's steely voice prompted Collin to continue.

"To find me," Kyreen answered. Her mind raced back over the last few weeks. Everything had been a lie. These days, supposedly her happiest since leaving the castle so very long ago, had been falsehoods. Nothing she had experienced had been real.

Kyreen looked squarely at Collin as though seeing him for the first time, stating, not asking, "You did not just happen upon that road outside of Wentworth."

Slowly Collin shook his head. As he opened his mouth to explain, Kyreen turned her back to him and looked at Aren. "I know I gave my vow, Aren, but you know I cannot leave Engla with that mercenary. Neither can I take the stallion to Markku. This is my fault and it is my responsibility. I alone must make amends. Can you persuade the council to postpone until I return?"

Aren looked at Kyreen, then Collin and finally at Stian's wounded face. Was it not just a short fortnight hence that she herself stood in Kyreen's position? Begging her friends to accompany her back into Myrddin to rescue her daughter? How could she raise objections? She could not. Finally, she nodded her ascension.

"I will do my best to delay the attack," she paused, looking as though she wished to add more. Finally, she simply hugged Kyreen, whispering into her cousin's ear, "The stallion will remain here. I will have Gunda fetch your gelding. Safe travels, my cousin."

Chapter 38

The trio rode hard through the night without talking, their mood pensive. When they stopped just before dawn, the silence remained heavy upon them all. After taking care of her horse, Kyreen rolled up in her blankets, but sleep remained evasive. She felt Stian's anger toward her like a hot poker burning, but strangely his mood towards Collin was neutral.

Engla must not have told him yet about her and Collin. Collin. Try as she might, Kyreen could not prevent her thoughts from circling back to him. Though the hurt still burned raw she longed for his embrace. It was in his arms where she had been able to forget.

Forget the past in Hanoria. Forget the present worries of her people. Forget the battle looming in her future. In his arms, all conscious thought had faded away. She had simply been. Been herself. Been a woman. Not the princess returned. Not the oddity from Jorn's farm. Not anything or anyone particular. She had never felt so alive or free as the moments she spent with Collin. Tears threatened again and she angrily shook herself from her reverie. Determinedly she shut out all conscious thought, silently repeating her mantras until sleep finally arrived.

The following afternoon found the group approaching the outer walls of Myrddin. Collin was the first to break the silence. He pointed to a narrow, almost invisible path leading away from the main road, saying, "We should not take the front gates into the city, at least not by daylight."

Not happy trusting him, but having no choice, Kyreen answered, "True enough. There is a place to stow the horses?"

Collin nodded and led them off the road. Stian followed the other two without comment. Kyreen worried about her friend. Instead of dissipating, his anger had continued to burn deep and hot. Would he hold up long enough to rescue Engla? Kyreen wondered watching his stiff back as he rode ahead of her. She knew her words would not help, so she remained quiet and turned her attentions to the woods around them. Nothing but wildlife noises and the sound of the horses' muffled hoof beats. Eventually the path emerged in a small clearing, shaded by a canopy of trees looming overhead. The smell of salt mingled with the scent of pine.

From somewhere beyond the vegetation on the far side of the clearing, waves crashed upon rocks. Her stomach tightened as she dismounted. Positioned this close to the sea, presumably a rocky coast from the sounds of the surf, and surrounded by dense foliage with the single pathway in, she felt trapped, cornered.

Collin did not dismount, instead he turned the gray back towards the path. "I will speak with the guards. See if they are on watch for you."

"Your clearing here, it is ideal for an ambush," Kyreen pointed out, loosening the cinch on the gelding's saddle, jerking with a little more force than was necessary in her agitation.

"This is perfectly safe and secluded," Collin countered, reining back around to look down on Kyreen.

"Safe for whom?" she asked, purposely refusing to look at him, avoiding his gaze, continuing to care for her horse. "Leave us here while you fetch your friends?"

Collin clenched his jaw. "That is not my plan. This is my city, Kyreen. I grew up with most of the guards. I want to find out what, if anything, they know about Markku and if Falk has alerted them."

He thought she flinched at his mentioning of the mercenary's name, but still she refused to look at him. When she answered, her voice was low and hard. "More like inform them of our location, I wager. No doubt my head carries a pretty price with the Faldorian. Is that not what you do, Collin? Find people for money?"

Collin jumped off his horse and closed the short distance between them, his arms stretched out. He was not sure what he had planned to do once he reached Kyreen—strike her, shake her, pull her close—but before he can do anything, Stian spoke out sharply.

"Stop it! This is my sister's life you risk! Even if Engla is not dead already, she could be... Markku... they..." Unable to voice the possibilities, his voice faded to a whisper, "Ye both know these men are nay nice people."

Kyreen had not flinched or moved a muscle when Collin had started towards her. As Stian's words died in the breeze, she stared at Collin, the man she had been falling in love with, the one whom she had thought had been falling in love with her, her expression unreadable. Then she pushed by Collin and walked to Stian, who had dismounted and was now standing beside his mount. After his outburst, he had covered his face with his hands.

She now took Stian's hands in hers and lowered them so she can gaze into his face. His expression of remorse and sorrow reminded Kyreen of that spring day they had first met so many years ago, only this time it was she not he who had committed the foul. She squeezed Stian's hands and ducked down so as to look up at his face. "Stian, it is me that Falk wants. He will keep Engla safe until I arrive."

"But ye know Markku," Stian replied. His angst flowed over Kyreen, a javelin striking through her heart.

Though she did not agree with Hanorian tradition, that culture flowed through Stian's veins and shaped his entire existence. He took seriously his duty to protect his sister from harm. These many hours of uncertainty and inaction had coiled up inside of him, twisting into hard knots of doubt.

"Markku is but a bully," Kyreen reminded Stian. "And a bully is nothing but a coward with power. He will not risk a confrontation with the likes of this Faldorian mercenary. We will get Engla back. Safe. Stian, look at me," she paused until the Hanorian lifted his head and, holding his gaze firm in her own, repeated, "Safe. You have my word on that, my friend."

The two stared at each other for a long while. Then, his expression still distressed, Stian finally nodded his understanding.

Kyreen looked across to Collin. "Go. Do whatever needs to be done to get us in without warning Falk. If you care for Engla half as much as you profess, you will do right by her."

Collin returned her nod, acknowledging the warning in her tone.

Knowing there is nothing he can say to regain her trust, he leaves in silence.

The wait was agonizing. Kyreen's nerves tensed with every noise from the surrounding trees. She busied herself with the horses, and eventually, out of other tasks, she began cleaning tack as the sun continued its downward crawl. What was normally a calming act was now an opportunity for her mind to race around the possible scenarios of the impending confrontation. With that final chore completed, there was nothing left to do but wait.

When the clearing was bathed in purple shadows and the sun, long out of sight, was almost completely set Kyreen felt Collin's return long before she heard his horse on the path. Noticing Kyreen stand, Stian also rose to his feet.

Dismounting, Collin quickly reported that the guards had not received orders to look for or detain anyone fitting Kyreen's description. He had gone to the guild house and again, everything there was quiet. It did not appear the general ranks knew about the Faldorian in the keep.

"You are sure they are not deceiving you?" Kyreen asked, trying to suppress the anger from her voice.

"There is a chance someone lied," Collin admitted. "But I know these men, Kyreen. Most of them grew up here, with me, on the streets of Myrddin. Besides, as ye said earlier, it is my job. I know how to get information."

Kyreen glared at Collin for a long moment, unable to clearly discern his emotions through the cloud of her own. Finally, not wishing to stress Stian any further with another confrontation, she bites back her retort, asking instead, "What is the plan?"

"Guard changes just after dark, and Gethan promised me the gate would be unguarded for a few minutes during that time. We'll be able to slip in then," he said, "Glain's place will not be safe and, although he assisted us before, I do not trust the stable master Ifor. There is, however, one person I know will aid us and will be of great help. I have sent word to have him meet us at dark."

Thus, a short time later, Kyreen stood inside the training room of Collin's guildhall. In the clearing, after hearing Collin's idea, she had suppressed her instincts to challenge Collin and now she regretted that decision. She did not trust Collin, his friend Rhun, or this plan, but once more her options had tapered down to trusting strangers. As Collin and Rhun talk quietly near the doorway, she appraised her surroundings, reluctant to admit this place was more than acceptable.

When they had first entered this building, located deep inside the city walls, Kyreen had harbored doubts. Towering several stories tall, this was the guild headquarters, housing several dozen of Collin's guild mates. Additionally, somewhere within this vast edifice waited Falk and, with him, Markku and Engla.

Kyreen had been surprised with this cavernous room, which was situated underground. Collin had explained it was used for large gatherings as well as combat training. The length of this room would permit archery while the ceiling rose three stories tall, more than enough room to permit plenty of maneuverability whether with a sword, a staff, or even on horseback. Currently, the center had been opened up with all the equipment pushed against the walls. The pungent aroma of sawdust, strewn across the earthen floor, filled her nostrils. Considering the narrow city streets and the tight quarters she had experienced at Glain's house, Kyreen realized this was probably the most ideal location she could have asked for to meet with Falk and Markku. Anticipating the confrontation, her hand moved to the tri-colored hilt of her sword, fastened to the belt now draped over her shoulder.

"I will need to take that," Rhun stated quietly. He and Collin, their conversation ended, were walking towards Kyreen.

To the side, Stian leaned against a large archery target. Since his earlier outburst in the forest, he had not uttered a single sound. Kyreen wondered once more at his stability. As long as she had known Stian, he had been susceptible to Markku's bullying. With Engla's safety in question, would he be able to confront Markku when the time came? She sincerely hoped so, for both his and Engla's sake.

Kyreen turned her attention to Rhun, her hand still resting lightly upon her sword hilt. "You expect me to hand over my sword?" she asked. Although her tone is neutral, her eyes challenged him to attempt the act.

Collin interceded, "Rhun needs to take something to Falk. Show him proof that you are here. What better item than your sword? It will convince him not only of your identity, but also of your surrender."

Kyreen's gaze never left Rhun's face, but she relented. Pulling the sword out, she handed it, hilt first, toward the tall ebony-skinned man.

Although her actions went against everything she had ever learned, her instincts were telling her that Rhun could be trusted. The conflict she sensed inside the man had nothing to do with her and this situation. She hesitated a heartbeat longer before releasing the weapon.

"I will be getting this back," she said, "one way or another."

Rhun nodded, a shadow of a smile almost crossing his solemn face.

He knew the woman standing before him was not someone with whom he wanted to cross weapons. Her feelings about him had been correct.

Kyreen's current dilemma had nothing to do with Rhun's. It was, however, offering up an opportunity for him to rectify a sticky situation.

Like Collin, Rhun had been recruited into the guild at a young age. Unlike Collin, he had no other family. His father had abandoned the family when Rhun was five, leaving Rhun's mother, a sickly woman, alone with three young children. As Rhun's mother's health had declined, so had her children's. Malnutrition and lack of care left the two younger children vulnerable to illness. Rhun's days had been spent scavenging the city to feed his younger siblings, but it was never enough. Within two years, his mother had succumbed to the coughing disease eating away at her frail body. Once their mother was gone, with no other family to be found, Rhun and his siblings had been taken to the orphanage. Later that winter Rhun's sister passed on, followed in the spring by his brother. With no one left to hold him there, Rhun ran away from the overcrowded institution. It did not take him long to join the guild where he thrived under the routine and discipline offered there. Collin's father, the lieutenant over new recruits had made sure the boy had a bed and food, even though Rhun had been too young to officially join the guild. Eventually, Rhun had begun accompanying Collin's father home, becoming best mates with Collin's brother. Rhun had worked his way up in the guild, content with his position, even happy.

Everything changed last year when Dwyn had become the guild leader. While the guild did operate along the outer shadows of the law, the vast majority of their dealings were legitimate. Most guild members had been dockworkers employed by the dock master. Shortly after taking over the guild, however, Dwyn had managed to lose the contract there, a contract that had been in place even before Collin's father had been born. Shortly afterwards the ships stopped hiring sailors from the guild. Several members were still under contract with shipping companies, but all knew they would lose those jobs once the contracts expired. When Dwyn had joined the likes of the Faldorian mercenary and Falk had told his tale of the hunt for Tyra and her child, Rhun had known something must be done about Dwyn and had begun to act covertly, gathering supporters, making arrangements to unseat Dwyn. Kyreen's and her friends' presence here now had merely accelerated those plans. Pushing these thoughts aside, Rhun replied, "I am not your enemy here."

Kyreen nodded, but her expression did not change. She still did not like having to trust Collin and his friends. She worried about the plan. So much could go wrong and she had many concerns for her friends. Engla and Stian hailed from a farming community which had not seen war for many generations. Aside from petty arguments and general acts of bullying, mainly from Markku's family, these people were not accustomed to violence. Kyreen refused to think about anything violent happening to either of her friends. She glanced at Collin. His concern for Engla was apparent in the emotions radiating from him. Kyreen clamped down on her own hurt, realizing the two men were gazing at her expectantly.

"What now?" she asked, intuitively knowing she would not like the answer.

Collin and Rhun exchanged glances. Collin finally answered, "Falk would expect you to be…restrained."

Kyreen inhaled deeply, knowing her irritation was more towards Collin than the situation. "Fine," she replied, turning around and pressing her wrists together behind her back.

Rhun stepped in to secure Kyreen's wrists. As Collin walked away, the tall man leaned close to her ear, his words quiet and quick, "When Falk arrives, he is yours. Do not worry about the others. Nobody…," Rhun paused and Kyreen's gaze moved to Collin busy tying Stian's arms, "Nobody will interfere until the deed is finished."

With a final tug, Rhun stepped away and Kyreen looked over her shoulder at him. Though they had just met and barely exchanged words, Kyreen suddenly understood from his expression that she did not head into battle alone. While she questioned Stian's ability and Collin's allegiance, this tall brooding man, as he had stated, was not her enemy. In that instant Kyreen recognized Rhun to be an ally. She could…she would trust him.

Kyreen tested the bindings. Although they appeared tight, she felt plenty of give within the rope and knew when the time arrived she could easily free herself. By way of thanks, she inclined her head towards Rhun and maybe saw a smile lift at the corners of his lips.

Hoisting the sword to his shoulder, Rhun looked over the trio before saying, "I shall not be long. They have been already been alerted to your arrival."

Once Rhun was out of sight, Collin guided Stian over to Kyreen in the middle of the large hall. Turning to face the doorway, he instinctively rested his other hand against Kyreen's elbow.

Instantly she flinched away as though burnt. "Do. Not. Touch. Me." she ordered quietly through clenched teeth and settled her gaze upon the door to wait.

Chapter 39

The tension between Kyreen and Collin continued to swell, but, true to his word, Rhun was not gone long. As she felt their approach, all thoughts of Collin faded, all traces of anxiety fled. For better or worse, for good or bad, the wait was over and this defining moment–sixteen years in the making–had arrived.

Rhun pushed open the heavy door, standing aside as Falk entered. Though Kyreen focused her gaze upon the Faldorian, she still registered the rest of the party trailing in behind him. The small bow-legged man with shaggy dark hair and a tankard of ale in one hand must be Dwyn, the guild leader. Markku entered next, dragging Engla beside him. The strut in the bully's step was not quite so pronounced and the glint in his eyes not nearly as confident. Kyreen reckoned Markku may have met his match in Falk. It was doubtful Markku's father's power would influence the Faldorian much, if at all.

As soon as Markku crossed the threshold, Rhun eased the door shut, silently clicking the bolt into place. Kyreen suppressed a predatory grin.

No reinforcements or help would be arriving. Just as casually, Rhun leaned Kyreen's sword against a straw bale, before taking his place just behind Collin and Stian. The dark man's expression remained disinterested, as though he were merely an observer of the events.

Falk honed his good eye onto Kyreen, his hate washing over her like a toxic cloud. He began to stalk towards the waiting trio and Kyreen felt Collin tense beside her. As the Faldorian's hand rose, she braced herself for the blow that never arrived.

"No!" Collin yelled, stepping between Kyreen and Falk.

The man paused, towering a full head over both Collin and Kyreen. The single malevolent shiny eye studied the young man standing between him and his prize.

"Dwyn," Falk growled, "Yer pup here tis in my way."

Rhun, continuing his charade, glanced nonchalantly at Dwyn. "Shall I get him, boss?"

At Dwyn's nod, Rhun moved over, taking Stian and Collin by their arms and steering them towards Markku and Dwyn. Engla, her hands bound and a rag in her mouth, watched the proceedings with tearful eyes.

Kyreen wished her friends did not have to be present for this confrontation and, with a silent prayer to whatever lords or goddesses who may be listening, begged forgiveness. She then pushed all other thoughts away, focusing all of her attentions to the man standing before her. The man who had attacked her people, then chased her and her mother through dozens of provinces for two years, eventually torturing and killing her mother.

Something in her steely gaze must have registered with the predator in Falk for his hand faltered just a heartbeat before he swung a meaty backhand into her face.

While Rhun's placement of the sword might have appeared haphazard and casual, Kyreen had realized the tall Myrddinian's genius the first time Falk's hand had been raised to strike her. Now, all the young woman had to do was allow her body to flow, to be carried by the power of Falk's blow and roll towards the blade resting against the straw bale. The bindings unfurled as she rolled over, bouncing up to her feet with the tri-colored hilt of her mother's sword resting easy in her now unencumbered grasp.

Taking a deep breath, Kyreen turned to face her enemy. Collin's concern washed over her and, from the corner of her eye, she saw Rhun restrain him. The sergeant-at-arm's words from earlier rang again in her head—"Nobody will interfere until the deed is finished"—and Kyreen returned her focus to the mercenary.

The surprise registered in the Faldorian's face quickly fled, replaced with rage. "D'ye think ye can best me, whelp?" he growled, drawing his own black longsword, the blade almost as long as Kyreen was tall.

Kyreen appraised the vicious looking weapon, noting the flanges protruding just below the guard, Falk's grip on the waisted-handle, his index finger of the lead hand wrapped around the cross-guard and yards of sharply honed steel glinting in the dim lamplight. For all its appurtenances, the weapon was, in Kyreen's opinion, as garish and offensive as the man wielding it.

She centered her own sword as she faced the man responsible for so much heartache in her life and those of her people. Suddenly the blade in her hand not only felt natural and balanced, it became a part of her, an extension, but even more. This blade had been crafted by a master smith many generations ago, shortly after the small province had been created and shortly before the first invasion from their Galorian neighbors. Though deadly, the sword had never been wielded in war. No, this was not a tool for the battlefield. That work was better served by spears or axes forged for that specific task. This was an intimate device, meant to be seen up close by one's foe. The ancient runes etched along the length of the blade, the tri-colored handle, the carved pummel shaped like a rose, the intricate brass guard, all served to send a message of authority and power. The bearer of this blade was not only a member of the royal family, and the blade was much more than a representation of the province. The bearer and this sword were Calan.

All of this knowing flowed in and out of Kyreen's consciousness in an instant as she assumed her battle stance. Below all of this understanding, however, Kyreen also recognized the sword was not simply a symbol. It was, after all, at its very core, a weapon. Before being adorned with all of these symbols it had been created for one purpose: killing. This sword was by its design a practical implement of violence, an instrument of death.

Like other finely crafted instruments, this sword had performed its duties extremely well over the years.

Even though Kyreen did not know the sword's history, the blade in her hand had touched her life even before her birth and the flight from her homeland so many years ago. In the hands of a Calanian traitor, it had slain her grandfather, King Roland. In the hands of a Galorian emperor, it had also ended the life of her father, Quillan, a Galorian prince. Tonight, as was the sword's vocation, once again would blood be spilled from its blade.

If Kyreen could have followed the golden thread of fate connected to this exquisite weapon in her hand, if she could have seen the future, foreseen the deaths to be brought about by this blade, if she could have prevented the violence to come, would she have? These were thoughts and questions that would haunt her for many seasons after tonight, when she raised the sword in combat for the very first time.

Falk towered over Kyreen by a full head, outweighing her by double. Though his strength and savagery most certainly would profit him, Kyreen's dexterity and equanimity would be her advantages. The dull black armor fastened to the Faldorian's body covered vital organs while Kyreen felt unprotected and exposed, especially without the leathers she had become accustomed to wearing during her recent training sessions.

Falk grinned, a humorless lifting of his thin lips, his one good eye glinting malevolently. "Are we here to battle or dance, wench?"

In his tone, Kyreen heard the dismissal, felt his arrogance. She saw herself through his vision, not as a Calanian warrior, but a ragged little orphan girl and determined Falk's pride would work to her favor as well. The girl shrugged carelessly, her expression and posture daring him to advance, to strike the first blow. An instant later he stepped in.

The journey to this clash of blades had been a long one not just for Kyreen, but also for the Faldorian bearing down upon her at this moment. When Falk had led his men into battle at the Calanian castle so many years ago, he had been a young man with a remarkable climb in the ranks behind him and a great future ahead of him. Leading the Galorian's takeover of Calan was to be Falk's final active operation. The gold and gems offered by the Galorian emperor would make him rich enough to launch his political career. For Falk had harbored lofty dreams of running his own country Faldor, dreams which began evaporating that morning the queen vanished with her children. The plan, years in the making, had been simple. Emperor Dolan would leave the tiny province unmolested; lulling the Calanians into believing the war could be over. At the annual Spring Festival, three groups of Falk's men were to gain access to the castle disguised as merchants and peasants. One band of mercenaries would then assassinate the small contingency of guards and open the castle gates to the waiting Galorian troops, and another group would begin exterminating the sleeping Calanians while the third would seek out the queen in the castle keep, killing her and her bastard offspring.

Everything should have been straightforward and the country of Calan demolished quickly and quietly. Somehow, though Falk never learned how, the alarm had been raised with that first kill in the square. From that moment on, nothing seemed to go right for the Faldorian mercenary. It was as if at that moment, the fortunes which had so graciously accompanied him his entire life had simply faded away, or worse turned against him.

By the time Falk learned of the queen's escape through the tunnels and assembled a tracking team, the fugitives had almost a full day's head start. As days turned into weeks turned into months, the seasons changing and the miles growing longer, Falk's men had begun to lose faith in their leader. Doubts crept into their thoughts as this woman continued to evade capture.

Slowly the number of men surrounding Falk dwindled as loyalties faded and the nonbelievers snuck away under the shadow of night. As numbers dropped, the whisperings increased. Then, as the more tough and resilient men disappeared, stories of sorcery and bewitchment, wizardry and hexing, swirled around the campfire. Men began to worry that their comrades had not turned coward, but were being lured away into the shadows.

Though he tried to stem such nonsense, Falk continued to lose control over his men until finally only a small handful remained. This duplicity from his men coupled with the frustrations of tracking the Calanian queen had worn down the Faldorian. Falk had not even known for sure if the Queen traveled alone or had one or both of her children with her until that gray dawn when a child—this whelp standing before him now— had torn his face with a dagger.

All this played in Falk's mind as he thrust his sword forward with a mighty roar. Kyreen easily evaded his first strike, pirouetting away and settling back into the ready, her eyes never leaving the big man's face.

As he readied another pass, pulling back before thrusting a powerful stab attack forward, Falk felt no worry. The puny blade in the girl's hand was no match for his longsword. With the reach of his blade, there was no way for her to close in on him. Thus, he began to toy with his prey, feinting a thrust before slicing down. Kyreen continued to spin and twirl, stepping, turning, always moving just beyond the edge of Falk's nasty blade.

So intent upon his adversary was Falk that he did not notice Kyreen's path. From across the arena the onlookers watch, feelings ranging from terrified (Engla) to apprehensive (Collin) to intrigued (Rhun). The guild's second-in-command was the only person, besides Kyreen, to perceive that her evasions were carrying her closer to the stack of discarded training weapons.

Falk continued slashing and thrusting, keeping Kyreen on the move, forcing her to continually adjust to his attacks. Just as on that first night of sparring in Calan against the youth Ebbe, Kyreen was unable to switch from defense to offense. The major difference in this fight, aside from the fact Falk was intent upon killing her, was the reach of the Faldorian's blade. No matter how Kyreen quickly evaded, she could never gain respite.

Again Falk stepped in, cutting down diagonally from left to right. The tip of his blade barely paused before he rotated the hilt, lifting the weapon straight back up to deliver a thrust towards Kyreen's midsection. Perhaps it was the distraction of the practice shield almost within her grasp or simply a lapse in concentration, but no matter the reason when she twisted away Kyreen failed to evade the sword's razor edge. But providence—either in her favor or against the Faldorian—prevented the blade from sliding in a fatal strike. Instead the sword tip bounced off a rib. Kyreen dropped to the sawdust and rolled away, but not before bright crimson red stained her tunic.

Chapter 40

"Kyreen!" Collin could not repress his shout. He struggled against Rhun's grip as Kyreen continued to roll away from Falk.

Markku also made as to step forward, but instead found a dagger pressed to his throat. While all attention had been trained on the deadly clash, Stian had only had eyes for the Hanorian bully holding Engla. As Kyreen had been avoiding Falk's blade, Stian had loosed his wrists from the ropes. Now he stood behind Markku, the tip of his dagger poised on the other man's pulse point.

"Release your grip upon my sister," Stian growled. This interaction distracted Collin from Kyreen. He immediately wrested himself from Rhun in order to liberate Engla from her restraints. Rhun let the younger man go. So long as Collin's attentions are on Engla and not on assisting Kyreen, Rhun did not care. For Rhun alone seemed confident that this battle, while not concluded, was nonetheless over and Kyreen the victor.

Dwyn for one was confident in Falk's victory. Though his eyes followed the action, his thoughts were on the gold he would receive, on the trade contract with Galor, on the power he will wield. So, the guild leader's disappointment was especially deep when Kyreen rose to her feet, her short sword in on hand, the wooden practice shield gripped in her other hand.

Falk's gaze narrowed as the girl squared off before him. The shield would make no difference. He was still in control. His single eye flicked to the blood seeping through her tunic and his stance relaxed.

In that instant, in that minuscule lapse of concentration, Kyreen took her opening. Leading with the shield, she closed the distance between her and Falk, raising the shield high above her head in order to drive it down onto her opponent's face, breaking the bridge of his nose, blinding him as his one good eye involuntarily watered. When Falk stumbled back, Kyreen kept close, lowering her blade and swinging an upward diagonal cut catching Falk in the knee, slipping through the slender opening between his leather guards. Even as the big man howled his anguish—both physical and emotional—Kyreen spun around drawing up her sword this time for a downward slash to his other knee forcing the large man to drop to his knees. Again and again Kyreen whirled this way and that, around the collapsed man. The longsword dropped from his hand, falling to the ground when Kyreen's blade cut into his arm, slicing the tendons at the elbow joint. A nick to his shoulder. A cut along his side. Kyreen struck again and again without thought, slicing and cutting until Falk's kneeling body is a tangle of bloody gashes, crimson liquid pouring from a dozen spots.

At one point Kyreen vaguely registered through her battle rage that the man was incapacitated, and tossed away the shield, its usefulness spent. Even through the cloud of fury, she remained ever diligent, kicking away the long sword, then positioning herself in front of the mercenary down to his knees. So many thoughts swirled in her brain. So many words she wished to say to this man, this monster who robbed her of her childhood, her family, her country, who stole the lives, the homes, the dignity of all her kinsmen. Instead she thrust the Calanian blade forward, driving the tip of her sword into the man's left shoulder, pulling it out to again thrust the blade this time into his right shoulder, and again out, then again in, now to his chest. Kyreen stabbed blindly, over and over again until finally, as she withdrew the sword, Falk toppled forward, face first into the sawdust. Even then she continued piercing the shredded leather armor, over and over, again and again, until a gentle hand wrapped around her wrist, staying the bloodied sword high over her head as the woman prepared to once again plunge the blade into the body, an almost unrecognizable mass of blood and meat.

"The deed is finished," Rhun said, his voice even and quiet.

Groggily, as though being awakened from a deep sleep, Kyreen looked up at the man. In the moment it took for her to recognize him, he slowly lowered her arm and extricated the blade from her grip. She glanced beyond Rhun's shoulder and spied Stian clutching Markku, his dagger still balanced on the bully's throat. Collin, at Rhun's suggestion, stood similarly positioned next to Dwyn. Engla, her eyes wide, face drained of blood, watched on in horror.

Kyreen glanced down, almost surprised to see blood seeping from her side. With difficulty, she trained her gaze on Falk's prone body. She still had work to do. Mentally steeling herself, she leaned over and tugging the bulging leather pouch of black leather from around the dead man's neck. From the contents within Kyreen pulled out a blood red gemstone, easily the diameter of a man's thumbnail. Drawing the bag shut once again, Kyreen proffered the pouch and its remaining contents to Rhun.

"This guild's contract with Falk, and also Galor, has been fulfilled and payment received," she stated.

Lifting the bag from her palm, Rhun nodded. "Acknowledged."

Crossing to Stian, his dagger still tight against Markku's neck, Kyreen chose to first address her friend, holding up the ruby. "This gem represents more money than Jorn ever earned working his farmstead. With it you should be able to make any necessary repairs or upgrades to the buildings, clear fields and plant wheat, alfalfa, whatever you choose. All I ask in return is that you buy back the herd Jorn sold," Kyreen's gaze moved to Markku's terrified face, her voice steely, adding, "For no more than ten percent over the price Soren paid."

As Markku opened his mouth to protest, she continued, "This is non-negotiable, Markku. You will convince your father it is in his best interest to sell. Stian will, of course, pay for any foals that may have dropped in the last moon, but not one dinar more."

Markku closed his mouth and Kyreen leaned in, her voice lowering so that her words could only be heard by the two men in front of her. "Should anything happen to Stian, Engla or their family I will hear about it and I will hold you responsible. Markku, believe me. I mean anything. If either of my friends catches a sniffle, twists an ankle, anything, it will be upon your head. I will find you and I will extract payment from your body. Know this, too. Should you choose to flee, no matter how far or to what remote reaches of this world you may run, I will track you down." The look in her eyes combined with the violence committed just moments earlier left no doubt in either man's mind as to the truth of her promise.

"Understood?" she asked.

His face deathly pale, Markku nodded. Stian lowered his dagger, but kept a firm grip upon the other man's arm.

Rhun, having unlocked the door to the hall, walked over with a handful of his supporters. He pointed Markku towards the door. "Someone is waiting to show you to your horse and escort you to the city gates. Do not return to Myrddin in the near future. Twenty or thirty years should suffice, eh?"

As Markku hurried out of sight and Stian embraced his sister, Kyreen turned to Rhun. "Thank you," she said to the tall dark man, who now appeared to be the leader of this guild.

Before Kyreen could continue, Engla threw her arms around Kyreen, who gasped at the pain in her side. Engla pulled back, blue eyes widening at the bright red spot staining Kyreen's tunic.

"It is nothing," Kyreen said, pulling her friend into a close hug on her uninjured side.

After a heartbeat Engla relented and leaned into Kyreen. For a long moment, the two women embraced, until Kyreen felt the trembling within her friend slowly fade away. Struggling to keep her own emotions in check, Kyreen glanced at Collin, who avoided her gaze.

Engla pulled back to gaze up at Kyreen. "Never before have I ever been so scared. I knew ye would nay abandon me. They did nay believe ye would show, but I never lost faith. I knew ye would rescue me."

"Just faith in Kyreen?" Stian stepped forward to once again hug his sister close. Although his tone was lightly teasing, Kyreen felt the underlying irritation and inwardly sighed. Sadly, even after all they had been through together, Stian held to his Hanorian roots. Kyreen hoped it would not undo Stian as it had Jorn in her foster father's final years.

Keeping an arm wrapped snuggly around his sister, Stian looked at Collin. "Tis something the pair of ye wish to discuss with me, is there?"

Engla blushed, slipping from her brother's arm and sliding into Collin's embrace. Before she can speak, however, Rhun stepped in, his hand light upon Kyreen's elbow.

"Please, excuse us. The lady here requires medical attention. We shall not be long," he announced, guiding Kyreen across the arena and into the hallway before anyone could protest.

Chapter 41

A short distance down the narrow passage way, Rhun turned into a small room, the center of which was monopolized by a battered wooden table. He motioned for Kyreen to sit upon the table as he moved to a cabinet on the far wall.

"Lie back," he commanded, rifling through a drawer.

Kyreen did as commanded, cringing at the pain as she settled back. Gritting her teeth, she lifted her shirt, wincing anew as the cloth pulled away from her torn skin. Rhun moved to her side, his eyes on the injury.

"Ye were lucky," he commented, fingers gingerly probing the wound. "How does it feel?"

"The cut does not hurt at all," she replied, "But I ache when I move, even when I breathe."

He nodded, picking up a needle and thread. "Your blood is still hot from battle. I wanted to stitch ye before that wears away. The sword nicked the bone, either a crack or a bruise. In either case, ye will ache for a while."

The two fell silent while he began to drag the needle through her flesh, pulling the ragged edges together. Kyreen winced with each poke, but did not make any sounds. From beyond the hall, she heard people moving up and down the hallway, though none paused at this room. She wondered to what business they attended. She wondered what her friends were doing. Unwillingly she wondered about Collin.

Rhun watched Kyreen's face as these thoughts flow through her mind. She was strong and the wound in her side was not deep enough to cause concern. He could not know for sure, however, about the invisible injury, the one she carried in her heart. Rhun recalled the first time he laid eyes upon Kyreen, in Glain's kitchen, not fooled by her disguise, having heard Collin's story of their travels. Somehow, he had known then that their paths would cross again. He had also known from the way she had gazed upon Collin that someday, sooner or later, his best mate's younger brother would break this girl's heart.

For years, Rhun had watched Collin seduce then shatter the hearts of maidens across this city…chambermaids, serving wenches, any young lass who spared a glance his direction. Collin had even wooed a nobleman's daughter once as she travelled to her wedding. That fiasco had almost cost him his freedom, maybe even his life. Rhun did not understand the attraction women had for Collin, for he was not the smartest, best looking, most charismatic, or richest of men. Yet he attracted them without effort. If any resisted his attentions, he would simply pour on the charm, but as soon as the thrill of conquest was over, Collin's attention would wane.

All this Rhun pondered as he bandaged Kyreen's wound, but he held his tongue. Now was not the time to discuss Collin. He doubted there would ever be a time he would want to broach that subject with this woman. As he tied the final binding, Rhun glanced at Kyreen's face, surprised to find her gazing thoughtfully upon him.

"You look distressed," she stated, feeling his concerns, but not realizing she had been the subject of his emotions.

He nodded, taking her face in his hand so as to inspect the swelling of her cheek and eye. "That is going to bruise, but no permanent damage. He swiped ye good there."

"I think mayhap Falk had struck a face or two before," she replied with a soft chuckle, wincing at the pain in her side. Glancing down, she made to sit up. "All done?"

Rhun assisted her into a sitting position. "Not too quick," he warned, holding up a hand when Kyreen began to protest. "Ye lost plenty of blood and are not ready to face your friends. Stay put whilst I gather clean clothes for ye?"

Kyreen frowned, knowing the man was stalling. Still her head felt light and her side had begun to ache so she nodded. Rhun stepped out into the hall, returning a few minutes later with clean tunic and undershirt.

"My apologies. We do not have any breeches that would fit ye," he said, handing the clothes to Kyreen and turning his back to her. As she pulled the bloody shirt over her head and reached for the clean garments, she heard the tinkling of glass.

"Thank you," she said, smoothing the tunic down and sliding from the table to her feet.

Rhun, turning with a glass in his hand, reached his free hand out to steady her. "Not so quick," he admonished again, pressing the crystal tumbler into Kyreen's hand. She eyed the amber liquid without conviction and took a sniff. The scent was heady and aromatic, much more appealing than the liquor Jorn used to bring home.

"Mead. Honey wine," Rhun said, gently tipping the rim of the cup towards her lips. "It will help take the edge off."

"The edge off of what?" she asked, eyeing him over the glass. Without waiting for his answer, Kyreen decided to continue trusting this stranger and swallowed the liquid, which exploded sweetly pleasant upon her tongue. She felt the alcohol traverse the passage to her stomach then a warmness spread from her center towards her extremities. Not a heartbeat later the trembling began and her knees buckled. Rhun rescued the empty glass from her hand and guided Kyreen back onto the table.

Without a word, he turned to pour another small portion of the mead, which Kyreen swallowed wordlessly as the tears began to flow. When she held out the tumbler, motioning for more, Rhun shook his head.

"Two is enough for now," he replied, setting the empty glass upon the counter before crossing over to slide the door shut, leaving a small crack through which a tiny amount of light may enter the room. Those tasks completed, Rhun took a seat beside Kyreen on the table and they sat in a companionable silence while her tears flowed.

Kyreen found Rhun's presence comforting, not at all presumptuous.

His mood was contemplative and supportive, making no demands, not expecting anything from her as the adrenaline drained away, leaving a huge void inside. Rhun knew the full impact of her actions would not hit Kyreen until later, maybe even months afterwards. For now, she simply needed an ally.

After several hours, or maybe just a few minutes, Kyreen's tears dried and she swiped a hand across her eyes. Wordlessly, Rhun passed Kyreen a scrap of cloth, upon which she dried her face and blew her nose. He slid off the table and turned, extending a hand to help her to her feet.

Together Rhun and Kyreen walked back down the hall and returned to the training ring. Falk's body had been removed, to be tossed off the city's cliffs to the rocks below for the crabs and other carrion to feast upon, although Kyreen did not ask and Rhun did not comment. Additionally, fresh sawdust had been strewn about, obliterating blood or any indication of tonight's altercation.

"Will ye rest the night here in our hospitality or shall ye be staying with Glain?" he asked, reluctant to break the comfortable silence.

Kyreen looked over to Stian, Collin and Engla. The men conversed amiably; Engla between them, glowing with happiness.

"I think it best I leave now," Kyreen answered.

"I understand. I can take you to your horse and, by your leave, accompany you to the gates."

"Kyreen!" Engla spied Kyreen and ran to fling her arms around the taller girl's neck.

Kyreen winced and Rhun could not discern whether it was from the pain in her side or the shrillness of the tiny woman's voice.

Kyreen hugged her friend briefly then stepped back. "I must be leaving."

Engla looked up at her best friend, "Must ye always be leaving? I am to wed Collin. We plan to stay here in Myrddin with Glain for a bit.

She runs the boarding house, but Collin owns it. Please stay? I would have thought ye to be happy for me."

Kyreen's eyes moved to Collin, who was walking over with Stian. "I am happy for you, Engla," she replied cautiously, returning her gaze to Engla's wide blue eyes. "I will visit you, but right now there is something at home which demands my attention."

Drawing back, unshed tears shimmering in her eyes, Engla nodded her understanding. "I will miss ye, Kyreen. You are my best friend. Thank you for everything."

Kyreen squeezed her friend's hand, nodded her farewell to Stian, ignoring Collin, and turned back to Rhun who was waiting by the door. "I am ready," she said.

They made the walk to the stables in another companionable silence, which neither Rhun nor Kyreen felt the need to fill. The guild business swirled through the back of Rhun's thoughts as he watched the woman beside him. Kyreen was obviously preoccupied. Although he did not know her well nor possess her empathic qualities, he well remembered the first time he took a life. Then, as with tonight, there had been no other choice.

At the stables Kyreen was not surprised to find her gelding saddled and waiting for her, along with a mount for Rhun. The quiet continued until the riders reached the city gates, deserted this time of night save for the pair of city guards, who discreetly headed into the watch tower at a nod from Rhun.

Once outside Myrddin, Rhun continued with Kyreen for several hundred yards before reining to a stop. Kyreen pulled the gelding to a halt as well. Under the dark of the moonless sky, Rhun nudged his horse close to Kyreen, turning in the saddle to draw one of Kyreen's hands—her skin icy cold—into both of his. Squeezing gently, he peered through the shadows into her emerald eyes for a long moment before speaking, as though carefully considering his words.

"Do not consider negatively what ye did tonight. You acted with courage and without alternative. It is my hope your people and my guild may work together. Would you consider returning to Myrddin to negotiate a contract?"

Surprised, Kyreen nodded and they exchanged a genial smile of comrades. Both had seen a satisfactory conclusion to their dilemmas and a future deal between their groups was not out of the question. Until they could return to their home properly, Kyreen's people needed supplies that could not be secured while in hiding. Rhun's guild could easily negotiate and procure buyers for the items the Calanians had to trade, namely horses and herbs.

Rhun continued to hold Kyreen's hand and she sensed a conflict within him. He remained silent so long that she was on the brink of bidding him farewell when he said, "From a personal perspective, it would be a pleasure to see you again."

It took a long moment for the implication of Rhun's words to register in Kyreen's mind. When it did, her face flushed, and she managed another smile, this one much warmer than the previous.

Satisfied his message has been received, Rhun released Kyreen's hand and reined his horse back towards the city. The young woman lingered briefly before nudging the gelding into a slow lope down the road. Had Kyreen waited just a heartbeat longer, she would not have missed Rhun pausing, turning back to watch her disappear around the bend towards Calan.

Acknowledgements

Having carried Kyreen's story in my head and heart for fifteen years before finishing up the manuscript (which then lingered unpublished another eight years), I know there have been people along the way who helped and whose names I have forgotten. For example, my fellow classmates in that creative writing class at Imperial Valley College in the early 90's and from my novel writing class at Belmont University in Fall 2006. I will be forever grateful for their encouragement on my first chapters which was enough to keep the embers glowing.

To my mom, Nancy—thank you for enrolling me in that horse book-of-the-month subscription, which inserted my childhood obsession with horses into stories, igniting my love of the written word. Most of those books still sit on my shelf at home, having always made the cut (along with my Breyer horse collection) covering thirty-plus years, five states, a former US territory, and too many moves to remember. Also thank you for being one of my first readers and editors.

To my other first readers—Rebecca, Sasha, Joe, Wendi, Renee—thank you for your enthusiasm and excitement. Your response to *Kyreen* helped round out this story and gave me the courage to press on with the decision to self-publish. I promise you all have first dibs at reading the next novel. Additional thanks to Rebecca for her additional literary input and suggestions. I promise to put a map and genealogy chart in the next book.

To my children, Ryann and Kyle—thank you always for your unconditional love and support. Being your mother has made me a better person. Everything I do is for you. Much love!

And, lastly, to my husband, my partner, my best friend in all the world, and the first person to read my completed manuscript, Clark. Thank you for everything. For supporting me. For pushing me. For believing in me. Everything I am and all of my successes are because of you. I love you.

Look for the next Chronicles of Calan novel coming in
Summer 2017!